THE DOLCE VITA DIVAS

MADDIE PLEASE

Boldwood

First published in Great Britain in 2025 by Boldwood Books Ltd.

Copyright © Maddie Please, 2025

Cover Design by Head Design Ltd.

Cover Images: Shutterstock

A CIP catalogue record for this book is available from the British Library.

Paperback ISBN 978-1-83656-016-6

Large Print ISBN 978-1-83656-017-3

Hardback ISBN 978-1-83656-015-9

Ebook ISBN 978-1-83656-018-0

Kindle ISBN 978-1-83656-019-7

Audio CD ISBN 978-1-83656-010-4

MP3 CD ISBN 978-1-83656-011-1

Digital audio download ISBN 978-1-83656-012-8

This book is printed on certified sustainable paper. Boldwood Books is dedicated to putting sustainability at the heart of our business. For more information please visit https://www. boldwoodbooks.com/about-us/sustainability/

Boldwood Books Ltd, 23 Bowerdean Street, London, SW6 3TN

www.boldwoodbooks.com

For Elsie April Briar and Margot Violet
With Much Love
xx

PROLOGUE
THEN

I first saw Paulo on 16 September 1984. It was during fresher's week, in the student union bar. The soles of my shoes were sticking to the floor as I walked, and I glimpsed him across the room. Just for a moment. I stopped, wondering who he was, struck by his good looks, the easy way he stood there, sipping a pint.

He was wearing a clean white shirt that day, which stood out among all the grubby denim, and he looked slightly nervous but at the same time happy, approachable. So being me and, like everyone else, not really knowing anyone, I'd approached. I'd been like that back then.

Perhaps it was because I was a bit overconfident

and didn't really worry about much. And I'd also downed one pint already, which I wasn't used to.

'You look cheerful,' I said.

He'd grinned back at me. 'I am, why wouldn't I be? What's your name?'

Well, this had been a promising start. I took half a step, edging out a hopeful-looking blonde who had been inching closer to him.

'Joanna,' I said, holding out my hand, 'Jo Parkinson. From Worcester.'

He hesitated for a second and then took my hand. 'Paulo Massimo.'

I had dithered for a moment under the gaze of those beautiful brown eyes, and then of course I said something silly.

'Gosh, that's lovely. Are you Italian?'

'I'm from Capri. What gave it away?' he said, and we grinned at each other again.

Back then I wasn't entirely sure where Capri was, except somewhere off the coast of Italy. It sounded far more interesting than Worcester anyway.

The blonde gave a disapproving hiss and moved off. I felt a little swell of triumph.

After that we chatted quite easily, while around us the bar became more crowded and people nudged us out of the way, eager to get to the sub-sidised beer.

He indicated a space in one corner and we moved into it.

'You're new here too of course?' he said.

I nodded. 'I'm an English student. I didn't want to do that; in fact, I wanted to do History, but my parents thought English was a safer bet, so that's what I did. What about you?'

There was a burst of noise from a group of people next to us and I didn't really hear his answer, but I was so happy with the way things were going, I didn't want to ask him to repeat himself.

When the noise died down, he was still ex-plaining.

'...roads, that sort of thing. We are creative problem solvers. At least that's what it says in the prospectus.'

'Impressive. To be a problem solver.'

'I wonder if I could creatively solve a problem for both of us?'

'That would be even more impressive,' I said.

He took my empty pint glass from my hand.

'*Rimani qui* – stay here. And don't go away and I will creatively bring us back another drink, okay?'

'Perfect,' I said, and we smiled at each other.

It seemed there was already a definite connection between us. Wow.

I watched his broad shoulders moving through the crowds of other students and gave a happy sigh. Gosh, he was gorgeous. Dark curls, dark brown eyes, and he could have read out the fire escape plan notices on the wall and that wonderful accent would have made it sound interesting.

He returned a few minutes later, holding two more pints and two packets of crisps clamped between his teeth.

'Let's sit down,' he mumbled and jerked his head towards an empty table at the far end of the bar.

So we did, me pulling up two rickety cane-back chairs and him dropping the crisps neatly onto the table.

'*Eccoci qui* – that's better,' he said sitting down. 'So Joanna Parkinson from Worcester, tell me all about yourself.'

I was eighteen, and probably didn't have a lot that was interesting to tell him, but we chatted away quite easily. Me telling him about my rural childhood in a small village, my all-girls school, my wish to become a teacher, and maybe one day if I found out enough, a writer. He trounced all that with the fact that his family owned a hotel on Capri and he wanted to live in America, where he would build huge roads and bridges. Girls passing him almost did double takes when they saw him. It was like being out with a film star.

He drew me a little sketch on the back of a beer mat, showing me where Capri was and where the hotel was located. A place called Anacapri, which sounded even more exotic.

'*Sí*, it's beautiful. The sky and the sea go on forever, the sun shines and then people smile,' he said.

'So why on earth would you want to leave?'

He shrugged as though the answer was obvious. 'It is so small there and the world is big. I want to see it, all of it. I want to drive along roads that stretch towards the Rockies. Cross the Atlantic on a cruise liner. See the huge road trains in Australia. The temples in Thailand. The prayer wheels in Tibet. I want to see everything. Are you hungry?'

'Oh, I'm always hungry,' I said, spellbound by his passion and ideas. Perhaps I too wanted to see the world, all those things, those people and places that were out there. Back then I hadn't been anywhere much. Just Devon and Cornwall, where we had relatives. Once a school trip to the Normandy beaches as part of a History project.

He finished his pint and slapped his hands down on the table.

'*Eccelente*, me too. All this talk of travel and adventure. Let's get something to eat. My treat.'

Half in a dream to think that on my first evening out I had struck so lucky, I followed him.

We went out into the city, through the damp streets, where hordes of new students were rushing around, making a lot of noise. We eventually ended up at a small restaurant which was garlanded with Italian flags and skeins of plastic vegetables. There were empty wine bottles on each table with red candles stuck in them. The air was fragrant with herbs and garlic. These days there are places like that to eat in just about any small town, but that evening it was the first time I had been anywhere like it.

Paulo spoke to the owner in Italian, which sounded so sexy that my legs went a bit wobbly. Immediately, the boss came out from behind the bar to shake hands and hug us. We were his best, his favourite customers. Nothing would be too much trouble for us.

We had an excellent meal, hot and steaming in white china bowls. Pasta with some sort of spicy tomato sauce and a snow drift of parmesan cheese. There was garlic bread, red wine in a wicker basket.

All of these things were new to me, exotic and exciting, and Paulo made everything seem better; the lights in the restaurant were more flattering, the rustic checked tablecloth was charming and even the piped music was perfect. If this was what being an adult was like, then I was all for it.

We walked back towards the student union through darkening streets, our hands occasionally brushing. We passed more groups of young people darting in and out of pubs and fast-food places. They were just like us. But they couldn't have been as happy as us, could they? It wasn't possible.

'I must catch my bus,' I said with a regretful shrug. 'Thank you for a lovely evening.'

'My pleasure.' He smiled, and he pulled out a scrap of paper from his coat pocket – an old receipt, I think – and wrote down his address and phone number. 'This has been fun, perhaps we could... Call me. I'd like... but no pressure.'

We smiled at each other and he bent towards me, took hold of the lapels of my duffle coat and pulled me in towards him. And then he kissed me.

I think we both reeked of garlic but it didn't matter. He made my heart soar in a way none of my other boyfriends ever had. I didn't even care that I was wearing a duffle coat, which might have been my father's idea of a warm coat but back then was incredibly uncool.

He waited until I was safely on my bus, and we waved at each other, smiling through the windows, which were cloudy with condensation. I looked around at the other passengers, almost sorry for them because they weren't me. I wondered if they knew how happy I was, how thoroughly surprised and thrilled with life.

Back in my student hall of residence, I flopped down on my narrow bed, still in a bit of a daze. There was a knock on the door.

'Come in!'

The girl swung on the door, half in half out of the room as though unsure of her welcome.

'Hi, I'm your neighbour, Susie. Remember me from earlier when your dad helped me with my stuff?'

I sat up. 'Of course.'

'Have you got a lighter? Mine's run out.'

I didn't but she left the door open, trotted off further down the corridor to find one, and then came back.

'What's your name? Had a good night?' she said, opening the window a little and lighting her cigarette.

'Joanna, but call me Jo. And it was excellent,' I said, smiling.

Eccelente. That was how Paulo said it.

Suddenly I didn't want to talk about him to her or to anyone. I wanted to keep him to myself just a little longer.

'How about you?'

Susie leaned her elbows on the windowsill and fluffed out her hair, which was curly, slightly wild and past her shoulders.

'Okay, I've been unpacking. I couldn't be bothered to go out, this damp weather does terrible things to my hair. These rooms are tiny, aren't they? I'm planning to move out next year into a shared house. My cousin just graduated. She knows a great place, down by the railway line, and it's much cheaper than here. You ought to think about it too.'

I wasn't really listening, I was still remembering Paulo, the way he had looked, how he had kissed me. What a fantastic start to my grown-up life.

Fidgeting, Susie sat down in the only armchair and then stood up again and went back to smoke out of the window, looking out into the dark night.

'Have you been eating garlic? I can smell it from here. My cousin says if you want to meet boys you should join societies. Rugby or squash. Not to play them, obviously. I mean, me with a squash racquet in my hand would be asking for trouble.'

'I've met someone actually,' I said, unable to keep quiet any longer. 'He's really lovely. He could be... you know... the one.'

Susie looked at me with astonishment, eyebrows raised.

'Blimey! That was quick work. You've only been here five minutes. Where does he live? What does he do?'

I fished in my coat pocket for the scrap of paper, and then in the other pocket. And then in my bag, which I tipped out on the bed. And then I searched again. Panicking, I even went out into the hallway and the stairwell to see if I had dropped it there.

'He gave me his number and his address, and I've lost it!' I said.

The disappointment was hideous. I felt almost as though I might throw up. Should I retrace my steps outside in the drizzle to the bus stop? Should I ring the bus company?

'Never mind, I expect you'll bump into him again,' Susie said reassuringly. 'What's he studying?'

'I don't know, he did tell me but I didn't hear. Something about roads,' I said miserably.

'That makes it more difficult. If he's doing engineering, they study at that place out of town, don't they. Near Ashwood? Or is it Ashton? Ash something anyway. Has he got a car?'

Back then, hardly any student I knew had a car so I thought this was unlikely.

I was busy searching my bag again and wasn't listening.

How could I be so stupid?

'You'll see him again in the union bar I bet,' Susie said, stubbing her cigarette out on the wall outside the window. 'No harm done.'

'But I was supposed to ring him and now I can't,' I said, the full reality of this fact dropping into my brain.

'It's always good to keep them waiting in my opinion,' she said, 'and anyway, you are too young to start having thoughts of anything other than fun. And certainly far too young to be talking about meeting "the one". I mean, really! Are you mad? There are four times as many boys here than girls. That's one of the reasons I applied.'

I supposed she was right. If only I had known how long I would have to wait.

1

When I was a child, birthdays always seemed to take forever to come round. But as the years passed, time appeared to gain pace. Then one year, about five minutes after my last birthday, another one was hovering into view and this time it was a really big one. Sixty-five.

I knew people usually talked about the big 5-0 or 6-0 as being significant, but at my age every milestone had begun to count. Being sixty-four had enjoyed some slightly comical connotations thanks to The Beatles. *Will you still need me?* Well, at sixty-five it felt like no one actually did. And it didn't really feel funny at all.

I hadn't really minded the previous significant

birthdays. Forty just proved I really was an adult. At fifty I was still working, fit and active, had grown-up children forging their futures and their relationships but still coming home for Mum's cooking, and I still had Greg. As I looked into the face of turning sixty-five, a lot of things were different.

Everything that was important in my life had changed and none of it had really been in my plan, such as it was. It made me realise that a lot of the things I had done in my life hadn't really been my idea either, and that really annoyed me.

I'd had to have a knee replacement (fell off a pavement), I'd been made to retire (cutbacks in the budget and the ever-present improvements that never seemed to improve anything), our daughters, Jessie and Katherine, and our son Alexander had all married and left home for jobs in London, Birmingham and Reading. The girls had produced children of their own (two granddaughters, Violet and Maudie), and Greg had flown the nest too (new wife in Dublin – Thin Blonde Trollop, or TBT as I preferred to call her).

Which left me on my own in a quite nice house in a small town, with a garden that, if I was honest, was a bit too big for me to manage, and a granny flat over the garage where ten days ago my son Alex had moved back for a 'short time while everything is sorted out' following the inevitable breakdown of his marriage. And to be fair, he hadn't been any trouble so far, so I really couldn't complain.

I had a reasonable pension from my years as a teacher too. So I couldn't exactly say I was suffering. But my goodness, even knowing Alex was in the self-contained flat nearby, I was lonely. And sort of rudderless. This wasn't what I had expected.

But what had I been anticipating for my – what were they called – golden years? I supposed a home together where Jessie, Kat and Alex came to visit us with their families. Where Greg and I would be the focal point of family events and celebrations. A couple of older, wiser, cuddly people that the younger generations respected as they sat around us, faces glowing from the firelight as we dispensed good advice after yet another of my marvellous Sunday lunches.

Greg and I would live out our days with each other, getting used to being older, overlooking each other's irritating habits and perhaps coping with life together.

Nope.

That wasn't how it went.

Greg left the day after my fifty-eighth birthday

with the TBT (initially dismissed by him as being rather young, too thin, obsessed with horses and a bit neurotic) who had been mentioned in passing over the last two years. A great PA but, as Greg said, a bit ditzy. What did that even mean?

I looked it up on Google once. She was either scatterbrained or was covered in a pattern of small, random motifs, typically flowers. Maybe she was both?

Apparently the last time Jess had seen him, Greg had been complaining about the cost of keeping TBT's small but high-maintenance horse in a livery stables, not to mention the price of snaffles and leg bandages and whatever else it was that horse needed. Kat had once shown me a picture on Facebook, where Greg was hanging on to the horse's bridle while TBT held up a red rosette in triumph. He looked slightly terrified, and she looked about twenty-one. Heaven knows what she saw in him. Jess said every time she saw him he was grumpy and dissatisfied and complaining about food allergies. She tried to be kind and wondered if he had IBS, and Alex asked her if she meant Irritable, Boring and Selfish. No comment.

After I retired, I'd filled my days with routine. Cleaning, social media, laundry, although there wasn't much of it those days, occasional lunches with friends, letter writing, gardening. But I began to realise that being out in the garden sometimes made me sad. Every little blossom, resurrected plant and border were things only I saw. No one but me exclaimed in delight when the lilac bloomed or the tree at the end of the garden finally produced apples after sulking for two years.

I didn't want to live like this, on the edge of everything. I hated the thought that maybe the most exciting part of my life was behind me. 'The best years of your life', that was a phrase I sometimes thought about. Was the best really behind me? How incredibly depressing. And I'd hardly done any of the things I'd meant to do. I'd just done what had been expected of me, what was right. I'd wanted to make other people proud of me, but was I proud of myself? I wasn't sure.

In fact, I wondered if I had got to the stage in my life when I was just taking up space rather than contributing to anything.

I'd had a good career working as a teacher, ending up as a headmistress of a small village school, so that was worthwhile. I had a decent pension, which Greg's lawyers had not gone after as Alex had threatened that if he did, he personally would never speak to him again. There are occasions when one's children can be surprisingly supportive.

So on the surface I had nothing to complain about. But apart from feeling in control of things, I wanted to feel needed. Included. Proud of myself. And sometimes I didn't feel any of those things.

I had people to talk to though, neighbours and ladies who worked in the little local shops, occasionally visits from past pupils and colleagues, and of course news from my two friends from university days. Ellen and Susie. I had Juliette too, who was my nearest neighbour. She lived in what would have been called the big house when I was a child. A rambling old rectory which backed on to my garden. The fence dividing our plots had blown down the winter after I had moved in, and rather than either of us mending it, Juliette had taken to just wandering in unannounced, usually with a cake so she was always sure of a warm welcome.

Then suddenly I reached the time in life when illness and deaths and funerals were things that happened to people I knew, contemporaries with whom I had worked, not just to other people's parents or older relatives.

Ellen – talented, bright and beautiful – who sadly after months of an unnamed ailment, which she had dismissed as nothing particular, died five years ago, and by then I hadn't seen her for a long time thanks to the travel restrictions, except on Zoom calls, not since she'd gone to live in Italy.

And now Susie wanted to celebrate my birthday. Was being sixty-five something to celebrate? Well, I supposed it beat the alternative.

She had been most insistent. She had been going through problems with her partner Simon for some time, but even at sixty-three she could still think of reasons to have fun and excuses to behave in a way people would not expect of women our age, which I was beginning to see was an excellent mindset. Despite the lessons we should have learned from the scrapes we had got into when we were younger.

Dressing downs at university when we had been caught doing something wrong – as we always were. Later on, parking fines when her assurances that 'no one ever comes to check this street after six o'clock' proved to be repeatedly inaccurate. Dreadful hangovers from homemade wine. Photographic evidence that although Madonna might have been able to pull off ripped jeans, lace mittens and bits of ribbon tied everywhere, we hadn't. Perhaps Ellen had, because she was an art student and naturally stylish. Susie back then was little and blonde and had the ability to look both innocent and dangerous at the same time. I had just looked like a crazy bag lady.

Since then, the three of us had gone our separate ways but with Ellen away in her home on Capri, Susie and I tried to meet up every few weeks, leaving our significant others and my children at home while the two of us went to a wine bar to eat over-priced salad and catch up with each other's news.

Over the years, the topics had changed from the excitement of getting married, having babies – or in Susie's case not getting married or having babies – the terrible twos, house moves, Ofsted inspections, annual work appraisals, relationship problems, travel adventures and exam results, and then the topics sliding away into empty nesting, random health scares, grandchildren and cholesterol levels. Far more things to worry about it seemed, and looking back, it was much more fun being young. Adulting is a heavy load.

'It doesn't have to be,' Susie said when I voiced that opinion one Friday evening as we finished a chilled bottle of Chablis. 'We can still have fun at our age, just more carefully so we don't hurt ourselves.'

I looked across the table at her. Sometimes, she didn't seem to have changed at all since the day she had swung on the door of my student room, asking if

I had a cigarette lighter. Yes, her hair was grey and her face more lined, but I'd read that wrinkles are where the smiles have been, and Susie did have a very smiley face. And sparkling blue eyes. Two things which had got her out of trouble or into an exclusive club on more than one occasion.

'And we can afford to do things, some things anyway. I'm not up for a world cruise. Jo, you are going to be sixty-five next month. I think that calls for a celebration, don't you? I think we should have a mini break. Somewhere lovely, without Simon, where we can get a massage or something. And we don't have to cook anything or clear up. I'll sort it out,' Susie said, as she had many times over the years. When she was younger she had always been up for a party, a festival or a concert.

'As long as you don't get a lot of grief from Simon when you get back. I know what he can be like.'

'Oh, him,' Susie said, pulling a face. 'I'm beginning to realise we might not go the distance after all. I know we've been together for a while but recently I've realised I have more fun without him. Is that very disloyal of me?'

'No,' I said, secretly relieved that perhaps Susie was seeing what everyone else had thought for years. 'But is being sixty-five really something to celebrate?

And what about Alex now he's moved back in with me? Do you think I should leave him on his own?'

'Yes,' she said firmly, 'he is after all a grown-up with a job and solicitors fees to pay, and he's not exactly mooning around the place being miserable, is he? And never mind him, remember poor Ellen. She died at sixty-one. Far too young. I sometimes forget, and think about emailing her, and then I remember all over again. But we are still here, like Elton says, still standing.'

'I can now I've had my knee replacement,' I said. 'Modern medicine is marvellous.'

Susie held out her phone to show us a picture.

'Anyway, back to our mini break. This place. It's only twenty minutes away from my flat, holiday breaks for over 55s.' I went over there to take a quick look.

'There are no kids dive bombing the pool, no toddler tantrums at the next table, and the chicken nuggets are called goujons. There's a spa where we can have treatments, and most importantly they don't use paper robes that tear down the back when you sit down. I phoned them up to check. Remember last time we got a weekend away? My fiftieth when I flashed the whole spa.'

'It was probably the best thing some of them had seen for years,' I murmured, and she laughed.

She pushed her wild, curly hair back behind her ears. I'd never known anyone with as much hair as she had. When she was younger it was sort of strawberry blonde; now at sixty-four, it was a silvery grey. She looked like a tiny Viking.

'I don't seem to have a bottom any more,' I said. 'It's more like one of the cushion pads for garden chairs I bought off Amazon. Flat. Perhaps I should get implants.'

Susie looked worried. 'I've often wondered what happens if you sit down too hard on them. Wouldn't they burst?'

'Or they might make you spring up again unexpectedly, like sitting on a space hopper,' I suggested.

We thought about this for a moment and then we both laughed.

'I'm not going to, so don't worry,' I said.

We both peered at her phone, and I squinted a little.

'What does that say? I haven't got my reading glasses. Alma Cogan? Wasn't she a singer?'

Susie giggled. 'It's Alma Court. You take a look at the website and then I'll make the reservations and sort out two adjacent rooms. It will be like being back in halls of residence again.'

'Except no smoking, pot plants on the windowsill or throwing up in the sink,' I said.

'As if we would,' she said. 'We're grown-ups now.'

'What a bore,' I replied, shaking my head, 'I've been thinking about it and I'm beginning to wonder if all my best years are behind me.'

'Rubbish,' Susie said firmly. 'The best is yet to come.'

* * *

'Oh, of course you must go,' Juliette said a couple of days later when I mentioned the proposed trip. 'There's nothing better than a little mini break. I was talking to Matthew only the other day about us having a couple of days somewhere. I said Ibiza and he said Scotland. I said my piece about blackflies and the rain, which are all I remember about our trip to the Trossachs, and he went on about Maurice not liking it in kennels. I swear that dog holds more sway than I do sometimes. So in the end we didn't book anything. I'll have to work on him.'

She was sitting in her usual place at my kitchen table that afternoon, sparkling in a bright fuchsia top and blue trousers. I was in a rather dull but comfortable dress which I had taken to wearing rather too often. Both of us were enjoying some of her experimental ginger, rhubarb and cranberry traybake. I munched away for a moment, my teeth stuck together and then washed it down with a second mug of tea. When Juliette said she was 'just popping in', it was never five minutes. But then she was such good company that I didn't mind. It certainly beat doing the ironing.

'But sixty-five,' I said in a mournful tone.

Juliette flapped a hand at me. 'Is nothing, don't come crying to me. I'm nearly seventy and I've never been happier. I used to think life had passed me by and then I realised it hadn't and I'd better get stuck in. Take every chance you get, that's my motto. This cake is very odd, isn't it? Perhaps less ginger next time. And less rhubarb. And come to think of it, fewer cranberries. Still, it was a good try. Matthew will eat it regardless. He seems to think everything I make is wonderful. How is Alex getting on?'

'He's okay,' I said, 'although he does seem to think my fridge is his. I'm never quite sure what I will find in there these days when he has one of his raids.'

'Don't let him settle,' Juliette said wisely. 'I have a

friend who has been trying to get both her kids permanently out for over three years. The boomerang generation, I think they call it. No sooner does one find a new person to flat share with than the other one breaks up with someone and scurries back to Kim.'

Yes, she was probably right. Even after such a short time in residence, Alex had snaffled up my best towels, made requests for certain grocery items to be added to my supermarket shop and claimed his washing machine wasn't working properly, so could he use mine.

'You go,' Juliette said, 'and report back. I might even persuade Matthew to come away with me for a few days, if we can find someone to look after Maurice.'

'I don't know anything about dogs,' I said, 'but I would if you can't find someone else. He's only little. He can't be much trouble, can he?'

Juliette gave me a look. 'You would think. I never owned a pair of wellingtons before I met Matthew. That dog has gnawed through three pairs of mine since we got married. And don't talk to me about chew toys. There isn't one made he can't demolish. And heaven knows how many dog beds we have bought him. He just steals a tea towel from the Aga rail every evening, brings it upstairs and sleeps on that at the end of our bed. For such a small dog he takes up a lot of room. And he's very hot. Now then, I must be off. Matthew has been at a parish council meeting, so he will be in a bad mood. I will have to sweeten him up, but I don't think it will be with this cake.'

* * *

Alma Court was absolutely magnificent as we drove up the tree-lined drive four weeks later. It was an old Palladian mansion, golden stone glowing in the spring sunshine.

I'd read up a little about its history before we arrived. It had been built in the nineteenth century for some bewhiskered industrial magnate who didn't appear to have had a conscience about his ill treatment of his workers and wanted to showcase his wealth to the world. And then, when wars and death duties ran a coach and horses through that, it was eventually bought by a faded sixties pop star who mistakenly thought it would cement his next incarnation as a respectable country squire, although hedonistic parties, raids by the vice squad and cars being driven into the carp lake didn't exactly help.

Eventually, after many years of neglect, it was brought back to life by a hotel chain, which had installed proper plumbing, fitted carpets and new lighting, and restored the lofty, plasterwork ceilings to their former glory. It must have cost a fortune.

We trundled our suitcases up to the reception desk, which had been installed in the massive entrance hall, and waited while a white-haired couple in front of us checked in. Then, having been reassured that a young lad called Jordan would bring their luggage up to their room, they went off, pushing matching Zimmer frames in front of them to find the lifts.

The receptionist turned to us with a bright smile.

'Welcome to Alma Court. I'm Tracy. How can I help?'

'Joanna Dawson,' I said, 'two rooms, two nights.'

Tracy did some busy typing on her keyboard and frowned.

We exchanged a look and Susie cleared her throat, tapping on the desk with her fingernails.

'Ah yes, of course, there you are. Joanna Dawson and Susanna Fellowes. I was looking in the wrong place. I thought you'd be in the new wing, the bit that isn't still cordoned off, but you're in the main building. Because of the *incident*. And you did request two rooms together. And we managed to do it. At this time of year, we're not booked solid. A lot of our clients don't want to deal with the stairs, which is why the ground floor rooms are always taken first.'

'Hang on. What incident?' I said.

Tracy wriggled uncomfortably in her seat.

'Nothing to worry about. Just a bit of drama.'

What could that be then? A fire? A murder? Blood splattered up the walls?

Susie plonked her handbag down on the desk and leaned forward.

'Do go on,' she murmured.

Tracy's eyes glittered with excitement, and we waited.

'Well, I shouldn't really, but there was a bit of a thing with three couples who were here with a coach party from the Midlands, part of a ballroom society, and some medication. *Unprescribed* medication. The sort you get from non-residents, if you catch my drift. A chap who, shall we say, is known to us. And the police. He shouldn't have even been on the premises but...'

'Drugs?' Susie breathed, absolutely delighted.

I think at this point her hair gave a little shiver of its own and I stifled a snort of laughter.

Tracy gave a tiny nod and chewed her lower lip,

obviously reluctant to say more, but her willingness to gossip got the better of her.

'Police everywhere,' she hissed, 'a fire engine *and* an ambulance parked outside just in case. And sniffer dogs. I've never seen anything like it. It was only yesterday they took down the blue and white tape. It was terrible trying to keep the other residents away. And Mrs Wilkins was trying to give the police sniffer dogs ham sandwiches because she thought they were looking for food. My word, she got shouted at and no mistake. People wanting to take photographs and see the room. I'd have thought people of that age would know better but of course everyone has mobile phones these days.'

'Was someone hurt?' I asked, not daring to look at Susie in case she made me laugh.

Tracy shook her head. 'Oh no, nothing like that. But as my boyfriend says, if you're not used to it, you shouldn't take it. And a place like this, people don't want to have fire alarms pulled when they're waiting for their starters, and it was prawn cocktails too that night, which are always popular. And they *definitely* don't want to see naked people in the dining room doing the conga when they're waiting for their Cumberland sausage surprise—'

Susie let out a snort of laughter at this point and I pretended to be fiddling with my handbag.

'Anyway, here are your room cards. Top of the stairs and turn left, or you can wait for the lifts down there by the bust of Margaret Thatcher.'

She gave us a brilliant smile and we left her to the next couple who had just ambled in, dragging cases and a picnic hamper on wheels behind them that clinked suspiciously as though it was filled with bottles.

'Mr and Mrs Bulstrode! How nice to see you again...'

Susie and I exchanged a look and both of us started giggling.

'Oh my stars this is going to be an absolute hoot,' she said.

'When she mentioned the Cumberland sausage surprise...'

'How surprising can a sausage be?'

'I do hope we find out,' I said, wiping my eyes.

There was no doubt about it – we were going to have fun.

2

Far too excited to join the queue for the lifts, we dragged our cases upstairs. The staircase was a thing of great size and beauty, carved and decorated with swags of leaves and bunches of grapes and wide enough to accommodate a car if one could have got through the new fire doors.

Ahead of us stretched a long wide corridor lined with massive portraits of stern-looking women in elaborate dresses, and at the end we found our rooms.

With mounting excitement, we went in and then came out again like over-excited kids to look at each other's. Our rooms were huge, high ceilinged, and each had gigantic beds, massive mahogany wardrobes, a television and a dressing table. There was also a mini fridge in a cupboard and on top of that a kettle, coffee maker and a wicker basket filled with cookies and bags of crisps. Each room had its own bathroom with complicated lighting that came on automatically, and there was an assortment of toiletries on a shelf in front of a massive ormolu mirror. It was all looking very positive indeed.

'Well, this is great,' Susie said, coming into my room a few minutes later. 'Much nicer than I thought. I'm guessing these were the posh people's bedrooms back in the day. I've even unpacked my stuff properly and put it all away. I don't usually bother. I feel quite grand.'

I went to look out of the bay window and down at the sweeping expanse of lawns beyond the driveway. A coach had just arrived, and a harassed-looking driver was encouraging the passengers off, while another man was lugging their cases out from the storage area at the back. After a bit of jostling, some of them reclaimed their walking sticks and frames and went inside.

'There's a whole coachload of trouble just arrived,' I said. 'About forty people. Do you think they will be trying to score drugs too?'

'I do hope so,' Susie said, coming to stand next to

me. 'I've never tried cocaine and often wondered about it. I mean, I wouldn't obviously, but perhaps people their age – pensioners – think, what the hell.'

'What do you mean, people their age? *We* are pensioners. They are probably the same age as us!'

'No, people my age look much older than me,' she replied, shaking her head. 'We are never going to be old. I've decided.'

'Too late,' I said, watching as a sprightly grey haired gentleman slapped at the coach driver's hands as he tried to help him down the steps.

I smiled at his obvious indignation and his determination not to be treated like an old person. Perhaps I could learn something from that.

'Isn't this lovely?' Susie said after a while. 'Shall we go downstairs and explore? It's four thirty. Perhaps we could have afternoon tea.'

'Or cocktails?' I said. 'If we are going to have fun, why shouldn't we start immediately?'

Her eyes brightened. 'Good idea, if the bar is open.'

'With this lot? I'll bet you ten quid it is. I'll just send Alex a text to let him know we got here okay. He said he might have a friend from work over this evening.'

'New girlfriend? Well, that's nice,' Susie said. 'Anyone you need to know about?'

'I don't know, he was a bit vague about that,' I said. 'Probably not. Alex has got very secretive since he broke up with Tallulah.'

Susie bent towards me. 'You can tell me now they are getting divorced – that's not her real name, is it?'

I chuckled. 'No, she's actually called Bertha, after a great aunt. Something to do with a will.'

'I thought as much.'

* * *

The bar was in the grandly named Sir John's Library and was decorated with big armchairs, stuffed pheasants in glass cases and wallpaper printed with old books. There were already a few people sitting around the tables; the men with pints of beer and their wives nipping excitedly at schooners of sherry.

At the end of the room were two small sofas, too big for one but not big enough for two, which no one wanted to sit in, possibly because they were too low to get out of easily, so we nabbed those and almost immediately a girl dressed in a grey polo shirt and black trousers came over to ask what we would like.

'Two cosmopolitans,' Susie said, without any hesitation, and the girl smiled her approval as she put down paper coasters.

'Start as you mean to go on, ladies,' she said, 'and it's happy hour too. Much more fun to have a half price cocktail than a half price pot of tea.'

'Happy hour. How marvellous,' Susie said, hitching herself back into the sofa so her feet didn't touch the floor, and she sat with her legs dangling like a child.

'Actually, it goes on until seven o'clock,' the girl murmured, 'otherwise the people who arrive late start kicking off, so no rush.'

She returned a few minutes later with our drinks and a bowl of Doritos.

'I'll be just over there, ladies. I'm Lisa, just give me a nod if you need anything. Anything at all.'

'I wonder if she would go back to my house and do the ironing,' I said, 'or water the pot plants on the patio.'

'No need,' Susie said, looking out of the window, 'it's raining again. Honestly, the weather this year has been terrible. What happened to the lovely spring days we used to have?'

'This modern weather is rubbish. I blame the government. Anyway, here's to us.'

We clinked our glasses in a toast. It felt really marvellous to be doing something different, just for us. To be with my friend not having to anticipate another quiet evening on my own.

'Thank you for thinking of this. It was a great idea,' I said.

'It was, wasn't it, and it's your birthday tomorrow too. What would you like to do? There are lots of activities,' Susie said, rummaging around in her handbag. She brought out a sheet of paper. 'I've written everything down because otherwise I'll forget something. The story of my life at the moment. I've already booked us into the spa for facials, my treat. And then in the afternoon there is a mixology class. We can learn how to make three cocktails with head mixologist Tim, who apparently learned his trade in the world renowned Hôtel de l'Excès in Scarborough. Then every evening there is dancing in the Lady Mary ballroom, followed by a show with St Vincent and the Grenadines. Marvellous name. Easy listening and pop, so no head banging or crowd surfing. It says they are just back from a successful gig in Latvia.'

'Well, we can't miss that,' I said.

I sipped my cocktail, enjoying the sweet tang. It tasted dangerously drinkable. I wondered why I hardly ever had them, and then realised there wasn't much fun to be had making cocktails on my own. Still, tomorrow was my birthday, and I was looking forward to it tremendously. Probably more than I had for years. Even though it would mean that I would then be hurtling towards the next significant milestone of seventy. Crumbs, that really did sound noteworthy. But then I remembered what Juliette had said, and she was so full of enthusiasm and spirit that I thought perhaps I should take a leaf out of her book.

'We are booked in for dinner at six thirty,' Susie said. 'The early sitting at five o'clock was full, but that's okay, isn't it?'

I agreed it was and insisted I wouldn't want to eat that early anyway.

I didn't like to admit that many times I had eaten earlier than that, had sometimes skipped dinner altogether, didn't often cook any sort of meal, and had recently become toast-reliant.

Toast had become a very quick, adaptable and reasonable substitute for actual food. It was like fast food without the drive or the queueing up. Or much washing up afterwards.

And yet, in the past when I had a houseful to deal with, I'd been a good cook, and I'd loved doing it too. Sourdough loaves, cake decorating and a freezer filled with meals ready for unexpected visitors. In this bit of my life, I missed being the provider of complicated curries, themed Italian or Greek nights and of course Sunday lunches. My Christmas dinners were still marvellous though; even I had to admit that. They were one of the few times of the year when everyone in the family seemed to be available at the same time.

My kitchen cabinets held a lot of gadgets I didn't need any more, so many huge casserole pots, saucepans and roasting trays that once I had used all the time.

Why was I denying myself such a pleasure? Interesting food was one of the few indulgences left in life as far as I could see. Instead, I had got into the habit of just refuelling myself at odd hours with dull snacks. Eating something out of boredom or just so that I didn't feel hungry rather than for enjoyment. I should do better in future, I resolved. In fact, at that moment, I almost felt in the mood to chop some onions or make some bread. Or a curry. I'd loved those.

There were jars of herbs and spices in a special drawer that I hardly opened. I made a mental note to go through them when I got home and throw out all the jars past their sell by date.

In fact, I had already made a half-hearted start doing the same thing to all the other rooms. Throw away the things that didn't 'spark joy', wasn't that what I was supposed to do? So far all I had thrown out was Greg's old bank statements, a pile of gardening magazines and two uncomfortable bras.

Then there was all the other stuff that Greg hadn't wanted to take with him, although he had taken the barbeque, the garden chairs and the television. Things that I had bagged up and dumped in the garage. The dozens of pairs of socks, bobbly sweaters that he had insisted on keeping for when he was gardening, although he'd never set foot in the garden when we were married unless he was carrying a bottle of wine and some glasses. A treadmill which he had used twice and dismissed as being faulty, wine-making equipment which had produced wine so acidic it could have stripped paint, not to mention tooth enamel. All those things were still languishing in my garage, home to spiders and probably mice if I looked too closely.

There was also the baggage our children had left behind in the attic and the garage. Shelves filled with books I would never read again. Apart from anything else, the size of the print seemed smaller than I remembered, or perhaps it was my eyesight?

I was reluctant to admit how far I had slipped in the Domestic Goddess stakes. Even to my closest friend. Was that pride? Foolishness?

'I went to look at the menu,' Susie said. 'Sounds good although quite predictable. I don't care as long as I don't have to cook it. Do you know I hardly bother cooking these days. When Simon's away and it's just me, it doesn't seem worth the effort. My signature dish these days is beans on toast.'

'If I'd given Greg beans on toast he would think I'd gone mad, and now Alex has moved into the granny flat, I sometimes get the urge to cook something more exciting, but so far he's hardly ever around.'

'How's his divorce going?' Susie asked.

I shrugged. 'Progressing slowly. I don't ask too much these days. He seems okay about it all. He says they are going to sell the house and split the proceeds. Thank heavens there are no children involved. Still, it's sad when it all started so well. Tallulah seemed very nice at first.'

We were now old enough not just to be divorced ourselves, but to have divorced children. A sobering thought.

Susie finished her cocktail and put the glass down on the table with a decisive clink.

'You mean Bertha. Let's have another,' she said. 'That didn't touch the sides.'

'Tequila sunrise,' I said, finishing my drink. 'I used to love those, and I haven't had one for years.'

We called Lisa over and she replaced our empty glasses with two full ones. Then she leaned down conspiratorially.

'Just a head's up. Apologies from Chef. There was supposed to be bread and butter pudding on the menu this evening, but the dance society from Walsall have pre-ordered it all. So there will just be ice cream or Eton mess. I hope that won't spoil your enjoyment of your evening, but it's as well to be prepared.'

'I made that for Greg once. When we were first married,' I said. 'He told me it was okay but not as good as his mother's. So I never made it again.'

'Don't blame you,' Susie snorted. She screwed her hair up into a bun and secured it with an elastic band which had been looped around her wrist and then shook her bundle of papers at me.

'So tomorrow we are booked in for breakfast at eight – all the later spaces were taken – and then for a facial at two o'clock and mixology at four thirty with Tim. Then perhaps we could have a walk around the grounds. They really are splendid.'

'If the rain stops,' I said.

We looked out at the darkening evening, where we could see two hardy types, a couple with big waxed coats and umbrellas, walking along beside the house, heads slightly bowed against the wind.

'I expect he says they have to do their ten thousand steps before they are allowed any dinner,' Susie said.

'Well, I don't even have a proper raincoat, never mind any wellingtons,' I said.

This too reminded me of Juliette and her problems with Maurice, and for some reason it made me feel happy. Susie was fun, but Juliette could easily be an inspiration.

'I hope you have some sparkly tops,' she said. 'A lot of the ladies here are looking very swish.'

'I didn't realise we had to dress up for dinner,' I said, 'but it beats something on a tray in front of *Pointless*. I'm usually shovelling in cheese on toast and shouting at the contestants most evenings.'

Susie held up her tequila sunrise for a toast.

'Well, not this time, there is a three-course dinner for us, followed by a show. Cheers!'

'But no bread and butter pudding,' I added.

'Bonus round, I'd call it.'

I took a sip of my cocktail, and for a moment the taste catapulted me back to the days when I had been younger and carefree, and yet it hadn't all been wonderful. There had always been the problem of Paulo, which I'd never solved.

3

The dining room was absolutely magnificent, as one would expect in what was basically a revamped stately home. High ceilings, beautiful, moulded plasterwork swags around the doors, and yet more very grand portraits of fierce-looking people hanging on the walls. The tables were mostly set for two, with dark-red tablecloths and sparkling cutlery.

Feeling very jolly, probably because of our two cocktails, we were escorted by one of the very young waiters to our table in the middle of the room. Around the edges stood several other waiting staff, all dressed in their rather unimaginative uniform of grey polo shirts and black trousers. None of them looked more than eighteen, so perhaps these were after-school jobs. Anyway, they were very keen and willing to help the people who didn't know what to do with their walking frames and sticks, and very patient when they came to explain the menu to people who had mislaid the right spectacles or forgotten to turn on their hearing aids.

'The chap on the table next to us just said he is exceedingly disappointed about the dessert menu. He's come all the way from Croydon,' Susie hissed.

'Perhaps he is a member of the bread and butter pudding appreciation society?' I whispered back.

When it came, the food was good but under seasoned, and I caused a bit of a stir with the waiters when I asked for a pepper mill.

'Perhaps my taste buds are old and battered,' I said, 'but that lasagne didn't taste of anything in particular.'

'Was everything okay with your meals?'

It was our waiter, Kyle, who hovered uncertainly beside us, his polo shirt coming untucked from his trousers. I felt rather sorry for him. He looked like he needed a good meal and a decent night's sleep, and I wanted to be kind.

'Lovely, thanks, Kyle,' I said with a meaningful look at Susie.

'Compliments to the chef,' she said cheerfully.

'Have you been told about the problem with the desserts?' he murmured, looking anxiously at the couple at the next table who had just caused a lot of fuss. 'The bread and—'

'It's fine. We wouldn't want it anyway,' Susie said loudly.

His worried little face cleared, and he started stacking out empty plates.

'That's a relief. After all, it's not my fault the Walsall Waltzers got to it first. You'd think there was a world shortage. Have you finished your wine? Would you like another bottle?'

'Better not, Kyle,' Susie said kindly, 'we're going to the show afterwards.'

'Nice, you'll enjoy that, and my advice is don't sit next to the dancefloor or you'll get trodden on. Once these couples get going they don't stop for anything. Go at least three rows back. And then St Vincent won't pull you up on the stage and sing 'What's New, Pussycat' to you. I'm just saying. I've seen it happen more than once.'

By the time we had finished it was only seven o'clock. Evidently the clientele didn't like waiting for their meals and the clearing away was incredibly efficient. Or perhaps Kyle needed to get home to do some school coursework, so we went back to our rooms to 'get a bit of sparkle on', as Susie described it.

Sitting on my bed, I eased my shoes off and wondered what I would be doing if I was back home. Probably putting on my dressing gown and hoping no one would ring the doorbell and make me lie that I'd been about to have a bath. Or wondering where Alex had got to. Certainly, I would not be thinking about changing into a sequinned blouse and evening trousers. Good. It made a nice change. I'd almost forgotten what it felt like.

I rummaged through my makeup bag to find a lipstick which would suit my pink top, and as I went into the brightly lit bathroom to apply it, I paused for a moment to look at myself.

Did I look sixty-five? What did that look like anyway?

I could remember my own grandmother in her sixties, probably the same age as I was now. She had been a small, white-haired woman in hand-knitted cardigans who looked ancient and seemed elderly. She had always been old to me. And yet had she felt that way?

Perhaps in her head she had still been a laughing girl, with tumbling curls and a ready smile as she had been in the formal portrait of her that my mother had kept in a special frame on the sideboard.

And my own mother at the same age had seemed much the same to my careless gaze, but she had been young in the fifties and sixties, the decades when teenagers had been invented, of miniskirts, the sexual revolution and The Beatles. At my christening she had worn a Mary Quant mini dress, with navy blue polka dots and sheer sleeves that my grandmother hadn't approved of in a church. My father had kept up a running joke for years that the headmaster of my school was in love with her, but perhaps he had been?

Was that why I hardly recognised myself when I caught a sudden glimpse reflected in a shop window or in a family photograph? Who was that nondescript, grey-haired woman who stood beside her little granddaughters? What age was I inside my head? Thirty or perhaps thirty-five on a bad day. So what had happened to the thirty years in between when I had been ageing and changing? A wife, then a mother, then a grandmother. Where had that time gone? Why had such a large part of my life blurred into insignificance?

* * *

By the time we reached the Lady Mary ballroom, the seats surrounding the dancefloor were all taken, and the place was full of pensioners doing the foxtrot. We found a table, the recommended three rows back, and watched, fascinated. Couples who it seemed could hardly walk unaided sprang into new vigour on the dancefloor. Heads lifted, arms raised, feet positively twinkling. The magic of dance, we supposed. It was rather inspiring. No wonder groups of them went around the countryside on coach tours, if this was the effect it had on them.

Susie, looking rather splendid in a patterned wrap dress with her hair bundled away into a thick plait, nudged me, raised her voice above 'You Make Me Feel So Young'. 'That's the man who made all the fuss at dinner about his roast potatoes being soggy. He looked like he wanted some cocoa and an early night. Now look at him.'

The man in question was out there in the thick of it, dressed in beige slacks and a shiny blue blazer, with his partner, a rigid-looking lady decked out in green sequins. Like the others in their group, they knew exactly what they were doing. It was terrifically inspiring, and I wished I could join in. Perhaps I would learn.

There was a young woman with a cackling laugh

and a name badge – Poppy – who we guessed was the entertainments manager. She moved around the tables and seemed to know all the names of the elderly dancers, calling out to them with encouragement.

'That's it, Sidney, it's going to be a tango next, and you know you like those. Just a warning to those of you who've had hip replacements, no need to stamp too hard. You want to be careful with that titanium. We don't want anything falling off, do we? Hahahah! Lovely to see you again, Denise.'

'How do they know all these different dances?' Susie wondered.

'Years of practice, I suppose,' I said. 'They are certainly enjoying themselves.'

The pre-recorded music stopped, and Poppy sprang up to the microphone.

'The moment you've all been waiting for. We love them, don't we, ladies? Take a breather, all you dancers, and sit back and enjoy the fabulous, the foxy – St Vincent and the Grenadines!'

The velvet curtains behind her swished open to reveal a chap with carefully coiffed hair and a nod to Elvis in his sparkling stage outfit and glittery sunglasses. He raised his hands to acknowledge the polite applause, and behind him three more soberly dressed musicians took up their instruments. Two guitars and a drummer.

'I know what's coming,' I said, 'I can feel it.'

'What?' Susie said.

'"Hound Dog". I bet you a fiver.'

'Thank you very much, thank you very much for that great welcome,' St Vincent said with an unexpected Memphis twang. He flashed his bridgework at the audience. 'We're thrilled to be back here again; I think I can see some familiar faces too. Now then, more about us later, let's get the party started with that great old favourite. "Hound Dog"!'

'Told you,' I said.

Actually, they were really good. St Vincent did some passable hip swivels for which he was rewarded with some shrieking from a party of six at one of the front tables, and the Grenadines kept up a good beat.

'Latvia. What a beautiful country,' St Vincent said when they got to the end and he had got his breath back. 'We were headlining on three river cruise boats. Such a great way to travel, and what lovely people. A Latvian invented blue jeans, they love beer, and they have the fastest broadband speed in the world. And what's your name, sweetheart? Connie Jones? That's a great name. I'll remember that. It'll come in handy later. Anyway, let's get on with another great favourite of mine, "Build Me Up Buttercup".'

Poppy, up on the stage beside him, encouraged the audience to clap in time, which they did with great enthusiasm. At the table next to us I saw a sprightly gentleman turn off his hearing aids and smile.

After about half an hour, and a spirited rendition of 'Hunka Hunka Burning Love', which caused some of the ladies at the front to have hysterics, St Vincent had a brief discussion with the Grenadines and then called Connie up onto the stage and sang 'Me and Mrs Jones' at her, while she giggled and fluttered and her husband banged his palm down on the table and roared with laughter.

Across the table I saw Susie fiddling with her mobile and frowning. And then she looked up at me and mouthed 'Wow.'

'What?' I mouthed back.

She passed her mobile over the table and pointed with some energy at the screen.

Excuse me for contacting you so informally. I hope this reaches you. As one of Ellen's valued friends of so many years, I would like to invite

you and Joanna to join me as my guests with
the wider family at the Massimo Hotel for a
celebration on Capri in October. I'm sorry I no
longer have a phone number for Jo that works.
I sent a letter to her old address, but it came
back marked as not known. And I could not
find her email address. Please could you let
her know about this? Ellen's funeral five years
ago was very private, as you know, but we
wanted to have an event which celebrated her
life. And this year it will also be my mother's
eighty-fifth birthday. An event which deserves
celebrating. The family and I would love you to
be there as my guests. Kind regards Paulo di
Massimo. RSVP. I will send you more details.

I felt a jolt of something, that made me feel cold
all over for a moment.

Paulo.

I hadn't let myself think about him for a very
long time. Perhaps I had brainwashed myself into it.
Not thinking about him, not caring, not wondering if
my life would have turned out better or worse if we
had been a bit older, a bit more grown-up when we
met. What had happened to me in the intervening

years? And him, how had he changed? How many years was it anyway?

I tried to work it out, counting on my fingers under the table.

My mood had plummeted in a few seconds with that message. One minute I had been happily tipsy, filled with the enjoyment of being with my oldest friend, laughing and relatively carefree. The next it was as though I had been hit on the head with something. A rock or a baseball bat, and I was suddenly sober.

As a teenager, relationships had been almost stress free, so disposable because there was always another keen young chap knocking at the metaphorical door of my life. It had been easy to forget and move on from them. But with Paulo it had been something very different.

Susie and I quickly knocked back our drinks, collected our things and left.

We headed down the corridor and away from St Vincent's spirited rendition of 'the best Eurovision song contest winner of all time – who can forget little Lulu in that gorgeous frock? "Boom Bang a Bang"'.

I hurried after Susie, my unfamiliar heels

catching on the carpet. I thought for a moment I might be sick.

Paulo had been trying to contact me. Ellen had known my email address – why didn't he? Perhaps it was obvious.

'A celebration,' she said, blissfully unaware, 'and a birthday party. I don't suppose that would be very exciting, but isn't it nice to be asked. I remember Paulo's mother from their wedding, don't you? She was very imposing. Like Maggie Smith with a bit of Sophia Loren mixed in.'

I nodded, remembering that Paulo's mother had hardly spoken to me at that wedding apart from the usual small talk, but she had watched me from across the room, with eyes that seemed to know everything.

Back in my room I drew my curtains against the dark evening, but we could still hear the rain battering against the windows outside. Susie kicked off her shoes and perched on my bed, and I put the kettle on for some tea. How many times had I done that over the years?

After our first year at university, Susie and I had moved out of the halls of residence and into a shared student house as she had suggested. Such independence. That winter, the snow had piled up against the windows, and we had a log fire burning while we drank tequila sunrises and listened to slightly dated music on her portable record player. Billy Joel, Gordon Lightfoot, Steely Dan, The Doobie Brothers, Jackson Brown.

For a long time afterwards, I'd been unable to hear any of those songs without remembering. The emotional power of music when you least expect it can be terrible sometimes. I'd heard 'What a Fool Believes' once in the car when I was driving Jess and Kat to school and had to pretend I was sneezing to cover up the fact that I was crying.

After that first magical evening in September, when everything had seemed so exciting, so incredibly promising, I hadn't seen Paulo again until almost a year to the day afterwards, when he had arrived unexpectedly to take possession of the attic bedroom of our shared house with his girlfriend, Ellen.

I could almost remember the feeling as we stood looking at each other. I think I felt the blood draining from my face.

'You,' I'd said rather foolishly.

'You,' he replied, sounding equally shaken.

He had given me a lopsided smile as Ellen looped her arm through his and looked around our untidy sitting room with a small smile on her face, probably thinking Paulo had brought her to a slum, no matter how cheap it was.

Ellen had been an art student, always seeking colour in her life. Her clothes were bright and eclectic, the posters in their room a random mix of Michaelangelo, Dali, Giotto and Lautrec. I remembered her as always smiling, her cloud of dark hair framing a beautiful face. Definitely the most attractive of the Three Amigos, as we came to call ourselves.

After the shock of meeting her and realising she was someone important to him, I could see she made Paulo so happy. No one could ever have taken her place. We had made friends with her for his sake. It still seemed impossible to imagine that she had died.

The truth was, I had developed a huge crush on Paulo the first time I saw him. Dark curls, sparkling brown eyes and a wonderful smile. And we had been out together just once, a perfect evening when all sorts of possibilities stretched ahead. And he had kissed me. And then I had lost his address.

Any hope I may have had of any sort of relation-ship with him were dashed when we met Ellen. She had seemed so lovely, so sweet, so beautiful, that they made a perfect couple, and unlike many of us who had started and finished relationships during our university years, they had gone the distance. I'd bet she had been a much better wife to him than I could ever have been; I had to remember that. But the dull ache of remembering him, being so close to him and yet so far away, never being more than a friend to him, was still, if I dared to think about it, there. Just beneath the surface.

* * *

We sat rather subdued, drinking our tea, and I found some paracetamol for the headache which was looming because of all the unaccustomed alcohol.

'Can I have one? Just in case?' Susie asked, holding out her hand.

I laughed then at such a ridiculous situation.

'So in the past, some of the guests here might have been procuring illegal drugs from some shady character who shouldn't have been on the premises, and here we are sharing out paracetamol. Talk about living close to the edge. Do you think it costs a lot to go to Capri?' I asked after a moment. 'I've heard it's very expensive.'

I knew myself well enough to know I was starting to think of reasons for not going.

'I heard all the celebrities go there. But would we even know who they were?' Susie said. 'I would back in the day if it was Burton and Taylor. Or Audrey Hepburn. Johnny Depp at a push—'

'He's very charismatic,' I said. 'Wonderful cheek-bones, but he always looks like he needs a good wash.'

'—but I don't think I'd know any of the new ones. Most celebs on holiday like to hide way from people during the day or stay out on their yachts, and then only appear at night when they think everyone has gone.'

'Like woodlice?' I said.

Susie laughed and carried on talking about Capri, the things she remembered from her visit there. How lovely the hotel was, the food she had eaten, what a shame we had never been there to-gether, and after a while I realised I had been lost in my own memories. I didn't want to share my feelings with her, not then. So I forced myself back into the conversation before Susie noticed that I was sitting there, silent and thoughtful.

'If we go it would be in the low season, so perhaps there won't be any celebrities at all, which hopefully means the flights will be cheaper.'

'I would like to go but it might be too expensive,' I said. 'I've just had the bathroom done.'

'But it is a special occasion. You can't not go.'

Susie was looking at me with a stern expression, and I felt myself relent.

'Perhaps I could soften Alex up with a beef Wellington so he will look after the house while I am away, and not have any of his friends round for a rowdy party? That's always assuming he hasn't moved out by then. Surely he would have? It's nearly six months away.'

'We need to do some research and find out what we would be letting ourselves in for. And then I can formulate a plan. Leave it to me, I still have contacts at the travel agency where I used to work. But for now, I think I should go to bed,' Susie said. She pulled the band off her plait and tugged at it angrily. 'God, I'm sick of all this hair. I've got a good mind to cut it all off. But Simon likes it so... Look, it's been a long day, and I've drunk far too much. And it's someone's birthday tomorrow.'

I sighed. 'It's only ten o'clock. Remember when we were students? We would be up until three in the morning at some ghastly discos and still get into lectures at nine the following morning. I used to sit at the back and snooze, and was probably still wearing last night's makeup.'

'Gosh, me too,' she said. 'I couldn't do that now. My skin has been awful since I turned sixty. Every morning, I peer in the mirror wondering what I'm going to find. I thought we were supposed to be past all that.'

'Go on then, push off and I'll see you in the morning,' I said, yawning.

'Birthday girl,' Susie said with a grin.

She paused in the doorway and turned to look at me before she left.

'I've just remembered. How could I have forgotten? Won't it be marvellous to see Paulo again after all these years? You went out with him, didn't you?'

How did I feel? Slightly sick, if I was honest.

'Oh, you know, fine, and it was only once,' I said, fetching my dressing gown from the bathroom. From the heat of my face, I was sure I was blushing.

Only when she had gone could I change into my nightie, lie down in bed and close my eyes to remember.

Remember him.

It was awful; all of a sudden; it hurt. It had been so much easier to forget. And yet those memories were still there, impossible to really block out.

His wide easy smile. The way he used to sing while he cooked. His passion for all things Italian. Football. Pasta. Wine. The way his hair curled into the nape of his neck. How I hadn't realised how much I'd loved him until I lost him forever. And I didn't think he had ever suspected a thing.

* * *

The following morning, I woke at my usual time of six thirty, wondering yet again why I couldn't sleep in as I used to when I was younger. During my first year at university when we had been in a hall of residence, I remembered those weekends, waking up at midday, stumbling downstairs to the bar, where I would meet up with Susie and we would eat disgusting burgers, allegedly lamb, but who knows what they were, other than the perfect antidote to a hangover.

Thinking about it, I hadn't slept properly since the day Greg and I had brought our eldest child Jessie back from the hospital. Perhaps that was it.

Some primitive parental urge to be constantly on guard. It hadn't seemed to affect Greg, who had been able to sleep through our children's teething, colic, nightmares and tantrums.

I made a cup of tea, pulled the curtains open and went back to bed.

Out there it was still raining, probably harder than ever, the rain slanting across my view over the grounds. The avenue of trees that lined the drive were bending in the wind. Not the day for a lovely stroll no matter how glorious the gardens were.

Never mind; it was my birthday. I had things to look forward to. Not least of which was 'Mixology with Tim' later that afternoon. I wasn't going to allow myself to think about Capri, special celebrations or Paulo.

Susie came to bang on my door about thirty minutes later, carolling 'happy birthday' in a way that made me hope the other residents nearby had hearing problems.

'I have presents. And on top of that, I have news,' Susie added rather mysteriously.

'Please don't tell me Simon has moved back in?' I said.

Although she had never married, Susie had been in an on-off relationship with Simon for four years, a man who, whilst handsome and charming, in the olden days would have been described as a cad and a bounder.

'I don't want to talk about him. Much more interesting. Presents first,' Susie said, grinning.

She had given me the reliable gifts for someone my age: a silk scarf in my favourite shades of blue and white, and a delightful vintage brooch from an antiques shop with my name enamelled on it.

'Thank you so much,' I said, 'I love them. You're marvellous.'

'Did the kids remember?' Susie asked.

'They did, but I will have my things from them when we get back, when they come over for cake,' I said, 'which I expect I will have to make. Now, what is this news, Suz?'

Susie grinned, looking almost exactly as she had the first day I met her when she had charmed my father into helping her with her bags up the four flights of stairs to her student room.

'Well,' she said, 'this morning when I logged on to the internet, which by the way is pathetically slow – perhaps we should move to Latvia if what St Vincent says is true – I had a very exciting email.'

'And?' I said as Susie paused for dramatic effect.

'My friend at the travel agency seems to have

been up all night and has found us flights direct to Naples at a great price.' Susie held up a commanding hand as I drew breath. 'We are doing this. Stop trying to think of reasons not to go. We have been friends for so long, and Ellen was a part of that. And I think it's only right that we should have a really fantastic experience, spending lots of time together. *Together*, to celebrate over forty years of friendship. Paulo still runs that gorgeous hotel in Anacapri, you must remember it, and he says we can stay there as his guests so it's going to save us loads of money. It will be the low season by then, and I expect they will have plenty of rooms. And that's the end of the news, so just accept it.'

'God, you are bossy all of a sudden.'

'I was thinking about it last night. We've all had difficult things to cope with in the last few years. You with Greg behaving like a silly old fool, then you had knee surgery, and the builders making a mess for weeks, then Alex and his divorce dramas. And I deserve it too, because I realise I'm wasting my time with Simon and I'm not doing it for much longer. Come October we are both going to Capri, and that's an order!'

We started laughing and talking then and had a big hug to celebrate, and feeling very tearful, I realised how suddenly out of the blue rotten things could happen, but also so could great things and I needed to learn to embrace both, not just focus on the bad.

And then I thought how marvellous women could be and how lucky I was to have such a good friend, and I began to feel very excited.

A proper trip away, even if it was for a sad reason. Capri. Sunshine.

And Paulo.

But I'd forgotten all about him for years, hadn't I? Well, if I hadn't actually forgotten, I supposed I had filed his memory away in a safe, very secret place. After all, I'd married Greg, and Paulo and Ellen had married and had a son and been so incredibly happy. Ellen had told us they had been. And that was a good thing.

My life now since Greg and I had divorced was restricted to my house, my garden, my routine. The years before that had been filled with work, looking after the children and him. There had never been any time for me. It didn't have to be like that now, did it? It wasn't too late to spread my wings, was it? I could also have an adventure. I could do some of the things I had always wanted to do.

And Paulo? We were both adults now. We hadn't

seen each other for decades, and we were different people. We were both in our sixties, proper grown-ups.

Perhaps he had forgotten about the foot spa and the bubble wrap incident? Perhaps he had forgotten that evening when everything changed between us.

4

We went and joined in an Aquarobics class where we jostled for space with some other ladies and boogied along, up to our waists in water, to The Jackson 5. We caused a bit of a stir when 'Thriller' came on the sound system, and the two of us tried to do the zombie moves and I fell over and came up spluttering.

I had some cheerful congratulatory texts wishing me a happy birthday from Jess and Kat, a GIF of a zebra dancing from Alex, and an adorable video of my four-year-old granddaughter Violet singing 'Twinkle Twinkle Little Star'.

After a light lunch we had our facials in the spa when a sweet young thing called Gracie plastered my face and neck with unguents, and I went to sleep. Then we had Mixology with Tim later that afternoon.

Tim – who looked about fourteen – measured the ingredients for the cocktails into the shaker and rattled it above his head while we sat watching. He was then prone to muttering, 'Well, the bottle's nearly empty, might as well,' and adding a bit more, so by the time we had finished our session, we were feeling very relaxed from the massage, decidedly giddy from the alcohol and had to go back to our rooms for a little rest before dinner.

I had a nice snooze for an hour, before I was woken up by a text from Alex asking if I had any white spirit as he had spilled something on the carpet. Nothing to worry about, just a splash of curry sauce. And a tiny bit of red wine.

I wondered which carpet and how much wine?

Just as I was about to ring him to find out what the damage was, he sent me a second text to tell me it was all sorted and wishing me a happy birthday again. This time without the zebra.

* * *

After we had enjoyed some under-seasoned minestrone soup and steak and kidney pie for dinner, we were thinking about our desserts and whether to have apple tart or lemon posset, when Kyle triumphantly brought in a birthday cake shaped like a volcano with a lot of candles already lit, and the whole dining room sang happy birthday to me and waved their napkins, which was lovely, but slightly embarrassing.

Two old gents in tartan cardigans came over and insisted on kissing my cheek while their wives took pictures and talked about putting it up 'on the inter faceweb thing'. Or possibly sending it into *Great British Bake Off* to show the joy a cake could bring.

'That's it,' I said, laughing and handing out slices of cake, which looked as though it had been constructed from bits of other cake and covered with a lot of brown buttercream, 'no more birthday stuff. Now we need to think about Capri. Which is much more exciting!'

And the more I thought about it, the more I realised it was true. I wasn't going to make any more excuses. I was going to go for it.

* * *

'That place you went to sounds absolutely just the thing,' Juliette said a few days later when she came over for coffee, 'and a lot of fun. I shall get a brochure and leave it lying around for Matthew to see. Perhaps I will ring the place in red pen just to make sure.'

'And while we were there we had an invitation to Capri in October,' I said.

Juliette gasped and then sighed with pleasure.

'How marvellous. Somewhere I've always wanted to go. I went on a school trip to the Amalfi coast once and we were due to go to Capri, but at the last minute the teachers called it off. They said it was too foggy, which was an absolute lie. I think they were all hungover.'

'It's for a friend's memorial service. We were friends for decades. Ellen married another friend, Paulo, and his family owned a hotel there.'

'That's very sad, but on the other hand I wish I had friends like that, and Italian boys are so glorious, aren't they? Wonderful olive skin, dark eyes, absolutely charming. On our school trip we had loads of them following our bus around in little Fiat 500s. Was Paulo like that?'

'Oh yes, I suppose so, in a way. I really can't remember,' I said with a laugh.

Juliette wasn't fooled for a moment.

'You're blushing! Ah, so you had a crush on him, did you? I can see it in your eyes.'

'No, I didn't,' I said.

'Yes, you did. I can tell. You looked all wistful for a moment, and you've gone pink.'

'Don't be daft. It was so long ago.'

'Yes, but there is always something special about first love, isn't there? I was madly in love with a chap when I was at university, Russell Ham. Can you imagine the jokes if I had married him? Juliette Ham. No one would have believed me. He was a percussionist, in the same orchestra as me. He used to wash his drum kit in my bath. And dry his cymbals on my clean tea towels.'

I laughed and Juliette joined in.

'But I still remember him. I even googled him a couple of times. He's played all over the world; I wonder what life would have been like if we had stayed together? Terrible probably, he was a bit OCD when it came to his beaters and lugs. I used his snare drum stand to balance a tea tray on once. He went ballistic and had to wash it all over again.'

I laughed until I had to wipe away the tears at that point. How great if felt to be able to laugh at the past. Perhaps that was what I should do, instead of looking back with such regret. Such guilt.

'So?' she said, tilting her head to one side.

'A bit of a crush I suppose,' I admitted. 'Well, yes, a full-blown crush. He was absolutely gorgeous back then, but he had Ellen. I never got a look in.'

'I expect he will be bad-tempered and sloppy now,' Juliette said reassuringly. 'He'll have food stains down the front of his jumper and terrible shoes that he never polishes, and you'll wonder what you ever saw in him.'

'I hope you are right,' I said, but somehow I knew it wouldn't be like that. It couldn't be, could it?

'You must send me pictures,' Juliette said, 'so I can see what all the fuss was about. Now then, I must go and rustle up something for Matthew's lunch, but before I do, I'd better use your facilities. My mother used to call it a try and see wee, but these days it's one for the road.'

* * *

On the fourth of October we left Heathrow and flew to Naples, landing just after two o'clock in the afternoon. When we got there, Susie had arranged a taxi to take us to the Molo Beverello ferry port where we and all our luggage boarded for the hydrofoil trip to Capri.

We sat together, me by the window peering out through the salt fogged glass, and she hugged my arm with excitement as the boat left the harbour, past the cruise ships and out into open water.

'Aren't we lucky,' she said, 'to be here together, instead of having to be with *other people*, no names mentioned, who would be whingeing about whether the toilet would flush correctly or had I packed proper tea bags.'

I thought back to the first time Greg and I had tried having a holiday together after our children had left home, and he had done exactly that. We'd only gone to Normandy, but to him everything was dangerous or somehow substandard, and above all, *foreign.*

After three days we had been thoroughly irritated with each other and I couldn't wait to get home again, which was such a shame because I'd enjoyed everything apart from his company. He probably felt the same way about me if I was honest.

Without the children there as a buffer between us, I began to realise that we probably didn't like each other much any more. It had been a bit of a wakeup call for me as I watched him, his mouth turned down with dissatisfaction, prodding at the perfectly delicious risotto he had ordered.

It was such a lovely afternoon as our boat ploughed through the calm sea, the sky above the Mediterranean streaked with apricot clouds, and out of the haze above the water we could see the island of Capri coming tantalisingly closer.

Occasionally a speedboat whizzed past us, and a couple of times some bikini-clad girls waved at us. I wondered what they were planning to do with their holiday. Young, attractive and presumably wealthy with some equally eye-catching friends. How lovely. I wondered how they were feeling. Confident? Excited?

Why weren't they at work? Perhaps this was their work, being influencers.

I wished someone would pay me to influence, although my knowledge gleaned over the years was of less exciting things than yachts and makeup. How to make a pound of mince feed five people. Seating nine people around a dining table built for six. Teaching a class of twenty-seven children to read. Dealing effectively with a furious toddler.

I decided if there was such a thing as reincarnation, I was going to come back as a glamorous redhead. I would be slender and six feet tall with marvellous legs, not five foot five with the suggestion of a varicose vein on one thigh and a tendency towards middle-age spread that was only kept in check with much effort.

And why was it that those days there were so many treats I had been denying myself as I got older? There were loads of things. Smoking – well, obviously that was sensible – doughnuts, cream, alcohol, sugar, fat.

Just as I was getting on in life and had more time to fill, the list of things I needed to avoid, that might have cheered me up and made my existence bearable, grew longer. If it carried on, I would be existing on a diet of kale and oily fish. So not only might I live longer, but it would jolly well feel like it too.

'When we get off, Paulo has arranged transport to the hotel,' Susie said. 'At least I hope that's what he said. My Italian isn't nearly as good as it was. I don't think he realised that. And he did talk very fast.'

'I bet it will be fine,' I said. 'Better than fine. It will be brilliant.'

Would it?

It wouldn't be long now, and I would see him again, and I felt odd and slightly queasy at the prospect.

After what Juliette had predicted, I wondered what he would look like, how the years had changed him. Would he be bald and portly with a couple of missing teeth? Would I really wonder what on earth I had ever seen in him? But then, how had the years changed me? Would we look at each other and both be horribly disappointed? And did that even matter?

I smoothed down my new dress, chosen for comfort during the journey. Blue with white polka dots. My birthday scarf tied at a jaunty angle around my throat. White sandals. My toenails painted a defiant red. The warm coat I had needed in England was rolled up and stuffed in my cabin bag.

The boat pulled into the Marina Grande port, which nestled on the coastline beneath towering cliffs above. It might have been nudging into low season but there were still a lot of people about. There were ice cream sellers, little cafés and wine bars, each more appealing than the last. There were stalls with the most luscious fruit displayed under canvas awnings, and warning signs. *Non toccare* – don't touch.

We disembarked from the ferry and as promised, there was a man there, holding up a card with Susie's name on it. He didn't speak much, just a few encouraging nods and smiles, and he helped us with our cases to the parking area where we found a funny little taxi, part golf cart, part van, with *Hotel Massimo* painted on the side, and behind it a small trailer for our luggage. Within a few minutes, and with much tooting of his horn, we were out on the road, passing boat repair yards and high stone walls and speeding away from the ferry up a steep, winding road.

As we went higher, the view beneath us widened out into a fabulous panorama of blue sky which met the blue sea in a misty line, scoured with the white wakes of several speedboats. Further out there were a few enormous yachts and a massive cruise ship heading towards Naples.

I felt a huge leap of excitement, to be there, doing something so completely different, and it was made all the better because Susie was there too. Part of the enjoyment of that sort of experience was having someone to share it with, after all. Maybe that was the best part of having fun – laughing about it with someone else.

But then underneath my excitement I was still aware of that terrible anticipation, which still churned away in my gut. People did this all the time, didn't they? Meet up with someone who had once been important to them. And they coped with it; perhaps they even laughed about it.

Do you recall when…? What a long time ago that was. I can hardly remember, can you?

Then the view was obscured by trees and houses, which gradually thinned out again to reveal the crags of the mountain in front of us, and we went round hairpin bends and negotiated narrow streets, scooters and mopeds and distinctive orange buses. Occasionally there were tall gates at the side of the road, closed against our curious stares. I distracted myself by wondering who lived there, what sort of house was hidden from view. I didn't remember much of it from my trip all those years ago, but I knew it would be only a few minutes more.

The road grew steeper and even more twisting, one side bordered by a leaning stone cliff face covered in wire mesh, the other giving us yet again that dazzling view over the sea, the horizon shrouded in haze, the houses far beneath us like tiny white boxes. The edge of the road was protected by a low wall and some railings, and below was a dizzying drop to who knew where.

The two of us leaned to the left, drawing away from the possibility that our little taxi might suddenly plunge over the edge.

We passed a sumptuous-looking hotel, half hidden behind trees and fences, and then on past a petrol station, a small supermarket, people walking at the side of the road, a few shops and wine bars.

At last, with a satisfied nod, our driver turned right, through some high iron gates and into a courtyard.

'*Eccoci qui*,' he said. Here we are.

We had arrived. Of course, I remembered it now. How could I have forgotten?

I took a deep breath and opened the car door. I wasn't sure if I was still excited, or whether the fluttering in my stomach would mean I would be sick on the marble steps.

What would it be like to see him again? Was I going to be able to be sensible about this or would I make a complete fool of myself? In the past I had done both.

* * *

Hotel Massimo was a large impressive building, built into the side of a rocky promontory so that most of the rooms were on a lower level than the entrance. We walked through the reception area, which was lofty and cool after the heat of the afternoon. I gave a little shiver, which I was sure was nothing to do with the temperature.

I could vaguely remember it from my visit all those years ago, and yet it was not familiar; things had changed. It looked much brighter than I remembered, the decoration light, sophisticated and classy where once it had been dark and dated with heavy wooden chairs and tapestry curtains.

There were a few people about – two women talking to the receptionist at the desk, a waiter hurrying past with a tray filled with empty glasses.

Susie, whose command of Italian was rusty but still effective, had been sitting behind our driver on the journey and had discovered he was called Umberto. He put our cases onto a trolley and had trundled them after us.

'*Grazie mille*, Umberto,' she said with a sweet smile, and Umberto looked pleased. Susie had always had this ability to win people over in an instant. It was always very interesting to watch.

'*Piacere mio*,' he said, flushing a little. My pleasure.

One of the women in front of us was willowy in cream linen and did not look as though she had been travelling for the last day as I know we did. She sounded American and having finished asking about towels for the pool, she wandered off, talking loudly about finding her husband and a drink. The other slightly older woman trailed after her, clutching at a carrier bag.

As Susie – who by then had been appointed spokesperson – reached the desk, a man came into the hotel from the open doors which I think led to the gardens, and walked towards us, both hands held out in welcome.

And there he was.

It had been so many years since I had seen Paulo; Ellen had always come to visit us without him. She said he found it hard to leave the family hotel for other people to manage, and in a way I had been relieved. But that day, completely demolishing my earlier doubts, he looked almost the same as he ever had to me. Tall, handsome and tanned, he was the very picture of a casually elegant Italian man. For a moment the old attraction I had always felt for him rose up again, and annoyingly I felt my cheeks burning. That was a great start, blushing like a teenager.

'Welcome,' he said with a wide smile, which also showed he hadn't lost any teeth.

Did his gaze rest on me for a fraction longer than it might have? I couldn't resist sneaking little looks at him to reassure myself that he was still the same attractive and charming man I remembered. Could I recall how I had felt about him? Of course I could. Had he realised? Did he remember?

We did the usual round of hand shaking, polite cheek kissing, and small talk about the superb weather.

'I can't believe it's you. At last,' he said.

He was still holding my hand in both of his, and for a moment I didn't want him to let go.

'It's been years, hasn't it,' I said. 'Decades, actually.'

'And how are you?'

How was I? A bit lightheaded if I was honest. I seemed to have lost control of my senses. Did my feet still work? Was I able to talk sensibly any more? Or would I just stand there with my mouth unattractively open, dribbling and prattling a lot of nonsense?

'Oh, you know, fine,' I said at last.

'We have a lot of catching up to do,' he said, 'but first let me show you to your rooms.'

The next few minutes were spent with him taking charge and being generally hospitable. All the time I could feel the blood pounding in my ears, my heart thudding.

'I hope you will be comfortable here,' he said,

escorting me into a fabulous room with a view over the Mediterranean.

'I'm sure I will,' I said rather croakily.

'I will see you later,' he said, and we looked at one another for a few moments while I fidgeted and wondered if I could think of something sensible to say. I couldn't.

* * *

I had only visited here once, many years ago. Ellen had urged me to come because Paulo had been away on business, and although that part of it was disappointing, I went, on my own, much to Greg's annoyance.

I wanted to prove we were still friends, that everything was fine and there were no hard feelings.

On that occasion I had been in a small single room on the top floor and the streets of Capri had been hot and crowded. At this time of year, it was quiet. The wonderful views of the coast stretched on to infinity, and it seemed a splendid place to be. No wonder Ellen had hated to leave it.

This time our rooms had glass doors leading out onto a wide stone terrace, where there were terracotta pots of flowers and purple bougainvillea cascading around the windows. It was marvellous.

After unpacking, the two of us met out there, marvelling at the beauty of the place. How wonderful to live like this.

'Well, really, Ellen was a lucky girl, wasn't she?' Susie said a few minutes later as she leaned on the balustrade. 'I don't remember Paulo being *quite* so attractive, but then I was with Tom back then. And I didn't have eyes for anyone else. Who knew he was such a bore; it must have been my hormones. No wonder Ellen didn't like to leave Paulo for long. Isn't it annoying how men can look better as they age with no apparent effort? While women spend more and more on face creams and potions and talk about cosmetic surgery. And it takes hours and a lot of money to colour our hair, while men can do it in ten minutes while they shave if you believe the ads. Why is that?'

'The same reason we get cellulite and men don't. And yes, she was a lucky woman,' I said, 'and she thought the world of him. They thought the world of each other.'

I said it firmly, almost to reinforce the fact in my own mind, and at the same time to sort of punish myself for still finding Paulo attractive. What was the point, after all? We hadn't met for decades; life had moved on for both of us. I needed to remember that.

Susie gave a deep sigh.

'Latin looks and his own luxury hotel? It's like something out of a film. My life has been like something out of a film recently, but in my case it was *Fatal Attraction*. The last secret girlfriend actually stood outside my house crying, with a rock in her hand. And Simon told me she had a Fortnum and Mason hamper in the back of the car too. Which was very weird because it was half past three in the morning, so why would anyone need a Piccadilly Vegan Picnic for Two at that hour? And why did he feel the need to tell me anyway? Simon said she was confused and had got the wrong idea. He went out to talk to her and try and calm her down. Then he came in to get *her* a cup of tea. Can you believe it? And like a muppet I let him. Then all of a sudden I had a horrible Damascene vision of what the rest of my life with him was going to be like, so while he was out there I packed his bags and slung them out onto the pavement. Then I double-locked the front door. And I threw his Moroccan Neroli shaving oil out of the bathroom window and it smashed on the drive. The last I saw of him, he was getting into *her* car.'

I put an arm around Susie's shoulders.

'His loss,' I said.

'I was such a fool,' Susie said, shaking her head so her hair fell over her face. 'Never again. He tried to tell me she was just a friend going through a bad time, but then he kept on ringing me and texting me, trying to make it all my fault as usual, so I blocked his number on my phone and I haven't heard from him for quite a while now. Perhaps he's got the hint?'

'No dating sites for you then?'

Susie rolled her eyes. 'I am never going to talk to a man again. Unless I have to. And only in an emergency. Is Alex really still in your granny flat? I would have thought he would have moved out by now?'

I sighed. 'He's on the hunt for a place, now the divorce is almost finalised. Their house should be sold by the end of the month and then the financial settlement will come through. I don't know what all the delays have been. It seems to have taken forever.'

'Perhaps he's too comfortable where he is?' Susie said with a knowing look. 'Did you ever get that wine stain out of the stair carpet? Now then, I'm going to freshen up and then change into something a bit more glamorous. Just in case I do meet Joan Collins or Johnny Depp in the bar. And don't forget, Paulo has invited us to join him for drinks in the garden at six o'clock.'

Ah, yes. This was the time when we would chat and exchange pleasantries and not think about that time when we had been good friends. When we might have been more.

Back then, I had watched him and Ellen, their relationship growing stronger and more exclusive until it had been no real surprise when she had come in one day flashing an excited smile and a gigantic sapphire engagement ring that had apparently been a family heirloom.

We'd had a party that evening, and I had wrestled with being happy for them and despairing that my life would never be like that. I would always be making the wrong choices, allowing myself to be pushed around, and looking back, I'd been right.

5

After I had finished unpacking and put all my things away in the enormous baroque wardrobe, I changed into some new grey linen trousers and a white shirt, which back home had looked quite chic. I wasn't sure they did here.

I fussed about in front of the mirror and turned the collar of the shirt up, to try and look more like Jane Fonda did in the skincare adverts when she was trying to hide her perfectly acceptable jawline and neck, and then turned it down again because it just looked as though I had got dressed in a hurry. I added a chunky glass necklace and then took it off because it looked what it was – something I had found in a charity shop for three pounds. Then I put it back on again.

I peered at myself. I looked different here. Perhaps it was the light that was so clear and bright. It certainly was doing my wrinkles no favours. Where did they spring from all of a sudden?

I put on some makeup. And found a lipstick. And a small handbag I'd discovered at the bottom of my wardrobe. I'd last used it years ago at an evening wedding party and Greg had said it was 'a bit much', but here it seemed perfectly okay to go out with a scarlet bag decorated with a sequinned butterfly and some coloured feathers.

As I got older, I was beginning to see the appeal of handbags. Unlike shoes (I was sure my feet had been spreading) or clothes (sizes always unreliable), a handbag always fitted and never got too small. And that was somehow very reassuring.

I looked at my nails. I'd had a manicure, and for once they looked okay. Instead of being rather grimy from time spent in the garden, they were coloured a rather sexy crimson to match my toenails. They were the nails of a woman who was going out for drinks in the garden on Capri and was staying in a beautiful hotel with her friend. Not someone who didn't usually give her appearance much consideration. This could be something I did on a regular basis from now on. After all, if I didn't care what I looked like, why should anyone else? No wonder women like me were ignored or not even seen at all.

Manicures were another thing I was beginning to see the value of. The rest of me might be gradually looking older, but with minimal financial outlay, my nails looked okay. They could be the nails of a much younger woman actually if I held my hands out in a particular way to hide the age spots. Nails didn't wrinkle or sag like some bits of me were doing. Interesting.

Then I straightened my shoulders and stood up properly instead of slouching as I often did, taking a last look in the mirror to check. Much better.

There was a knock on my balcony door. It was Susie, looking very sophisticated in strappy sandals and a delightful cream cotton dress patterned with lavender wisteria, which made the most of her bosom.

'I couldn't decide between striped capri pants in honour of the location, or this dress. I was feeling in an Audrey Hepburn mood.'

'You have the figure for it,' I said. 'When I wear capri pants, I always look like I've been paddling. Or I'm standing in a ditch.'

Susie laughed and went to check her reflection in the mirror. Her hair was glossy and shining and pinned up into a messy chignon. The now permanently evicted Simon would have been kicking himself if he had seen her.

'It's a pity you decided to foreswear off men,' I said, 'because you look sensational.'

Susie blushed and fiddled with her straw bag, pulling out a pair of oversized sunglasses.

'Oh, you,' she said with a little smile, 'don't be daft. No one's going to notice me.'

I watched her preening in front of the mirror for a moment and wished that I could be more like her. More confident, sure of herself despite all the years when Simon had tried and failed to control her. Perhaps the effect was wearing off quite fast. She had such energy, and a poise that was very endearing, just as she had when we were younger. Could I do that too? Discard all the negative feelings I'd had about myself for so long, and believe in myself again?

We went down the marble staircase and out into the gardens below our rooms. Through a stone archway and some luxuriant swags of yet more bougainvillea, we found a small gathering of people clustered around a long table covered with a white cloth, where waiters were serving drinks.

'Ah, there you are!'

It was Paulo looking very elegant in a dashing Panama hat with a striped band. I felt a silly little thrill of excitement. On other men it might have looked as though he was umpiring a cricket match, but yet again, here things looked very different.

'At some point I must introduce you all to the family,' he said, 'at least the ones who are here. Firstly, let's find you some Prosecco.'

He held up a hand and instantly a waiter brought a tray of drinks. The place seemed to run like clockwork; it was very impressive.

How could he be so relaxed at meeting up again? Had he forgotten everything? Or had he really just forgotten all about me, the feelings I thought we had shared all those years ago?

It felt horrible to realise that, yes, he probably had. That he hadn't given me a second thought for decades, while I remembered him in so many ways. His birthday, the way he could throw on any clothes and still look stylish, the sound of him singing in the kitchen, his unwavering support for Inter Milan football club.

At that moment I wondered if he remembered anything about me at all.

'And now come with me. My son and his wife and my grandson are here somewhere, but for now I must take you to say hello to my mother and stepfather,' he said, and he gave a funny little grimace. 'Do you remember her? And please don't take too much notice of what she says. She can be a little outspoken these days.'

In the possible comments for 'how to put guests at their ease', this didn't work at all, but obediently we followed him through another stone archway to a little pergola where an elderly but very elegant woman was sitting in a comfortable-looking chair, holding court to a group of young people.

She looked up as we approached.

'Paulo, *eccoti finalmente.*'

'She said "There you are at last",' Susie murmured.

I caught my breath. Ah, yes, I did remember her. This woman might have been my mother-in-law if things had worked out differently. I had met her at Paulo and Ellen's wedding, a rather intimidating but striking figure in a blue outfit, loaded down with jewellery. Next to her sat an elderly man in a dark blue blazer and cream trousers with a sunhat tilted over his eyes, who looked like he might have been in the middle of a nap.

The group of young things parted respectfully, and Paulo bent to kiss his mother's cheek.

'Mamma, *questi sono gli amici de Ellen*. Do you remember Jo and Susie? These are Ellen's oldest friends. From England.'

'It might be true but I'm not sure I like the use of the word "oldest",' I murmured.

Paulo darted a look at me and laughed. 'Okay. Some of Ellen's dearest friends.'

Susie giggled and stifled it with a cough.

We shuffled towards her rather nervously, although at least we did resist the temptation to push each other forwards. It felt almost as though we were meeting royalty. Or our old headmistress. Should we curtsey? It almost felt appropriate.

For heaven's sake, we were mature women in our sixties, not timid schoolgirls.

'My mother, Contessa Carolina,' he said, 'and this is my stepfather Conte Frederico di Genovese.'

The elderly man woke up with a start and looked around him, rather confused.

'I wasn't asleep, I was just resting my eyes,' he said, and then he stood up, took off his hat and bowed charmingly over our hands.

'Please call me Freddy,' he said.

'A pleasure to meet you, Freddy, and happy birthday, Contessa,' I said, and I handed over the birthday card and the gift we had bought.

Susie and I had debated long and hard about this. What did you give a wealthy woman for her eighty-fifth birthday? We had no idea of her taste, her colour preferences or indeed her health. Perhaps the glamorous box of Charbonnel et Walker truffles, striped and tied with a satin ribbon, would be acceptable. We had stuck to the classic milk chocolate version; personally, I think there are far too many sea salt and caramel versions of things. All older women liked straightforward chocolate, didn't they? Or perhaps our gift would be the one thing that would send the Contessa into a diabetic coma and then we would get the blame.

Freddy perked up at this and held out a hand.

'Shall I look after those for you, *mia cara*?'

The Contessa dipped her chin and gave him a glance that said no, and he shrugged good-naturedly. Then she looked up at us imperiously with dark, curious eyes and watched us for a few long seconds.

I remembered that look from years ago. She would have been a good interrogator for the FBI. No one would have been able to stand up to her for long. And then unexpectedly she smiled, and her face softened into beauty again.

'Thank you. These are my favourite. You may call me Ceci,' she said. 'All these birthdays and titles are nonsense these days, unless we want tickets to the opera, or a free flight upgrade. Which we often have in the past, haven't we, Freddy? But not so much these days, now I am old and *decrepito*.'

Frederico flapped a hand towards her in disagreement, and to be fair, Ceci didn't look decrepit to me. I did some rapid mental maths. Paulo was my age, so Ceci must be in her eighties. What had he said in that message? Eighty-five? She didn't look it. She sat ramrod straight in her chair, still beautiful, with fine brown eyes and thick silvery hair swept up into an elegant chignon, and Frederico watched her with eyes that clearly adored her.

She waved a hand, weighed down with a massive emerald ring, towards us, beckoning us forwards to sit next to her.

'You must tell us all about yourselves,' she said. 'I am sure I must have met you at Paulo's wedding, but that was so long ago, and I am *smemorata* – forgetful.'

'That's nonsense,' Paulo said. 'Your mind is still as sharp as ever.'

'If I choose,' she said with a wicked smile.

Now that we had passed the initial scrutiny, I was beginning to warm to her. She might have been portraying herself as an old woman who needed her husband to fuss over the cushions behind her or worry about freshening up her drink, but I had the feeling there was far more to Ceci than that.

'Ellen spoke of you often,' she said. 'She was very fond of both of you and your times together. Am I saying this correctly? My English is not good. Freddy is far more fluent than I am. He speaks four languages.'

'Your English is excellent,' I said, 'and Ellen was a good friend to us. We had fun over the years and saw each other through some difficult times too.'

'Fun,' Ceci said mournfully, her gaze drifting off to the horizon, 'there is not enough fun these days. People are so angry, so busy with being offended. It tires me. You know the best weapon? Laughter. Laughter and tiramisu make everything better.'

I nodded then because I couldn't argue with that, and then Ceci looked at Paulo hopefully and raised her eyebrows.

He took the hint. '*Sì*, Mamma, I will fetch you both some tiramisu.'

'Not for Freddy, he has had some already and I am keeping an eye on his diet.'

'You're not as much fun as you used to be,' Freddy grumbled.

'You may be able to speak four languages, but you can't say no in any of them,' Ceci said.

She rewarded Paulo with a lovely smile, and he wandered off, ducking through the archway, the fronds of bougainvillea brushing his broad shoulders.

'*Bene allora*, tell us about yourselves, it might keep my husband from dozing,' Ceci said. She pointed at Susie. 'You are Susie. I met you more recently, didn't I? I think you are the one who travelled? I remember Ellen told me when you came here before. But I was only visiting too. I was living in Rome with my second husband. Never mind, *è stato un errore* – he was a mistake.'

Susie nodded. 'Yes, I did visit, but not for many years. I was making the same sort of *errore* too.'

'*Chi non fa non falla* – if you don't make mistakes, you make nothing,' Ceci said, 'and now we can laugh about it, can't we?'

She patted Freddy's hand affectionately and he smiled back at her.

'Nearly,' Susie said doubtfully, 'once I get the stink of Simon's shaving oil off my driveway. I threw the bottle after him when he left.'

'And you are Joanna. Ah, yes, I remember you,' Ceci said. 'I believe you were the one who caused the most trouble.'

'No, I was the one who was caught,' I replied, wondering how much she knew about me, 'because I was the oldest, people assumed I was the ringleader.'

Ceci chuckled approvingly and then waved a commanding hand at the young people, and they obediently moved away and started flicking their hair and taking selfies. Then she motioned us to sit down.

'Young people,' she sighed, 'look at them. They all think they are so different, but they are all the same really. They wear the same clothes; they pull the same foolish expressions when they take pictures of themselves. And why do they do that? Do they really believe that this magnificent view over the Bay of Naples is improved if they stand in front of it pouting? Last year one of my god daughters visited the Taj Mahal, but you can hardly see it. She and her girlfriends were standing in front of it, all with the same silly eyebrows and inflated lips. Giulietta is the prettiest girl, but she said she needed "starter surgery". Have you ever heard anything so ridiculous?'

'In which case I probably need finisher surgery,' I said.

'Giulietta has her father's nose, that is the problem,' Freddy said. 'It would take a lot of work to sort that out.'

Ceci laughed. 'You are mean, Freddy.'

'Well, it looks all right on him. Perhaps she will grow into it?' Freddy muttered.

Paulo returned with a little plate of tiramisu and a lace-edged napkin. Freddy's eyes followed it sadly as it was placed on the table in front of her.

'I need another drink,' Ceci said, holding out her empty glass towards him. She looked around the table and then added, 'Never mind that, bring us a bottle.'

'I thought you insisted you were staying for only one drink and then leaving?' he said, raising one eyebrow.

'Freddy and I have found amusing company,' Ceci said.

'I'm delighted to hear it,' he said. 'That means I can leave you both to enjoy yourself. I have things to see to.'

She took a spoonful of tiramisu and closed her eyes with pleasure as she tasted it.

'My doctor would be cross to see me eating this,

but at my age, who cares? This is almost as good as the one my mother used to make. One night when I was about seven, she caught me going downstairs in the dark for more, and I told her it wasn't my fault. I heard voices, and it was the tiramisu calling to me. She said it was strange how the tomatoes and the onions didn't call to me too.'

'It's calling to me too, *mia cara*,' Freddy said sadly. 'Why do I have to listen to my doctor, but you don't?'

We sat there in the dappled shade chatting and drinking some very fine wine, which was nothing like the rather acidic Prosecco I had been expecting.

Ceci was very chatty and, as time passed and the rosé went down, delightfully indiscreet.

'I was first married at nineteen to a man who fell in love with my feet,' she said, 'and the rest of me was *assolutamente bellissima* – beautiful at that age. I have the photographs to prove it. I must show you one day. He hardly noticed. I had a wonderful figure, a high proud bosom, a tiny little waist, but it was my feet he loved. He liked to paint my toenails purple, and then he could stare at them for hours, which didn't leave much time for anything else. We divorced when Paulo was five. Luigi had found a dancer in Paris with higher arches than mine. He wouldn't be so happy if he could see my feet now.

They have spread out like a duck's. I am sure if you threw me in a pond I would be able to paddle to the side in no time. My second husband was a gambler. I married him for passion. He married me for my money.'

I wondered how her current husband was taking all this, but he looked quite happy.

Paulo returned with an ice bucket and a new bottle of wine, which he opened with practised skill, and topped up our glasses.

'Mamma, are you boring these ladies with your stories?'

'Not at all,' I said.

'We are enjoying every moment,' Susie said, shading her eyes and looking out at the matchless views of the Mediterranean.

Paulo looked down at me then, a polite smile on his face, and there was suddenly an unexpected silence. The noise from the people behind us seemed to fade, and it was as though just for a split second, everyone stopped moving. It was just as it had been all those years ago.

I think if I had been in possession of a Geiger counter, it would have registered something. But I wasn't sure what it was. I was probably out of practise at recognising those moments. But there was definitely something. But then again, perhaps it was just me, and Paulo was wondering why I was looking so glassy-eyed.

'And my third husband, dear Freddy…'

'Mamma, you are a terror,' Paulo said, turning back to her. 'I'm sure Ellen's friends don't want to hear this.'

'You're joking,' I said, 'we absolutely do!'

Paulo chuckled and went off back to his other guests. I watched him, perhaps for longer than was strictly necessary. The years had changed him, of course, but I could suddenly remember him so well. How he laughed, how he always walked quickly as though he didn't want to be late for something, his ability to look as though he was having important thoughts, when in fact he was probably thinking about football.

Ceci sighed. 'I met Frederico in Monte Carlo. We had such fun, didn't we? Back then he played the piano and I would sing. I had the voice of an angel, didn't I, darling? We used to sing all the old songs. And we used to throw parties where one day would melt into another. Do you remember that wonderful time just after you had retired, when we went to Aix, and met up with all your old colleagues?'

Freddy looked thoughtful. 'I remember fragments. Something about trying to balance on two champagne bottles. Now then, we have this excellent wine, let's have a toast. To your birthday, my darling, and to Ellen, who we still miss.'

We clinked our glasses together and I took a sip. The new wine was icy cold and refreshing.

'And you, Jo. Do you have a husband?' Freddy asked.

'Not any more,' I said.

Ceci widened her eyes at me and held out a hand, rotating it slowly, encouraging me to elaborate.

'He had an affair with his secretary, and at one point he promised to end it if I would take him back, but I realised that I didn't much like him any more,' I said, feeling that my marital history was far less interesting than hers.

'*Bene*,' Ceci said. 'I didn't really like my first two husbands. I do like this one though. And when the first passions cool, that's the most important part.'

Freddy smiled happily and blew her a kiss across the table.

I thought about this. Yes, I supposed she was right. Every marriage went through difficult bits. The disagreements about the children, what colour to paint the bedroom. As I remembered, Greg and I had one of our worst arguments about that. How ridiculous.

If I was honest, the passion in our marriage had faded after about two years, and we had been married for over thirty. That was a bit sad. Particularly as when I looked at him in the cold light of day, it was true – I didn't actually like him much at all.

Ceci wagged a finger at me.

'You are thinking about that, aren't you? I can tell.'

'I didn't like Simon either,' Susie said, 'but he was so charming and handsome and very good in – well, never mind that. I forgave him for a lot.'

Ceci leaned back in her chair and stretched out her arms in front of her. A diamond bracelet flashed on one wrist. A tiny watch sparkled on the other. And I remembered the sapphire engagement ring Paulo had given to Ellen, 'a family heirloom'. Perhaps it had been one of hers?

'*Meglio soli che male compagnati* – better to be alone than in bad company. At my age there is nothing worse than being bored, and Freddy makes sure I am not, don't you, darling? If I was as young as you, or even ten years younger, I would want to have an adventure, but I have only recently had my cataracts done, and I am not supposed to do anything interesting.'

Freddy patted her hand. 'When you are properly recovered, we will go to Las Vegas, and you can gamble, and I can stay up all night and watch the showgirls.'

'That's a terrible idea on so many levels, and you hardly keep awake until dinner these days,' Ceci said.

I had a think for a moment while Freddy sneakily topped up our glasses again. It looked as though the bottle was nearly empty.

I couldn't come up with anything that someone as vibrant as Ceci might consider an adventure but one that didn't involve – what were people supposed to avoid after a cataract operation – bending over or weightlifting?

'Perhaps we should go shopping,' I said.

Ceci pulled a face, and her mouth turned down.

'I am done with shopping. I have too many clothes already...'

'You are right,' Freddy murmured.

'...things that remind me of the past, that hold so many memories. New fashions don't hold the same appeal to me now. Colours are so dull, *tessuti sintetici* – synthetic fabrics are so ugly. Perhaps I have lived long enough. I have done the things I wanted to do, seen all the places, been in love often enough. What is there left to do?'

'Have fun?' I said. 'My mother always said that when she got old she was just going to get into mischief. And I didn't really know what she meant, but just recently, I have been thinking I may well do the same.'

Ceci's face brightened. 'Yes. I like the sound of that.'

She finished her Prosecco, looked at the empty glass and put it down on the table with a grimace.

'I shouldn't drink this, *mi rende scontrosa.*'

Susie murmured, 'She says it makes her grumpy.'

'It's a bit late to tell us that now,' I muttered back.

'So, what will you do while you are here?' Ceci said. 'The event is the day after tomorrow. Ellen said it was not to be a sad occasion. She wanted a small funeral, and then a time later on, when people could remember her with joy, not tears. *Non sarà così* – it will *not* be like that for me. When I go I want the whole island to be there, lining the streets as my coffin passes, weeping and wailing and telling each other how wonderful I was. Everyone will wear black and there will be white flowers filling every balcony and vase. I've written it in my will.'

'I expect that will be quite an event,' I said.

Ceci smiled and leaned forward to pat my hand.

'Oh, you must come,' she said, 'you'll enjoy it. I've been to so many funerals and they are *sono insoddi-facenti* – unsatisfactory. These days there is far too much reserve, too much bravery when someone dies. We need to mourn properly and then the grief is gone, leaving only the memories.'

'Please don't die any time soon,' I said, 'just so we can come to another party.'

Ceci threw back her head and laughed, and her diamond earrings sparkled in the sunshine.

'I am in my eighties. How much longer do you think I have? Now then, back to now. What were we talking about?'

'What are the arrangements for the event?' Susie asked.

'You'll have to ask Paulo. I can't remember,' Ceci said, scraping up the last of her tiramisu, while Freddy watched her with the sad eyes of a spaniel. 'But I do know there is going to be a lunch and then just an informal gathering in the evening. I do not stay up late any longer. I need all the beauty sleep I can get. You must wear your best, most glamorous, most colourful outfits, if only to please me.'

Susie and I looked at each other, obviously

thinking the same thing. After a lot of phone calls and discussion, we had both packed something smart: black dresses and jackets. Dark tights and sensible shoes. Nothing glamorous or colourful.

'I'm not sure...' Susie said.

'I have a dark dress,' I added. 'It does have sleeves. I don't think I will need the jacket in this heat.'

Ceci picked up her empty glass, looked at it and put it down again.

'Well, *ovviamente* – obviously you can't come like that,' she said at last, with a nod towards our outfits.

I thought we looked okay, actually. Quite presentable.

'Oh, I don't know, darling, they look charming to me,' Freddy said kindly.

'Freddy, every woman over twenty-one looks charming to you,' Ceci said, rolling her eyes.

'But none as beautiful as my wife,' he responded gallantly.

'What sort of thing did you have in mind?' I said. 'Perhaps we should go shopping.'

I said this quickly, trying not to remember that we had not seen any shops other than high end designer boutiques and famous labels as we drove through the town. I didn't think my budget would stretch to those unless they were prepared to sell me a glossy carrier bag.

'I'm sure something can be arranged. For young women like you, it's much easier. It's the shoes I have trouble with. Back then I could dance all night in stilettos. These days, I wear them only to sit down in. Freddy calls them my barstool shoes. In an ideal world I would be carried from my car in a litter. *Sono stanco adesso,* I'm tired. I will go to my rooms now,' Ceci said.

She stood up and tapped Freddy on the shoulder as he looked as though he was nodding off again, and then as he reached behind his chair for his walking stick, she waved a hand to catch the attention of a silver-haired, very distinguished-looking man who was standing a little way away, talking to another dark-haired chap who could have been, but probably wasn't, a Mafia Don.

'Raimondo. To me if you please.'

Raimondo put his glass down and offered Ceci his arm.

'Raimondo is my—' She looked up at him. 'What are you? I can't remember.'

'*Sono il tuo figlioccio* – your godson,' he replied with a charming smile. 'Your favourite godson.'

Ceci made a dismissive noise. 'He can't be my

favourite until he gets married again. It's ten years since his wife died. A man shouldn't be on his own. No one should. I don't know what Freddy would have done if I hadn't found him.'

'I would have thrown myself into a ditch and died of despair,' Freddy said dramatically.

'Yes, you probably would.'

Ceci tottered away, Freddy a few paces behind her, and then turned just before she went back under the archway.

'You may call on me tomorrow morning. At ten thirty. No, at eleven o'clock. I will see you then.'

'Flipping heck,' I said as we watched her slow progress, 'I feel like I've had an audience with the Queen. Or Bette Davis.'

Susie gasped. 'Oooh, I saw that only recently. *Whatever Happened to Baby Jane*. She was terrifying. Ceci doesn't look like that. She's rather gorgeous, isn't she?'

'I bet she was an absolute beauty in her youth,' I said. 'I'd love to see the photographs.'

Susie chuckled. 'Can you imagine Simon's reaction if I'd tried that with him? *Simon, to me, if you please.* He would have thought I'd lost my mind.'

Another waiter appeared with a silver platter filled with gorgeous-looking little treats.

'Compliments of Signor de Massimo,' he said, sliding it onto the table.

'What a way to live,' Susie said. 'I could get used to this. And what is it about Italian men? They are so incredibly attractive. Raimondo, for a start. What a hunk. You don't see many men like that in Somerset.'

'And from the way he looked at you, the feeling was mutual,' I said.

'Oh, don't be silly,' Susie said, blushing a little.

Suddenly a small boy came cannoning through the archway and skidded to a halt at our table.

'I'm hungry,' he said accusingly, a distinctive Texan drawl in his voice.

He was a lovely looking child, decked out in a Ralph Lauren shirt and shorts, but his expression was dark with anger. From my years of experience dealing with primary school children, I knew he was on the edge of a full-blown tantrum, something I had always wanted to avoid, and still did.

'Would you like something from here?' I said, trying to deflect him.

Actually, I didn't think there was much on the table that would appeal to a child. Kids seemed to have a whole new segment of the food industry devoted to them – cartoon characters and crazy shapes and packaging. Headache-inducing television ads and wild colours. I'd often wondered why they couldn't be encouraged to eat actual food? Oh well, perhaps it was just me who thought like that.

He looked at my plate, picked up a miniature blini topped with smoked salmon and shoved it into his mouth. After a moment he spat it out into his hands, wiping the cream cheese onto his shirt and throwing me an accusing look.

'What's that? And where's Andrea?' he said.

'I don't know. Is she your mummy?'

The boy evidently found this so funny that he laughed, doubling up so his head almost touched his knees.

'No, she's not my *mommy*. Andrea is my nanny.'

'Lucky Andrea,' Susie murmured.

I picked up a paper napkin and tried to wipe his hands with it, marvelling not for the first time how a small child's fingers could be so bendy.

A harassed-looking woman, who I recognised from the reception desk earlier, hurried towards us.

'There you are,' she said, her voice heavily accented. 'Where have you been? So sorry, ladies.'

'I was looking for fries,' the boy said, his lower lip trembling, 'and she gave me weird stuff to eat.'

Andrea looked at me with horror in her eyes, as

though I was a clear and present danger to her charge and she wanted to call the police.

'Come with me. Mommy is worried about you.'

He narrowed his eyes. 'Am I allowed fries as a treat if I do?'

Andrea took his hand, let go with an expression of disgust, pulled out a pack of wet wipes from her pocket and cleaned his hands properly before leading him away, murmuring in what I think was Spanish to encourage him.

'Well, he's a little charmer,' Susie said.

Seconds later the boy was back, flinging himself onto my lap where he buried his face in my neck. Andrea appeared a few moments later.

'You must come with me. You shouldn't talk to strangers. And Mommy will want you to change into clean clothes.'

'I don't want to,' he said.

Andrea threw me an anguished look.

'Do you have something special to wear?' I said.

The boy looked up at me, his huge brown eyes suddenly filled with the sort of tragic despair small children can project one minute, usually followed by unrelenting joy the next.

'I expect you are going to look quite the little

gentleman,' I added, 'and that shirt has cream cheese all over it.'

And come to think of it, so did I now.

He gave an enormous sniff and wiped his nose on the back of his hand.

'I'm looking forward to seeing you again later when you are all cleaned up,' I said, wiping a smudge of cream cheese off my face, wondering if I could peel his arms from around my neck without him throwing another tantrum. 'Now then, go along with Andrea like a good boy, quick as you can, and do as she says.'

Without a word, he slithered off my lap and onto the ground and wandered off, Andrea hurrying after him.

'Not lost it then?' Susie said. 'Those headmistressy tones still work.'

6

That evening after I had changed into a smart dress, Paulo led us to a wonderful table in the restaurant, where the matchless view over the bay of Naples was equally as delicious as the meal we were served.

He pulled out a chair between me and Susie and joined us.

'I should be in a hundred different places,' he said. 'There is always someone calling me away to sort something out, but I thought it would be more enjoyable to take the opportunity to talk to you all.'

'Marvellous,' Susie said. 'Everything on our journey here went like clockwork. And the island is just as beautiful as I remembered.'

Paulo gave a pleased smile. 'It is. Sometimes I

forget, or perhaps I take it for granted. Nowhere else has quite so much charm. So much of my family history is here. I hoped my mother and stepfather would join us this evening, but she is tired, and they will be eating in their rooms.'

'She's a fabulous character,' I said.

Paulo nodded. 'She is. I hope she didn't shock you. I think she likes to elaborate her stories.'

'Freddy seems a really lovely man too,' Susie said. 'Very distinguished with that silver hair.'

'He is,' Paulo said. 'It took some time, but in the end she found the right person to keep her happy.'

'I can't wait to chat with her again,' I said. 'She's an inspiration.'

At that moment there was a small commotion at the doors and the familiar sight of the same small boy from earlier, barrelling towards us. Or rather towards me. I braced myself for the onslaught.

He skidded to a halt in front of me and held out his arms for my approval.

His new outfit was probably the most impractical one any child had ever had. A white shirt with a little logo on the pocket in gold thread and white shorts. Even his trainers were spotlessly white. What was his mother thinking? At that age my children had been in T-shirts and jeans, and nearly always covered in mud or food.

'I'm so pleased to see you again. You look very handsome,' I said, 'and now you are the smartest boy in here.'

Actually, he was the only boy in the room; the rest of the tables were filled with hotel guests, all of whom were well dressed, and about our age.

Behind Paulo I saw a glamorous couple gliding into the restaurant, a tall handsome man who somehow looked familiar, and a beautiful blonde woman who was so tall and slim she was practically two dimensional.

Paulo stood up.

'Ah, there they are. Now then, may I introduce my son Leonardo, who I don't think you have seen since he was quite small. He has been working in Texas for the last twelve years, and this is his wife Raleigh, who is from Atlanta, Georgia,' he said. 'And you have met their son Eric already.'

Of course, Leo. I had known they'd had a son; I'd met him once, when he was about ten. Ellen had mentioned him in her letters and emails over the years. Sent pictures of him graduating from school, from university. How he had moved to America and found a new life there. How much she had missed him. Her delight when he had married Raleigh. Her hopes for grandchildren, which had seemed to be coming true.

So, Eric was the much longed for grandson, but had Ellen ever known the boy? Had he been born before she had died or afterwards? It wasn't the sort of question to ask, but I suddenly felt immensely sorry for her, that she had possibly never actually seen him except maybe in photographs.

We all stood up and were properly introduced while Eric stood at my side, tugging at my sleeve.

'Eric, darlin',' Raleigh drawled in an accent rich with shades of *Gone with the Wind* and the Deep South, 'don't do that. Come and sit by me and Poppa.'

Eric didn't answer but plonked himself on the chair next to mine, his mouth a grim line of determination.

'Looks like you made a fan,' Leonardo said, who sounded like an American but looked just like his father at the same age. He had the same dark eyes, the same height and build, the same easy manner. It almost took my breath away. 'Don't you want to come over here, buddy?'

'I wanna sit here, Poppa,' Eric replied.

'I'd be delighted,' I said quickly, before he could

cause any trouble, and I pushed his chair in towards the table, effectively trapping Eric there, his chin just over the level of the cloth. His eyes fixed on the glass jar of breadsticks in the middle of the table.

'Well, if it's no trouble,' Raleigh drawled, looking more than a little relieved. Evidently Andrea was having the night off. I hoped she had a comfortable chair in her room and a decent glass of wine to keep her company.

After the introductions and small talk was over we all sat down, and I gave Eric a breadstick, while glasses of water and wine were poured.

'I want soda,' Eric piped up.

He didn't make a request; it was more a demand, and it was all I could do not to say something.

'Now, you know what you learned about that,' Raleigh said, who had chosen to sit opposite me. 'You were talking about cola in school only the other day. What did you learn about cola, Eric?'

Eric thought hard.

'The Houston police use it to clean blood off the road after an accident?'

Raleigh looked shaken. 'No, that may be true but that's not what I meant.'

'If you won't let me be a cowboy I'm going to be a policeman,' Eric said. 'I'd like to do that.'

'I don't think—'

Mercifully, Raleigh was interrupted by waiters bringing us the first course, which were some tiny bruschetta, laden with miniature tomatoes, slivers of mozzarella cheese and a drizzle of balsamic glaze.

Eric, swinging his legs under the table, scraped off the toppings and ate the bread.

'What's your favourite food?' I asked him.

'Candy,' he said. 'M&Ms.'

'Yes, I like those too,' I said, and Eric smiled.

'I'm not allowed the blue ones.'

'We always take the blue ones out, darlin', don't we? We don't want a repeat of last Thanksgivin',' Raleigh breathed and favoured me with a slightly raised eyebrow. 'It was like havin' dannilburn in the house.'

We tutted and nodded together while I tried to work out what she had said. She then went on to mention The Alamo – not in conjunction with car hire but with reference to a site of historical importance. By a process of elimination, I realised she was talking about e-numbers and Daniel Boone the famous frontiersman, and I looked at Eric with new respect.

'I love your necklace,' she said, eyeing my charity shop bargain. 'Is it Murano glass?'

Doubtful, I thought.

'From a vintage shop back home,' I said at last, which seemed to satisfy her.

We then had crab claws the size of bicycle spokes arranged on a platter with lemon wedges and aioli followed by salad in frosty glass bowls with chilled forks.

Raleigh picked daintily at the meal, keeping up a thoroughly entertaining and censored stream of scandalous gossip, which was spoiled a little because I didn't know any of the people she was 'dissing'.

Someone called Clarke had run off with the pool guy and someone else called Jelly – although in retrospect it might have been Julie – was suspected of another 'enhancement'. Following some subtle pointing to her own nose, I guessed this was code for cosmetic surgery.

Raleigh looked at me thoughtfully for a moment and leaned towards me, tapping her upper lip with a manicured nail.

'I've discovered a wonderful lady back home. She specialises in threading.'

I covered my impending moustache with my napkin and wondered what it would be like to be one of those women who were constantly tweaking and titivating themselves, unlike me who thought applying body lotion after the occasional bath was a bit out there.

Raleigh then filled me in on her latest purchases from the mall where she liked to go with her friends, as the remains of the hapless crustaceans were cleared away and Eric lay on his stomach across his chair and pretended to be swimming.

Eric, his appetite blunted by breadsticks, picked at his meal with no great enthusiasm, having wrapped his napkin around his fork as he said it was too cold, pretended to sword fight with a crab claw and dabbed at his fantastically beautiful salad with a pout of dissatisfaction.

Lamb medallions arrived shortly afterwards – a mini work of art with the beans artistically arranged into a tiny log cabin. Eric demolished these with a sweep of his fork and asked for fries.

I wondered if his parents ever admonished him or tried to instil good manners into him. It seemed not.

Dessert was more fresh fruit cut into fantastic shapes as though a sushi artist had been let loose in the kitchen. Eric wandered off at this point to stare at some of the other guests.

'Hey, buddy, don't leave the table, come back and join us!' Leonardo called.

'We're not saying "No" at the moment,' Raleigh confided quietly. 'It's a new thing we're trying. It's called No No Parenting. It seems to be working.'

Oh really? Did she think so?

Leonardo looked up from his dessert and exchanged an eye roll with his father.

'We want Eric to find his own boundaries,' Raleigh continued with a confidence I thought was misplaced. So would she if she could have seen Eric behind her crawling under someone else's table.

'What if his boundaries aren't the same as yours?' I asked, unable to keep silent any longer. 'What if he wants to set fire to the curtains or smoke a pipe?'

Raleigh gave me a patient look and moved her fruit slices around her plate.

'He wouldn't because of mutual respect,' she said.

'Well, I'd prefer he get it sorted sooner rather than later,' Leonardo muttered rather testily, pulling the cheese platter a little closer. 'I'm not sure it's working.'

Eric came to sit down again and watched, mesmerised, as his father cut him some thin slices of cheese.

'Now, we all know little boys and girls who are

good get treats,' Raleigh said, bending towards Eric, who ignored her as he put about half a pound of butter on a bread roll and made a cheese and strawberry sandwich.

After Eric had messed about a bit more, ignored his grandfather's attempts to distract him by making animals out of his napkin, dropped some cheese on the floor and cleaned his knife on the tablecloth, he began to whine. A quick call from Leonardo's cell phone produced nanny Andrea from her room upstairs and she shepherded her grumbling charge away.

'So now then, you were going to tell me how the Hutchinson deal is going,' Paulo said to his son.

Leonardo began to elaborate on a brief earlier conversation regarding oil reserves in Arizona while Raleigh went back to more salacious gossip now Eric was out of the way. Someone called Kitten and a black-tie event where the waiters were topless and 'ver', ver', accommodatin' indeed.'

'It did cause quite a fluster, but they raised ninety thousand dollars for St Xavier's,' Raleigh said. 'It's the pre-school where Eric has been going. I've been helping with a lot of fundraising. It takes up a lot of my time.'

My mouth dropped open. When I'd been a headteacher we had thought ourselves lucky to raise a few hundred pounds for the school every year. What on earth did they need that for, and how on earth did they prise ninety thousand dollars from the parents?

'Ninety thousand dollars? What does his pre-school need? A private jet?'

Raleigh looked blank and then twirled the stem of her water glass rather pointedly.

'We want them to become the well-rounded citizens of tomorrow.'

'Yes, I'm sure they will be.'

I thought back again, remembering the stationery and little extras our fundraising had bought. What sort of life did they live? I couldn't imagine it.

Eric's return at speed to the dining room at that point, was followed a few seconds later by some shrieks of anger and a torrent of Spanish from his nanny.

'What on earth is the matter?' Paulo said.

Raleigh flapped a casual hand. 'Oh, he's just over excited.'

'In that case he's been over excited for about two years,' Leonardo said waspishly.

'Now, honey, you know what we said.'

Eric deposited a handful of rather sticky M&Ms

in front of me across the table. He'd obviously got some from somewhere.

'They are for you,' he said. 'You said you liked them.'

'How very kind,' I said, scooping them up. 'I'll have them later.'

Eric beamed at me and banged his hands down on the table, leaving smudges of chocolate and food colouring.

'Don't react,' Raleigh hissed.

So much to my disappointment, no one did.

Andrea let loose another anguished flood of Spanish.

'*Lo siento mucho, el esta peor que nunca, nose que le esta pasando y me tiene muy afligida. Ya he tratado pero el no lo nota. Que debo hacer? Soy una mujer.*'

And then she took Eric away. He turned at the door and waved at me and I waved back.

'What did she say?' I said.

Raleigh flapped a hand.

'Oh, nothing important. Something to do with it getting late. She's Spanish. She gets emotional over the smallest things.'

'Actually, she's from Venezuela. And she said she doesn't know what to do with him. So how long is this No No stuff going on?' Leonardo said, reaching for the wine. 'And why?'

Raleigh gave a patient sigh. 'No is a negatory word and we want Eric to be positive, don't we? I'm going to say yes as much as possible to him.'

'I don't mind trying that too, honey,' Leonardo muttered and took a bite of his cheese.

Raleigh didn't respond. Irony, sarcasm and humour seemed to pass her by unobserved.

She smiled, showing perfect teeth. 'I keep meaning to ask. I love the idea of spending one Christmas in Englandland? What's it like?'

I thought back to Englandland and conjured up a completely inaccurate but very pleasing picture for her of snow, sparkling winters, chestnuts roasting by an open fire, hot chocolate and, of course, rosy-cheeked carol singers at the front door.

'So you have Santa and presents and all?'

'Yes, and the true meaning of Christmas too. Happy Christmas, not Happy Holidays. The Nativity, the three kings, that side of things.'

Raleigh smiled. 'Yes, it's real handy the way it's all sorted at the same time, isn't it?'

I tried to get my head round the thought processes behind this and failed.

And was Christmas really like that? Probably not

if I was honest. What would it take to change things as far as that was concerned? To stop it being a mad, labour-intensive slog, which I was not sure anyone really appreciated. When people sat at the table with their phones next to them to see what other people were doing.

Just once I would have liked to have that picture-perfect event, with snow and sleigh bells and everyone being happy. A handful of glitter spread over my day, like an old-fashioned card with candles and lights and an advent calendar with pictures inside, not chocolate.

A new resolve grew inside me. That was something else that was going to change. This year I would switch off the Wi-Fi and confiscate everyone's phones as they came into the house. And we would do things properly and actually talk to each other and to me. Perhaps this would be my version of No No parenting.

7

Now that the first meeting was over, I began to feel rather more settled. I tried to sort out my feelings. My reservations and worries had obviously been for nothing. Paulo and I had known each other many years ago, which for a short while had been one of friendship and occasionally brotherly teasing on his part at least. Well, most of the time. But then we had parted, and he had found a life and happiness with Ellen. That left us then in the category of old friends, and nothing more. Perhaps that was the way to look at it.

And such a long time had passed. Perhaps I was the only one who remembered the feelings of that first evening? And the night of the party? Memories tugged at the back of my mind and I pushed them away with considerable determination.

But why could I remember parts of it in such piercing and embarrassing detail when at the same time I found it hard to even remember Greg's face? And we had been married for decades.

We sat there for a long time as the evening outside darkened into night. Through the window we could see the lights of a few fishing boats, and further out the flashier display of a cruise ship. We drank our wine and finished our meals and then at Paulo's insistence we moved into a little sitting area, where the comfortable armchairs were placed beneath open windows, and the scent of the sea wafted in on the evening breeze and mingled with the delicious aroma of the coffee which magically appeared.

'In England it will probably be raining,' I said, 'and the central heating would be on. It's nothing like this.'

'I have just bought a heated blanket,' Susie added. 'My circulation has got so bad, my feet are always cold.'

This continued into a discussion about English winters, and Raleigh countered with tales of tornados and thunderstorms and flash floodings in Texas, punctuated by the nailing heat of summer and the panic when the air conditioning had broken down the previous year.

'It does get colder here in the winter months,' Paulo said, 'and last February it snowed. For half an hour. It caused a lot of excitement. Not like in England. I remember one winter when I was a student; everything shut down, the roads were blocked, and the trains didn't run.'

'I remember that too,' I said. 'That was an awful winter.'

'Yes,' Susie said, 'do you remember, we found an old wooden pallet in the garden shed and broke it up for kindling.'

He nodded. 'Ah, yes, of course. There was frost on the inside of the windows. The only warm place was all of us huddled up in front of that fire under a blanket.'

He smiled and sent me a twinkling look. I felt my face flush with embarrassment, and I ducked my head towards my wine.

He did remember some of it after all. And so did I.

We had all worn coats and hats in the kitchen, where the single glazing and the warped door frame let in the cold. Paulo had bought a huge blue and grey checked blanket from a charity shop to spread over us all in the evening as we watched black and white films in front of the fire, delaying the moment when we would have to go to our cold bedrooms.

His hair had been longer then, and dark, almost black. I had brushed it out of his eyes, telling him he needed a haircut, and he had laughed at me... I could even remember the warmth of our bodies under that blanket.

I looked away then, feeling very uncomfortable.

Stop it.

I had been a bit crazy back then; I could see it now. Leaving home for the first time, the unexpected freedoms and opportunities. During my first year I had started to drink too much to hide my insecurity and party all night to prove to myself how many friends I had. Nothing had seemed to really matter. Life had been a long, careless, unending journey to be filled with excitement and fun.

Then the shock when the following September he and Ellen had appeared, brought in by friends of friends, and moved into the attic room under the eaves of the roof. Together.

We had lived in a chaotic, noisy house which backed onto a railway line where the trains thundered through our lives so regularly that in the end we didn't notice them.

People came and went, and sometimes we only knew because there was different food in the communal fridge with people's name written on it, or some new trainers at the bottom of the stairs to fall over. Ellen was different; she was calm and organised. She'd turned their drab room into a haven of colour and comfort. With her serenity and her kindness and her character, which was so much better than mine had been back then. No wonder Paulo had found peace with her, had been attracted to her. No wonder he had chosen her, fallen in love and married her.

I didn't react when I found them together, cooking in the kitchen, Ellen standing behind him with her arms around his waist, her cheek against his back, looking across at me with a slightly challenging, proud stare.

And yes, I had been horribly jealous. My own subsequent boyfriends who drifted into my life and then left just didn't compare on any level with Paulo. He was an unattainable, wonderful man who treated me like an occasionally irritating sister. Nothing more, and I had learned to live with it.

We had all gone to their summer wedding in Devon where there had been a barn decorated with wildflowers and hay bales. Susie and I had thrown a party for her the week before, with cheap sparkling wine and paper bunting I had made from old magazines; that's how well I had dealt with it.

At the evening reception I had wanted to find someone to partner off with. It had felt wrong to be alone, and I met Greg, who was a friend of someone's friend, and he had seemed like a safe haven. Which in the end, of course, he wasn't.

My parents loved him. He was a financial advisor, doing well and about to start his own firm. My father had urged me to marry him.

You're not getting any younger, and he seems a decent sort.

And so, I had.

'It's lovely here,' I said, forcing myself back from those far off days. 'I wish I had come back here before now.'

'I wish you had too,' Paulo said. 'Ellen talked about you a great deal in her last months.'

'She was due to come over to stay with me, and then she said something had come up and she would rearrange everything. She never told me what. I would have visited her, if I had known she was so ill,' I said.

Paulo shook his head. 'She didn't want that, for people to fuss, to see her so fragile.'

'I'm so sorry,' I said. 'It must have been difficult.'

Paulo nodded. 'She was only unwell for a short time. And she died very peacefully. But yes, it was a very sad few weeks.'

Raleigh, on the other side of our group, was talking about a Chinese therapist she had been seeing and complaining how bad the teas he provided tasted.

'But I'm sure it's doing me good,' she said at last. 'My inner tranquillity and sense of self is recovering. My inner child is blossoming again.'

Strange, I thought, looking at her, that someone so young and beautiful could have problems with her sense of self, whatever that was. Maybe I had the same sort of issues, but I doubted they would be cured by any herbal tea. I'd tried some rooibos and strawberry once and it had not improved my tranquillity at all. In fact, I'd had a bar of chocolate afterwards to take the taste away.

Did I have an inner child too? It was more likely I had an inner old cat, who was a bit antisocial, didn't like being cold and wet, liked going to bed early and occasionally hissed at things.

'Your grandson Eric is quite a character,' I said.

Paulo sighed. 'Children these days are different, aren't they? Constantly praised and rewarded for the smallest things. I'm not sure it's a good thing, but it's not my place to interfere. Do you have grand-children?'

'Two granddaughters, Violet who is four and Maud who is three.'

'So, we are both grandparents. *Mio Dio*. Where did the years go?' he said, shaking his head.

'I have no idea. One minute I am young, and life is a game, the next I am an old woman—'

I stopped, feeling awkward. I knew I was an old woman – one glance in the mirror every morning confirmed that – but perhaps I should have had enough pride to avoid voicing it.

Paulo laughed quietly.

'You haven't changed at all, Joanna,' he said, 'not to me.'

It was the first time since we had met up again that he had said my name properly, and a tingle went down my spine.

It sounded just the same as it had in the old days. Somehow different from the way anyone else said it. Softer, warmer and unmistakeable. I had wondered about this, how no one else in the world said my name as he did.

This was the moment when normally my nerves would get the better of me and I would allow myself to spout a lot of jumpy nonsense. I would say something self-deprecating and crass, pointing out my grey hair and wrinkles. The way my neck had started to sag, the beginnings of bingo wings which meant I never wore sleeveless tops, and T-shirts had to have proper length sleeves. I had often wished the person who invented cap sleeves could be put up against a wall and pelted with tomatoes.

Instead, just for once I didn't. If he wanted to remember me as a twenty something, then I wouldn't argue.

I looked across at him.

'Nor have you,' I said, and just in that moment I realised it was true.

Of course I could see the change in him, but at the same time, very oddly, he was exactly as I remembered him. Tall, broad shouldered, dark haired, and handsome. Yes, he had filled out and his hair had gone grey – he wasn't a young man, after all – but his kindness and his humour were still there behind his dark eyes.

For a moment I felt quite emotional.

I had never felt the same way about any other man as I had about him. Had it just been because we had been so young and unsophisticated? But as I got to know him, I had really liked him; that was the thing. He was a decent person, funny and thought-ful. I had been too immature to realise it at the time, but there weren't many like him.

* * *

At last, the evening drew to a close and we all made moves to go to bed. And then on the way out into the hallway, Raimondo appeared and made a subtle but definite beeline for Susie. They exchanged a few words, and he kissed her hand very elegantly before inviting us both back to the bar for a nightcap.

I might have been in my sixties and unable to remember to put the bins out on the right day, but I still knew how not to be a gooseberry.

I made my excuses and made my way to the staircase, watching over the edge of the bannisters as Susie hauled herself up onto a cream leather barstool and Raimondo presented her with the drinks menu.

'Goodness me, I think your friend has an admir-er,' Raleigh said cheerfully from behind me.

'Well, let's hope he's not like her last one. That man was so bad for her.'

'And I know you and my father-in-law are old

friends?' she added. 'I could see you were having a lovely chat.'

'Nothing particular,' I said. 'We were just talking about Ellen.'

And I think it would be very bad form to make any attempts to flirt with the widower just before an event to remember his wife.

'I'm sad to say I didn't get to know her very well. I only found out I was expecting Eric a few weeks before she died. She was so excited at the thought of being a grandmother. But then she was ill and died before Eric was born. Such a tragedy. Paulo said she wanted this event to be a celebration, not a memorial,' Raleigh said, 'but if you and my father-in-law are old friends, I hope you have photographs of the old days you can show us?'

Old days?

'Oh, not with me, maybe there are a few somewhere,' I said, trying to sound disinterested.

There had been photographs, of course there had, lots of them, but eventually I had thrown them away. Actual printed pictures from a roll of camera film, collected from a shop, showing moments when we had been in the same group, when our smiles had mirrored each other's.

These days pictures could be taken in an instant

and deleted with the swipe of a finger. Perhaps most of them were never looked at again. Not like the time when we had stored photographs in albums and actually studied them, showed them to other people. Searched for a face, an instant, an expression, a meaning.

It had been a significant moment when, a couple of years after I had married and we had been moving house, I had thrown those photographs onto a garden bonfire, the broadness of Paulo's smile the last thing to disappear as the flames curled around the picture, and I'd supressed a moment of panic, wanting just one last regretful look. If only I could remove my memories quite so easily.

* * *

When I got back upstairs, panting slightly because I was quite full from the meal, and let's be honest, not used to quite so many stairs, my room was a haven of cream and gold, lit then by tastefully placed lamps. The bed had been turned down and there were bottles of spring water and a golden box of Gianduiotto chocolates on the bedside table. I felt quite the film star as I pulled on my M&S nightie. Maybe I should have brought something rather more glamorous?

And some feathered mules, although the one time I had tried them I had fallen off them and hit my head on the bedside table.

I was tired but I didn't want to miss anything of this wonderful place, so I got back out of bed and padded barefoot out onto the balcony. Susie's room was still in darkness so I assumed she was still downstairs with Raimondo, flirting and being charming as only she knew how.

Outside, the night was dark, just a few lights showing from further along the coast and the ships out at sea. There was hardly a sound. It was very unlike life at home, where the buses passed the end of my road, car horns sounded at odd hours and the village schoolchildren stuffed empty crisp packets into my hedge on their way home. What must it be like to live here?

I took a deep breath and closed my eyes. There was a certain undeniable magic there. No wonder it had been a favourite of some of the Roman emperors, although from what I knew, they hadn't exactly covered themselves in glory with their behaviour. Hadn't one of them pushed his enemies and some of his unsatisfactory slaves over the soaring cliffs? I really should find out.

I got back into bed and sent some photos and an

email to Alex, Jessie and Kat so they could see what a lovely place this was. And then I sent Juliette a photo of Paulo, taken when he was laughing at something Leo had said, and then I turned off the lamp.

Much to my surprise, because he wasn't the sort to be communicative, Alex replied almost immediately with a text, asking if there was any washing up liquid in my kitchen as he had run out. And did I mind if he had a friend over to stay the night as they'd both had a few drinks. As it was by then past ten o'clock in England, I thought it might be a bit late to ask. I replied telling him where to find my cleaning supplies and repeating my insistence that no one use my bedroom. I had a smiley face emoji by return which didn't exactly reassure me.

At first it was completely dark. Then my eyes grew accustomed to the dim light from the lights from the garden below. And I wondered again what Susie was up to.

She always had been a bit of a flirt, bright and interesting, and had attracted a lot of male attention over the years until more recently when Simon had gradually squashed her spirits and made her doubt herself. Perhaps this was a new beginning for her, now that she had finally got rid of him.

She hadn't had the same assault on her figure

that most women have from pregnancy and chil-drearing. She was as trim as ever, a striking woman, intelligent and well-travelled. Why wouldn't any man find her attractive?

Women of our age might not have the supple-ness and taut skin of women like Raleigh, but we... what was it? We knew *things*. Important things about life and other people. We might not be young any more, but we still had value. I liked the thought of that. But did the broadness of our experiences count as much these days as a size six figure and thousands of followers on social media?

And then I thought about Paulo.

After a few minutes, I stopped myself. Raking over the past was not a good idea. Paulo had invited us here for Ellen and Ceci and that was all. I would not allow myself to travel back in my memory and, even worse, to wonder what might have been.

A ping from my phone woke me just as I was drifting into sleep. It was from Juliette.

> That's him??? Good grief, what a looker!!!!! I bet you still fancy him something rotten!! Send me more tomorrow. X

8

The next morning, I woke at seven o'clock feeling rested and much calmer than I had expected.

Since Greg and I divorced I had found it hard to find any sort of peace of mind to allow me to sleep properly. I suppose in the middle of those wakeful hours I had rehashed all his lies, the deceit and the disappointment so many times without ever finding satisfaction.

The same questions over and over again – why did he do it? And had he actually found happiness? And worst of all, was it somehow, as he had suggested, all my fault?

I honestly thought over the years I had done my best to support him and take on all the domestic tasks he refused to do, but whatever it was he wanted, it wasn't me. I could still remember that bitter insult he had thrown at me the last time I had seen him: *You're fifty eight, face up to it, no one else is going to want you.* Was that true?

And yet that night I had slept better than I had for years. I would not waste any more time thinking about my failures. There was a whole day ahead of me, a new day filled with new experiences. I would not just deal with mundane domestic chores, perhaps go to the supermarket to buy dull things. We were going to see the Contessa at eleven, and I had the feeling that if she said eleven o'clock, she meant it.

Meanwhile there was breakfast to think about, and what was I going to wear? I had bought a few new things in honour of the occasion, and I had deliberately left behind all the things I usually packed.

The safe, navy blue trousers, several washed out shirts and sweaters, all rivals in dreary predictability, and some dreadful shoes with (utter shame) Velcro fastenings, had all been dumped in the clothing recycling bin at the supermarket and instead I had splashed out on some maxi dresses and pastel trainers, which I saw were all the rage in the fashion magazines at my hairdressers. I might be past middle age, but that didn't mean I had to dress like an old woman.

In the end after several false starts, I chose a smart pair of dark trousers and teamed it with a blue and white striped shirt and a bright blue sweater, which I tied around my neck. These choices were so unlike me, and I spent several minutes preening in front of the mirror, wondering why I didn't dress like this at home. Why was I still keeping new underwear and clothes 'for best'? What was the point of that?

Perhaps it was the weather here that made me feel so light hearted and optimistic, the sunshine and the clear air, plus of course the wonderful feeling of being on holiday and having few responsibilities.

Downstairs I discovered breakfast set out in the dining room and it was a splendid-looking buffet, with helpful handwritten labels, jugs of chilled fruit juice and artistically arranged ham and cheese platters. Outside, the sea sparkled and shone in the morning sunshine. The sky was forget-me-not blue and cloudless. It was perfection.

Susie was already there, sitting at a table by the window drinking coffee.

'Oooh, hello. Sleep okay?' she said. 'I was out like a light the moment I got into bed and didn't stir until seven thirty. Perhaps it was because Simon wasn't driving the pigs to market next to me. Thank heavens I don't have to put up with that any longer.'

I laughed. 'Separate bedrooms, that's all the rage these days.'

Susie wrinkled her nose. 'I don't think I would like that. But I'll give that some thought. Although as I said, I have absolutely no intention of ever speaking to a man ever again.'

'Apart from Raimondo?'

'That doesn't count. And I'm sure I didn't say that. I was just being polite to a fellow guest.'

'And do you intend being polite to him again?'

Susie blushed. 'Stop making something out of nothing. Have you seen the buffet? I thought I would wait until you came down before I attacked it.'

'Come on, I'm hungry,' I said, 'and how did your evening with Raimondo pan out? You definitely said you weren't going to talk to a man again, except in an emergency.'

'Don't be silly, and it's none of your business,' Susie said firmly, 'but I can see some fabulous pastries over there.'

There was fresh fruit, teas, and coffee. Bread and rolls of all sorts, including sweet Italian bread labelled *maritozzi*. Golden, glazed croissants, or as we were in Italy they were more properly called *cornetti,* some plain and others filled with custard or chocolate. Thin pastries filled with ricotta called *sfogliatelle.* Baskets of almond biscotti to dunk in our coffee, slices of a majestic panettone studded with candied fruits, a tray of *bomboloni,* doughnuts filled with whipped cream. Little tarts, or *pasticciotto,* filled with lemon custard. The choice was impossible.

'There's about nine million calories on this table,' Susie said as we stood clutching plates in front of the display, dithering. 'How do we decide?'

'Let's just go for the naughtiest-looking ones. We are on holiday, so the calories don't count, and I bet the coffee is fantastic.'

Choices made, we returned to our table.

'This is such a treat,' I said, slicing into a *bomboloni.* 'I must say, this beats a full English every time, or toast and Marmite which is what I usually have. I wonder what Alex is doing?'

'Forget about him, I'm sure he will cope without you for a week,' Susie said.

'Probably, and I did tell him not to have any parties while I was away. Although he did have a friend from work staying last night.'

'New girlfriend?'

I poured some coffee and took an appreciative sip.

'He didn't actually say. I'm sure it will be fine. And I can't do anything about it after all.'

'Of course it will. So what are we doing today?' Susie asked.

'Going to see the Contessa at eleven. And then I have no idea. Perhaps for once we don't need to do anything? No one to worry about, no one to entertain. We could even sit in the garden and read. An actual book. I haven't done that for ages.'

'I read a lot these days,' Susie said. 'There's nothing on television except reality shows and endless repeats and politicians shouting at each other.'

'Perhaps we could just sit and think,' I said. 'I haven't done much of that either. And sometimes I need to think more. About important things – what next, life and everything.'

'No, nor have I,' Susie said, looking pensive.

Yes, at the beginning I had entertained endless theoretical arguments I would have with Greg if our paths had ever crossed since he had left me. Which they hadn't. I'd formed all sorts of withering put-downs and accusations ready for the eventuality. But that morning I realised it made things a lot more pleasant to just forget about him. Life was so much simpler without him, and quieter without his end-less complaints about the council or the neighbours.

But in the past I had been lonely. There was no disputing that. And I had at least got into the habit of daily activity, but never really doing much different. Just doing what my mother would have called keeping body and soul together.

'Are you really not going to tell me about Rai-mondo? I'm terribly curious.'

'I can't think why, nothing happened. He's very charming and a good listener, which isn't something one finds very often in a man these days. Raimondo and I had a brandy and a nice chat and then I went to bed. On my own, before you get any funny ideas.'

'That's disappointing,' I said. 'I thought you and he had a definite, you know, connection.'

Susie pushed her wayward hair out of her eyes.

'Well, we did, but I'm not that sort of girl. I might see him later on today, and of course at the celebra-tion lunch tomorrow. Or I might not.'

I made a childish *oooh* noise and Susie clicked her tongue.

'I could just ask you the same question about Paulo,' she said. 'All those lingering glances and meaningful silences. What's going on there, if we are talking about connections?'

'You're imagining it,' I said. 'Lots of water under lots of bridges. There's nothing to tell. We are just old friends.'

Susie took a sip of coffee and put the cup down in the saucer, and then she leaned a little way towards me.

'I remember the night of that party. I. Don't. Believe. You.'

For a moment I wondered if she was right, and I couldn't help myself; I was pleased. But also a bit rattled.

* * *

At ten to eleven we went to ask the receptionist where we might find the Contessa.

'We have been invited to her rooms,' I said proudly. 'We're just not sure where to go.'

'Please, let me help you,' said a voice behind us, and there was Paulo, looking ridiculously handsome in a white shirt and dark jeans. My heart gave a little unexpected flutter of excitement.

Had he looked that elegant when I knew him all those years ago? I didn't think he owned a suit. Or a tie. And yet there had been something about him that was inherently stylish.

And then there it was, that moment, the one I had tried so hard to forget over the following months and perhaps even years. Maybe it was the white shirt; he had been wearing one that night. His tanned neck rising so perfectly out of the unbuttoned collar.

It was the second term after Paulo and Ellen had moved into our house. A bleak, cold Saturday in January when we had used Paulo's birthday as an excuse for a fancy-dress party. I'd gone as Bo Peep in a blue linen dress and lace shirt. I'd had a toy lamb under one arm and a shepherd's crook made out of a broom handle and a wire coat hanger. Paulo had dressed as a gangster in a pinstriped suit, his hair slicked back and a terrible fake moustache he'd bought from the joke shop. The memory of that evening was one that suddenly seared through me like a blade.

We had been sitting next to each other on the battered sofa, where one of the legs had fallen off and been propped up by a pile of textbooks by the previous tenants. Everyone had drunk quite a bit by that stage; we certainly had.

'You look marvellous as a gangster. Happy Birthday,' I'd said, and I had reached across and flung my arms around Paulo and I'd kissed him.

I hadn't intended it, but suddenly that kiss had turned into something more. There was an unmistakeable and momentary magic between us in that moment, and I believed, I knew – he had felt it too. His arms had gone around me after a second, and nothing in that room had mattered as much to me as the feeling of his hands in my hair.

And as we parted, we had stared into each other's eyes. Neither of us seemed able to breathe properly; the noise from the party had faded away and then I had looked over his shoulder to see Ellen, frozen in the doorway from the kitchen. Her face, normally so serene and composed, had been a picture of anger and disbelief.

She had mouthed something at me. *Don't you dare.*

And then the moment was broken when we realised Paulo's fake moustache had fallen off and landed on my cleavage, and he had laughed. I had laughed. And mercifully after a moment everyone joined in. All except the young man who was supposed to be my boyfriend at the time. I couldn't even remember his name.

He just looked at me, utter disgust on his face, snarled some insults in my direction and then he had grabbed his coat and left, slamming the front door behind him.

What have you been doing? How did that moustache get there? What a funny thing to happen. People laughed some more.

I looked again and Ellen had left the room as well. Moments later, Paulo went after her. I'd had another drink then from the punch bowl. Heaven knows what was in it, but it didn't dull the utter despair I felt that evening.

* * *

I met up with him in the kitchen the following morning, both of us in need of coffee and an Alka Selzer.

'I'm sorry about last night,' I said, just as he spoke.

'Joanna...'

'Is Ellen very angry?'

'Ellen is never angry.'

I tipped a load of foil cartons into the bin liner and started clearing the table, which was littered with empty bottles and the remains of a messy birthday cake.

Paulo took hold of my wrist and we looked at each other.

'Why didn't you ring me? After that night?'

'I lost your address,' I said miserably.

'I looked for you.'

'I looked for you, but I never saw you until that day you turned up with Ellen.'

We stood in silence for a few minutes, both of us thinking.

'Joanna, Jo, do you want me to—'

I interrupted him, terrified of what he might say. Was he going to offer to end their relationship? Tell her he had feelings for me?

I felt bad enough about what had happened; I didn't want to make it any worse. And I had a pounding headache that meant I could hardly think straight.

'I don't want you to do anything. Ellen's lovely.'

'She is,' he agreed. 'I don't want to hurt her. But you and I...'

'Then don't,' I said, pulling away, 'don't hurt either of us. I couldn't bear it. Forget it. I just want things to go back to how they were. For Ellen to forgive me.'

Had she ever forgiven me? Perhaps it was a case of keeping one's friends close and one's enemies closer. She never mentioned it again and nor did I. But I remembered it.

Had I been right not to listen to what he wanted to say, to find out what he thought? Had I turned my back on something that could have been so important?

The toy lamb had been found weeks later under the sofa, the moustache stuck to its face.

* * *

I took a deep breath and steadied myself against the wall for a moment, a bright smile plastered on my face.

We followed Paulo down a long corridor and he knocked on a door at the end. After a moment he went in, beckoning us to follow him.

'*Sei pronto*. You are prompt,' Ceci said with approval. 'I like that.'

She was sitting by the open window, elegant in a silk dress, a cashmere wrap around her shoulders.

'Come in. I have ordered coffee; it should be here in a moment. Freddy has gone off for his morning walk. Paulo, you can leave us. Yes, off you go. If you see Freddy loitering by the kitchens, hoping for treats, you have my permission to shoo him away.'

Coffee? What I needed was a strong drink. Something like bourbon or Polish vodka, although I disliked the taste of both of them. I imagined myself for a moment, propped against a dark bar somewhere, downing a shot, wincing as the alcohol burned its way down.

'My hairdresser will be arriving soon, but for now, come and sit down, tell me about yourselves. I never get the chance to find out about young people these days, and my hearing is poor, so when I am in company like yesterday I prefer to talk about myself. Then I don't have to listen.'

Young people? It was a long time since we had been referred to as that. It made me feel unreasonably pleased.

'We are loving being here,' I said, 'it's absolutely beautiful. The only thing that could make things better would be if Ellen was here with us too.'

Ceci nodded, looking thoughtful.

'She was an extraordinary woman. So calm and always so composed. Nothing seemed to upset her, which in a family like ours was strange. When I was younger there was always someone arguing about something. The house was filled with the noise of me and my sisters fighting. When I was bored as a child I used to pick fights with the two of them just for the fun of it. And so did they. We still do. Ellen would leave the room if people argued, if she thought the atmosphere was difficult.'

Yes, I remembered that aspect of her character only too well.

'But what are you hoping to do while you are here?'

'Just meet Ellen's Italian family and friends. And relax I suppose and enjoy the scenery. There is something about overlooking the sea that is so wonderful and restful.'

'I must warn you, my younger sisters Sylvia and Lucia will be arriving sometime today,' Ceci said, and she gave me a look. 'That will be interesting. There is nothing restful about them, I can assure you.'

'How do you mean?' I asked.

'Sylvia is *una donna molto anziani* – a very old woman,' Ceci replied after some thought. 'You will see.'

'Brave of her to make the trip then,' Susie said, 'if she's that old.'

Ceci snorted. 'She is three years younger than I am. But every time I see her, in her head she is an invalid. Always fussing and complaining. Wanting attention. Too hot, too cold. Feel my hands. Do I look pale. Where are my pills, my medication. No way to be. There is a cliff not far from here, *Salto di Tiberio,* where the Emperor Tiberius threw his enemies off, so that their bodies were smashed on the rocks below. After five minutes Sylvia makes me feel like that. I must take her up there one day. She is also colour blind. She will be wearing turquoise, although she thinks it is orange, I can guarantee it. It's bad enough losing my youth, I refuse to accept old age as she has. Not yet anyway. You must keep her away from me, in case she depresses me.'

'We will do our best,' I said. 'What about Lucia?'

'Now, Lucia was the baby of the family and she was always very silly. She still is. You will see. It will take her perhaps five minutes to throw a tantrum about something, and she's seventy-eight and should know better.'

Susie and I exchanged a delighted look. This sounded very promising indeed.

A waiter came in with a tray of coffee at that point, which he settled on the sideboard.

'Leave it, Mario. We can manage,' Ceci said, and he left with a little bow at the door.

The next few minutes were taken up with serving the coffee and remarking on its wonderful taste.

At last, Ceci patted my hand. '*Eccelente*. Now then, what to wear tomorrow. I would like your opinion. Although I may ignore it. I have a choice.'

She stood up with none of the usual effort of accompanying noises that many older people make and led us towards her bedroom where several very flamboyant cocktail dresses were hanging from the picture rail on padded coat hangers.

'Wow, these are lovely, so bright and vibrant,' Susie said, reaching out to touch them. 'This beading is wonderful.'

'I refuse to wear black. It drains all the colour from my face, and I look like an old crow,' Ceci said. 'I am much more myself in bright things, pretty things. They lift my spirits and my soul. People wear too much black and call it fashion. Chanel had a lot to answer for. It's lazy. Black is for mourning and death. And pretending one is svelte when one only has to look properly in the mirror, preferably side on, to see one isn't.'

'This red cocktail dress is gorgeous,' Susie said.

'Valentino,' Ceci said with a wistful sigh. 'I wore that to a party in Rome where I met the Conte. He loved that colour, but I don't wear it now. I just like to look at it. It's a work of art. I was very poor when I bought it.'

'I don't think you can have been,' I murmured.

'Poor in money but not in spirit,' Ceci said firmly.

Thinking about it, there wasn't much spirit displayed in my choice of clothes. Even with my new purchases; they were pretty safe. I was never going to sashay into a party and catch the attention of a titled nobleman.

'You should wear it tomorrow,' Ceci said, her face brightening, 'that would be fun.'

Susie gasped. 'I couldn't possibly, it must be worth a fortune. It should be in a museum somewhere.'

Ceci snorted. 'So should I. But that's foolish. And I think it would suit you. You are not fat like so many women these days.'

We all stood up a bit straighter then and pulled in our stomachs. That was something else about Ceci: her posture. Not slumped over as we often were. I would try to do something similar from now on. I was aware that I had adopted a rather round-shouldered look recently. Was this because my muscles were slack or because I was old and lazy? Probably the latter.

There was a timid knock at the door to Ceci's apartment and she motioned me to open it as I was closest. It was a small worried-looking woman in a floral overall, whose face tensed up at the sight of Ceci holding court to guests.

'*Signora, posso tornare se non è conveniente?*'

She was clutching a canvas holdall, which she held defensively in front of her.

'Nonsense, Gina, it is perfectly convenient,' Ceci said, 'and as I am now in the mood to have some fun, I have *una sfida* – a challenge for you.'

The woman looked even more worried at that point, and well she might.

9

We finished our coffee soon after that and I went back to my room to have a look through my wardrobe for suitable degrees of glamour that Ceci might find acceptable.

Susie, meanwhile, was held back by a crooked finger and a knowing nod from the Contessa, which brooked no disagreement.

'You will see,' was all she said. 'I know what I am doing and so does Gina. *Ci divertiremo,* such fun. You can go now, Jo, yes now, and I will see you later.'

Mystified, I obeyed and went back to my room to rummage unsuccessfully through my clothes, realising that new shirts, dresses and trousers from chain stores in the high street were no match for Valentino originals.

I sat down on my bed, suddenly remembering a dress I had bought for one of Greg's work parties, just after we got married, in Schiaparelli pink. Greg had taken one look, smothered a laugh and made me return it to the shop. I'd really liked it too. Why had I done that?

Still, I did have a sparkly skirt I had seen and coveted for months in Jigsaw. But I hadn't bought it until it was in the sale. How typical of me. And I had a top that could go with it, although I would have to push the sleeves up as they were a bit long. If I just turned up in my black outfit, Ceci would have given me one of her looks.

What did she want Susie for, I wondered? What sort of fun was she planning? Perhaps she wanted to dish the dirt on Raimondo? Warn her off because he was another of the caddish sorts to which Susie seemed to be attracted. Maybe he had a mistress in a penthouse flat somewhere in Naples that he thought Ceci didn't know about. And he was keeping it quiet in case she wrote him out of her will.

But I had to be honest, he was very handsome. There was something about a lot of Italian men that was very attractive. I always did have a bit of a soft spot for Robert de Niro. And Al Pacino. And John Travolta. It's something about the eyes.

Perhaps Ceci was persuading Susie to try that dress, and Susie was resisting because she didn't have decent underwear on, and she was trying to make excuses so she could go back to her room and find her Spanx?

Don't be daft. Why would she buy shapewear? She certainly didn't need them.

And why were some women trying to make their bottoms look smaller, and the other half trying to make them look bigger? Life could be very confusing sometimes.

Having decided what I would wear, I realised I was hungry. It would have been nice to have a car; well, a theoretical car, because there was no way I was driving on those narrow roads, and then I could go out somewhere and find a café or a wine bar. Instead, I would have to stay in the hotel, which of course was no hardship.

And I was sure someone could rustle me up a couple of sandwiches if I asked.

* * *

I made my way to the garden terrace and a few guests were already there, murmuring and chuckling and drinking chilled white wine and eating elegant little lunches. It looked like just the sort of place I wanted to be. Out in the clear air but shaded under a cream canvas canopy from the sun.

To one side outside the open kitchen doors, a little girl was playing with a skipping rope with painted wooden handles. The hotel cat was taking a siesta in the dusty shade of a lemon tree.

A waiter came to take my order; I explained I was waiting for Susie and – unwilling to leave me with nothing – he brought me a carafe of iced water to be going on with.

I sat fiddling with my phone for a few minutes, wondering how long Susie was going to be, and then I wished I had something to read. Even at my age I felt slightly uncomfortable, firstly because I was alone, and secondly I was doing absolutely nothing.

Perhaps I could understand why my mother had always taken her knitting bag along with her. My abiding memory of her was her hands being busy. Mending, sewing, darning socks. I mean, who even darns socks these days? Even at my age, our generation of women seemed to have an underlying inability to do nothing, to be seen – by someone – as idle. Even if I was watching television, I would usually be doing something else at the same time. Ironing or scrolling through my phone or making a shopping list.

I glanced around. There were a couple of middle-aged men sitting on their own just looking at the view. They didn't seem at all bothered. Maybe they were captains of industry who felt they deserved a break and were taking one?

Perhaps it really was just women who felt they needed to be occupied all the time? And what did we do now? Checked our emails or messages. Watched television while dusting it or sorting out the messy drawer in the sideboard. And who put all those things in there in the first place because they couldn't be bothered to actually put away all those cables and useful gadgets?

I once pondered if all the Christmas presents children bought for their fathers over the years ended up dumped in drawers like that around the world. The sets of Allen keys, the handy magnifying glass on a keyring, the perpetual brass calendar that always broke. Novelty coasters and executive desk toys.

Just as I was wondering if I could have a glass of wine, a woman came and stood next to me, and I looked up, doing a double take at the sight of her. It was Susie, but I hardly recognised her.

In all the years I had known her, Susie had always had a mane of untameable hair which had been a constant source of anguish to her.

Now she stood in front of me, looking pleased but also slightly embarrassed. Her hair had been cut into a short bob just below chin level and her tousled curls were framing her face in a way I had never seen.

'Good grief!' I said, almost dropping my water glass in shock. 'What did she do to you?'

Susie ran her fingers through her hair nervously.

'She insisted. As soon as you left the room, that woman, Gina, had a long discussion with Ceci, and then she pushed me into a chair, wrapped a robe around me and before I knew what was happening, she had got her shears out and they were flashing around my ears like Edward Scissorhands. I didn't dare move. What do you think?'

'You look marvellous,' I said, 'absolutely amazing. I don't know why you didn't do that years ago.'

'I was too chicken,' Susie said. 'It seemed easier just to tie it back out of the way. But now, I think I love it. My head feels so much lighter.'

'You look about ten years younger too,' I said,

'absolutely glorious. I think you deserve a drink to get over the shock. I think we both do.'

Seeing me looking round, the waiter hurried over and in moments had brought us two large glasses of chilled Pinot Grigio.

Susie and I chinked our glasses in a toast of celebration and then she gave an embarrassed giggle.

'Actually, I just saw Raimondo in the bar. He said I look *stupenda,* and he has invited me out for a drive and a late lunch on the other side of the island. Near Marina Piccolo. Do you mind if I go?'

'What, now?'

Susie nodded and took a big gulp of her wine. 'Dutch courage,' she said. 'It's a long time since I've been out with someone new.'

I felt a bit disappointed at the thought of being left on my own again. She had said we were going to spend lots of time together on this trip, but she looked so excited and happy that I didn't have the heart to say so.

'So this never talking to a man again isn't really working out for you, is it?' I said with a grin.

Susie shrugged and pulled a funny face.

'Oh, you know.'

I insisted that I didn't mind one bit and also made some rather pointed remarks about her not being out too late and behaving herself. And then she took another quick sip of her wine, grabbed her handbag and hurried off again.

I didn't think I had seen her looking that animated for a very long time. And I really was pleased for her.

But should I have given the dashing Raimondo a stern warning before they left? Perhaps I should have got him alone behind the bins, holding him up against the wall by his lapels and threatened him with a damn good thrashing if he upset her?

I watched her retreating back for a few moments. And then I carried on looking at the place when I had last seen her, rather thoughtfully. How exciting. And how marvellous that she at last had someone to take her mind of Simon who had successfully gaslighted her for so long.

I half wished it was me, rushing off for a date with a dashing man, but then, thinking about it, the whole thing, even the prospect of it, was so exhausting.

I thought about what it would take to get to know a new man – exploring their character, waiting to see if they had any unpleasant habits. Did they understand about laundry baskets or was the floor an equally suitable alternative? Did they pay their bills on time or, like Greg, hide them unopened in the vegetable rack? What side of the bed did they sleep on? What was that song? *How do you like your eggs in the morning?* I really didn't think I had the energy. And did I really need that anyway?

'I am sure she is more than capable of looking after herself,' I muttered under my breath.

But then, was she? Susie had waited hand, foot and finger on Simon. She even used to organise his car servicing and top up his washer fluid, and if that wasn't a reasonable thing to expect a man to do for himself, I didn't know what was.

'Madam?'

It was the waiter back again, his young face anguished, probably at the thought of me sitting there without any food.

What did I want? Well, actually I was getting hungry so I ordered a caprese salad, with bright basil leaves, succulent tomatoes and slices of wonderfully fresh mozzarella. The whole thing was garnished with a balsamic drizzle and chunks of focaccia bread in a little basket.

So now I wasn't just a woman sitting alone in public, I was also eating alone. This wasn't something I had done for a very long time. But should that matter? Who had even noticed me; an older, grey-haired woman was someone that was easy to miss. And suddenly I didn't want to feel like that.

Who cared what other people thought? I had taught thousands of children to read and write and add up. I'd paid my taxes and not broken any laws. I didn't even have any points on my driving licence. I had as much right as anyone else to be there, enjoying the sunshine, the experience, just living. I didn't need anyone to validate me.

I took a deep, brave breath, sat up a bit straighter and concentrated on the view, the warmth of the October sunshine and the clear, sea-scented air. This day was mine. And so was tomorrow.

And I made myself eat my salad slowly, appreciating the flavours, and not rushing to get through it so I could escape somewhere else.

Feeling rather pleased with myself, I waved the waiter over and ordered another small glass of wine and asked for the dessert menu. If Ceci thought tiramisu was the secret to happiness, then who was I to argue?

* * *

In the end I stayed there for ages, allowing myself to

relax, happy to be sitting in the dappled shade of an Italian sun.

I already felt different in this place, where the warmth and the sunshine and the break to my routine had made me see that there was indeed life outside my small existence. My ordinary house in the everyday town where I had settled seemed a long way away. Not just in miles, but in the experience of life. While I was plodding on with my steady routine, other people out in the wider world were experiencing life properly. Perhaps they were going out to dinner, travelling, meeting new people, making friends who had nothing to do with their children's activities. I wanted to do that.

After about half an hour, a couple of very chic young women at the table next to mine, who had been talking in French about someone called Hector, who had obviously upset one of them, wandered off, leaving behind a copy of some French fashion magazine.

I went and grabbed it and, leafing through the glossy pages, I began to wonder if I lived on the same planet as they did. The thing that struck me was how miserable the models looked. If I was that young, slender and attractive, I would probably spend my life whooping for joy and grinning at myself in the nearest mirror. But how did they actually get them-selves into those complicated swimming costumes with all the straps and buckles that lay smoothly against their skin? If I tried that I would probably look like a string bag of potatoes, with my sixty-five-year-old body bursting out of it.

I was squinting – because I had left my reading glasses in my room – at a picture of a thin, de-pressed-looking girl in a gingham playsuit (€1057) wearing the ugliest shoes I had seen in a while (€758) and wondering why the prices in those magazines were always so peculiar, as though someone had just picked them out of thin air, which possibly they had, when I heard a familiar voice.

'There you are, I was wondering how you were getting on.'

It was Paulo. I looked up, screwing up my eyes even more because the late afternoon sun was be-hind him, dipping towards the sea.

'Hello,' I said, trying to sound casual, although my heart did do a little flutter.

He put a hand on the chair next to me.

'*Permesso?* May I?'

'Of course.'

I closed the magazine rather clumsily, so it fell on the floor, and he bent down to pick it up.

'How are you?' he said.

'Fine, absolutely great,' I said, wishing that there weren't quite so many wine glasses on the table. Two of mine and one of Susie's, which I had finished off. He would think I was a complete lush.

'That's good. And where has Susie got to?'

'She has gone off for a trip with Raimondo to have lunch somewhere. He is safe, isn't he? I mean trustworthy.'

Paulo laughed. 'Safe? Of course, and I am glad if they are enjoying each other's company. He has been on his own for many years.'

'So has Susie. Well, not actually on her own. I mean, she did have other partners over the years. The last one was Simon, but he was a classic narcissist so she might as well have been alone.' I needed to think of something sensible to say. 'Is everything ready for tomorrow?'

Paulo nodded. 'I think it will be fine. Everything is very organised. My staff are busy setting everything up in the ballroom. It's not a place we use very often, unless we have a wedding party here.'

'That's great. And how many people do you expect?'

'Quite a lot. Ceci and Frederico still have many

acquaintances, and Ellen made a lot of friends here over the years.'

'Did she? Of course she did. She was a lovely person.'

My tongue was sticking to my teeth, my mouth was so dry, and it made me sound as though I was drunk or having a mild stroke. I took a sip of wine.

'This is great,' I said. 'I think it's the house wine.'

'Yes,' he said, 'I hope you like it.'

'Oh, I do.'

My goodness, this wasn't going well. I was asking dull questions and saying silly things. And all the time, I just wanted to ask him about what he had been doing with his life: had he been happy – yes, of course he had been; there was no way I wanted to eradicate that – but did he, like me, have the tiniest twinge of regret or curiosity about how things might have worked out between us?

I had been happy, on and off, I knew that. I'd had three healthy children and a good career which had brought me a great deal of satisfaction and pleasure. It wasn't that I wanted to erase all those years or re-gret them. I think the thing that was preoccupying me more than anything was – I'd been able to live my life for over sixty years, conforming to what people expected of me. Couldn't I just please myself for once? So what next? There had to be a what next, didn't there?

There was a long pause, which was beginning to get slightly uncomfortable when the silence was broken by the sound of china breaking from somewhere in the hotel. I resisted the urge to cheer as we always had years ago.

'It's great to see you again,' he said at last.

'Yes, it is, isn't it?' I replied. 'I mean, it's great to see you too.'

'You haven't changed a bit.'

'Oh, I'm sure I have,' I said. 'It's been almost forty years. If I hadn't changed at all you would think I had a portrait in the attic.'

Shut up, for heaven's sake.

'You look just the same too,' I added.

'So how has life been treating you?' he said. 'I often wondered about you.'

Really? I'd assumed that he had completely forgotten about me. I felt a sudden wash of happiness.

'Did you? Gosh. I married, had two daughters and then a son. I retired a few years ago; at least I have a decent pension. You hear such awful stories... and then I got divorced. And now I live in a little cottage with a garden. Just me and my wheelbarrow. Although my son has moved into the granny flat.

Just temporarily while he sorts out his divorce; at least, it's supposed to be temporary. He's been there for seven months.'

He looked out at the view for a moment and then laughed.

Why was he laughing? Was he realising what a good life he had enjoyed in comparison?

'I cannot imagine that,' he said at last. 'You were always so busy with friends and being sociable. The thought of you pottering around a quiet garden is very unusual.'

Hmm, what did that say about me?

If I thought about it, back then I had behaved in a way that I would not have found acceptable for my own daughters. The very thought of them smoking, dabbling a bit with cannabis and drinking pints of lager and snogging unsuitable young men on a regular basis was too awful. I had tried to find my place in the world, to feel good about myself. But that had led me to partying all night, stumbling into lectures, resitting exams when I failed them. Handing in work late, nearly getting thrown out altogether on one occasion when... well, never mind. Which really was tremendously hypocritical of me.

'I'm so sorry,' I blurted out.

Paulo looked surprised. 'For what?'

'That we lost touch.'

'Yes, it was a shame. I'm sorry too. I often wondered... Ah, well,' he said, *'non importa,* it doesn't matter what I wondered.'

So, was that it? Was that the final door closing on everything? I didn't want it to be, but it seemed it was. And what did he wonder?

'I must go and check on a few things,' he said, and he started to make the moves men make when they are about to leave. Looking at his watch, collecting up his mobile, checking in his jacket pocket for keys, his wallet, pulling out a scrap of paper and reading the message there before screwing it up and leaving it in the empty ashtray.

I watched him, studied his profile for a moment, remembering how much I had yearned for him once upon a time. How I had wanted to run my fingers down his jawline, through his hair. Wished that his eyes had brightened at the sight of me.

But then I remembered how often we had argued, shouting at each other about nothing. The washing up, the laundry drying on the radiators, books and paperwork strewn all over the table. Simply because we were both passionate, hotheaded people back then. But perhaps that was how

I had dealt with my feelings. Hidden my attraction for him with irritation and silly quarrels.

'I would ask if there's anything I can do to help,' I said, 'but obviously there isn't. After all, you have a very efficient staff.'

'Ellen trained them well,' he said, and then his phone buzzed with a text, and he studied it, looking worried. 'Oh dear.'

'Problem?' I said.

'It's from Leo. Eric's nanny Andrea is unwell. Apparently the travel has brought on one of her migraine episodes which can last two or three days, and Leo and my daughter-in-law are finding it... shall we say, difficult. One would not think Eric would be a problem for them, but he is. Between you and me, I am doubtful that their style of parenting is working but I'm reluctant to interfere. I'd better go and see if I there is anything I can do.'

'Perhaps I could help?' I said.

Paulo looked doubtful and then slightly puzzled.

'Surely one small boy doesn't need all of us fussing around him?'

I was inclined to agree, but then kids seemed to be treated differently from when I was young. Back then, they were on the edge of everything; nowadays, they seemed to be slap bang in the middle.

'He's been travelling. I expect he is jetlagged and confused about everything. There are such a lot of new things to take in,' I said. 'Different routine, and food, and a strange bedroom too. It's very unsettling when he is only five.'

'Yes, I suppose that's true,' he said, 'but you shouldn't be worried about that.'

'I am more than available to keep an eye on Eric. I'm happy to help if I can.'

He looked conflicted. 'Leo did tell me that Eric has taken a liking to you. Perhaps you are used to small children, you were a teacher weren't you, and then you had your own grandchildren – so I perhaps... At least you would be able to help keep an eye on him at the event tomorrow? If Andrea is no better?'

'I'd be delighted,' I said, my tone firm with confidence.

'Well, let's go and see, shall we?'

If I had thought about tomorrow at all, I had imagined myself wandering around, having miraculously found an elegant and stylish outfit that was not the black dress or the sale bargain items I had planned. If only Paulo had told us what the dress code was, we could have avoided this. But then men never seemed to worry about that. Unless it's a black-tie event, the big decision for them was either wearing a tie or not wearing a tie.

I had imagined myself newly confident, fake it till you make it, a glass of Prosecco in my hand, talking about Ellen, meeting some of her Italian family and friends and generally being a well-behaved guest. Enjoying some delicious canapés and feeling very happy to be in such glamorous and delightful surroundings that were so unlike my life back home.

Supervising a small boy who was the product of 'No No' parenting and wanted to be a cowboy hadn't been on my to-do list. But if Paulo needed my help, then of course I would say yes.

And actually, although I had taught for many years, I didn't know a vast amount about the modern methods involved in looking after small children. These days I only saw my granddaughters occasionally as their parents seemed to lead such hectic lives, and now Violet and Maud were finding activities and a social life of their own to keep them busy. There seemed to be at least one birthday party every weekend from what I could tell.

Paulo's confidence in my childminding skills was very far off the mark.

10

We found Leo and Raleigh in their suite. Leo was tucked away in a corner on his mobile having a rapid-fire discussion with someone in Italian, and Raleigh was standing by the window looking elegant but hopeless.

Her face brightened as we came into the room.

'Leo is on the phone trying to ring round the agencies to find a temporary nanny; so far he hasn't had any success. And now it's getting late and they are all closing for the day. We thought we might find a museum to visit, but of course it's too late for that now, so perhaps we could organise a little evening picnic in the garden, but Eric doesn't know what he wants.'

She threw a look at the door of the adjoining bedroom, and we heard the sound of a television volume being turned up and then down again, followed by a muffled thud.

'What's the problem?' I asked, feeling a bit irritated that she wasn't doing anything sensible.

'Oh, you know, Eric is such a bright boy. He is easily bored and distracted,' Raleigh said.

'I think all five-year-olds are the same,' I said. 'What about taking him for a walk around the garden? Looking for bugs or birds. It's a beautiful afternoon out there. And more importantly, how is Andrea?'

'She's got a headache,' Raleigh said. 'I mean, we all get headaches, don't we?'

'She has a cluster migraine,' Leo said firmly, ending his phone call. 'It's not the same thing at all. She's very unwell.'

'So where is Eric?' Paulo asked, sneaking a look at his watch.

'Watching television in our bedroom,' Raleigh said, nodding towards the closed door, 'but it's all in Italian. And his iPad has run out of charge and the cable is in Andrea's room somewhere.'

There was the sound of the door handle rattling, and a moment later Eric came out.

'I've been out on the balcony, watching a man washing the windows,' Eric said with an enormous grin of satisfaction.

Raleigh gasped with horror. 'On your own?'

'He was wearing rubber boots and a hat. And he had a bucket, and a spray bottle with blue water in it. I want to do that when I'm grown up. Or I'm going to be a cowboy.'

Raleigh looked a little shaken. 'No, Eric, you're going to Harvard Law School, remember?'

'And then can I be a man with a spray bottle?'

'Mmm, sounds a great job, buddy, everyone needs clean windows,' Leo said enthusiastically, busy doing his five-minute father stint. 'Would you like a drink of water?'

'I've had pink juice. The man gave it to me. He had a spare can, and he opened it for me.'

Raleigh clutched at her throat and gave a strangled cry.

Paulo looked at his mobile, obviously trying not to laugh.

'I'm terribly sorry, there is a problem in the kitchen, something to do with a delivery for tomorrow and a couple of waiters who are off sick. I must go and check.'

He gave me a grateful look and a wink and left.

'We can go out into the garden for a walk around before bedtime,' Leo said brightly.

Eric dropped his head back in the universal child language of acute disappointment and began to whine.

'That sounds lame.'

I held out my hand and went into headmistress mode, speaking in a tone I had used to great effect down the years with recalcitrant children.

'Perhaps you can go to the part of the garden where there aren't any lights and then we can watch the stars come out as it gets dark. That's what I used to do when I was your age. Let's give it a try. Hurry up and put your sweater on and some warmer trousers; it might get chilly as the sun goes down. There aren't a lot of streetlights here, so you will be able to see the stars far more than you can at home. And you never know, if you're lucky we might rustle up some fries.'

'Oh, okay,' Eric said quite reasonably. 'Are you coming too?'

'Well, I suppose I can if you want me to,' I said with a questioning look at Raleigh.

'You won't let him touch any bugs, will you?' Raleigh said, nodding. 'He had a worm in a matchbox once. I nearly fainted.'

* * *

We made our way to a delightful pergola at the far end of the garden, where there was a stone table and the sort of reclining chairs usually seen on film sets in Monte Carlo.

We got some drinks and Eric emptied his elegant metal cone of fries and then fidgeted around and dropped onto the floor where he scrabbled around for a while looking for a toy car he claimed to have lost. After a while he came back up and sat on the chair next to me with his legs sticking out.

'This chair is prickly,' he moaned as though he had been stabbed with a thousand knives.

'But, honey, it can't be prickly,' Raleigh said.

Leo took off his pullover. 'Sit on this, buddy,' he said, 'this is nice and soft.'

'Leo, that sweater is Hugo Boss,' Raleigh hissed.

'Well, does anyone have a cheaper one for him to sit on?' Leo hissed back.

I did but I wasn't going to admit it.

Eric struggled to get comfortable and in the process, he kicked me. He gave me a knowing look like a cat who recognises immediately the person in the room who distrusts it least.

'Honey, be careful, you'll hurt yourself,' Raleigh

said, looking at me reproachfully as though it was my fault.

The sun set and the daylight began to fade.

'Sit on my knee, Eric,' Leo said, reaching out a welcoming arm. Eric gave a babyish grizzle.

'No, want to sit there.' He pointed towards me, and I stood up so I could move out of his way. Perhaps I could walk around the back of everyone. Or maybe I could wander off to the bar, pretend to get lost and have a cocktail?

Before I could do either, Eric clambered heavy-footed onto my lap and settled down after turning round three times. Exactly like a blooming cat. There was something about that boy...

'Well, thank heavens,' Raleigh hissed. 'Keep still.'

Not sure if she was talking to Eric or me, I froze and gradually the light faded and the stars over the dark sea began to twinkle.

I could hear Eric's yawning somewhere below my chin. He didn't seem to weigh much but he was all angles and bony knees, and it took some time before he seemed to be comfortable.

'What's happening?' he said rather loudly.

'Let's be like little mice. Really quiet.'

Eric giggled and gave a squeak. He kicked out his feet, catching me a hefty whack on my leg.

I bit back a yelp.

'And really still,' I hissed.

'Or what will happen?'

'You won't see the stars, and neither will I,' I said.

'Tell me about the stars,' he said.

I dredged through my memory for information I had found for my own children when they were this age and prone to asking difficult questions.

Why doesn't glue stick to the inside of the tube? If a mermaid has an accident, does she go to the doctor or a vet? That sort of thing.

'Stars are giant balls of hot gas made up mostly of hydrogen and helium. Our Sun is a star.'

I heard Eric give a little gasp and miraculously he was still.

'If you look carefully, you can see groups of stars called constellations. And they all have different names. One of them is called Leo, like your dad.'

I felt him relax against me and I could just make out his profile as he looked up at the sky.

I managed to point out the Plough and the North Star, and then the W of Cassiopeia, and then Orion's Belt.

I was rather enjoying myself, despite the fact that my left leg was itching, and I couldn't reach it as Eric was in the way. Leo went off to answer a phone call at one point, and Raleigh wandered off too, murmuring something about finding another glass of wine, leaving me and Eric alone in the gathering darkness.

'Will the stars ever fall down and hit us?' Eric wanted to know. 'Like they did with the dinosaurs?'

'Very unlikely,' I said.

'You're sure?' He yawned again.

'Positive.'

'Did you ever see any dinosaurs?'

'No, I never saw one,' I assured him, wondering how old he thought I was.

A few minutes later, I looked down to see Eric had fallen asleep, curled up on my lap with his arm around my waist. I could just see the dark sweep of his eyelashes against his cheek and his chest rising and falling.

How many years was it since my own children were this small and came to me for comfort and advice? It seemed a long time and yet no time at all. Violet and Maud were this size. I'd enjoyed cuddles with them when they were babies, but more recently I hardly saw them. They lived hours away from me and like all modern parents, Jess and Kat had plunged into the world of children's activities. They were busy and happy and well cared for, but I was missing out. I needed to do something about that while they still fitted onto my lap.

What should I do? I looked around and saw to no great surprise that Leo still hadn't returned and nor had Raleigh. It was just the two of us sitting out there in the dark. For heaven's sake! What sort of parents were they? The minute they got the opportunity to connect with their child, they blooming scarpered. No wonder Eric was so confused.

I looked down at him and felt rather sorry for him. Actually, he really was a beautiful child with glossy dark hair and pale, almost translucent, skin. It had been many years since I'd had a child of my own asleep in my lap, but the feeling was the same. Comfort and a protective urge that would probably never fade, no matter how old my own children were.

So much ahead for this spoiled, amazingly privileged boy. And yet there were still reasons to feel sorry for him. Only five and his life was already mapped out. An incredibly expensive school with other spoiled kids who thought nothing of yachts in the Caribbean and ski lodges in Aspen. Clothes direct from designers, toys by the truckload, interior designers brought in to change his nursery into a proper boy's room. Perhaps he would have a hand-built bed in the shape of a rocket or an SUV. An artist would be drafted in at huge expense to paint a mural of planets or a jungle. Then onto Harvard Law School, development of utter self-belief and superiority and eventually marriage to a brittle little wife like his mother.

Perhaps at some point, Eric would stop whining and annoying everyone all the time and learn to be tolerable occasionally? Maybe? Well, he couldn't be five forever, could he?

Paulo returned and I felt his hand on my shoulder.

'Is he asleep?'

'Seems like it,' I said.

'You're very good with him. You must have been a great mother. Ellen never really enjoyed it. She was quite honest about it. One child was enough for her, although I would have liked more.'

I sat as still as I could, taking in this information. Something I hadn't known. But then when I had seen her with Leo, she had been curiously disinterested. Perhaps she had been the sort of mother to speak about her child and his achievements rather than be a part of them.

Eric gave a huge sigh. It was like having an unexploded bomb on my lap. I had the awful feeling Eric wasn't the sort to wake up chirpy.

I was right.

A few seconds later he began to wriggle, and he opened his eyes. He locked his gaze with mine for a moment as though he didn't recognise me and then he started grizzling.

I stroked his hair back from his forehead, feeling very sentimental.

'It's okay, Eric. You just had a little nap, that's all. Do you remember the stars coming out?'

He let loose with a wordless babble of protest and then slithered off my lap onto the floor and began to howl. After a moment I realised things were worse than I had thought, and he had peed on me. The sweet, lovely, sleeping child was gone and Eric was back.

* * *

I went back to my room to change my damp clothes and as I opened the doors onto the terrace outside, Susie appeared.

'I've got something for you. Why are you wet? Did you spill something?'

'Don't ask,' I said. 'I've got to get changed. So, what have you been doing?'

Susie looked dreamily into the distance for a

moment.

'I had a lovely lunch at a gorgeous little place overlooking the sea, then I came back and had a little snooze. These beds really are comfy, aren't they? And then the Contessa rang me and invited me back to her room.'

I went into my bathroom, took off my clothes and put on my dressing gown.

'I'd better have a shower,' I said.

'Well, before you do, come and see what I've got.'

Susie led me to her room and pointed with some excitement at some cotton clothing bags hanging from the curtain rail.

'Ceci said we could borrow these. She got them in Paris about a million years ago. Heaven knows what they're worth. Just take a look.'

She unzipped the bags to reveal four cocktail dresses, each more dazzling than the last.

'She did say she had gone through a phase when she was bigger than she is now, which I think was her way of being polite about the fact that we are both fatter than she is. I'm going to wear the red one, so you can choose one of the other three.'

I reached out to touch the silky fabrics, one heavily embroidered with leaves and flowers, the other two beaded and shimmering with each movement.

'I can't wear something like that,' I said. 'I'd be bound to spill something down myself. And considering Eric just peed on me, I'm not going to let him anywhere near them.'

'He didn't?'

'He fell asleep on my lap. I feel quite sorry for him actually. His parents are lovely, but they obviously don't have a clue how to handle him, and now Andrea is out of commission for a couple of days, you would think their world had come to an end. I've offered to keep an eye on him.'

'And this is the thanks you get?'

'Look, I'm going to have a shower, and then I will come and have a closer look. So, you had a good time?'

Susie gave a happy sigh. 'I really did. Raimondo is such a gentleman. We had a meal down by some little harbour. Everything tasted so wonderful, and then we just sat and chatted, and he drove the long way home, so I got a chance to see the scenery. And then we stopped for coffee at some out of the way place with Roman ruins in the garden. This glamorous life is marvellous, isn't it? I've had more compliments from him in the last twenty-four hours than I had in four years from Simon.'

'I often think that when I am getting into bed at seven thirty with a cup of tea and a Penguin to watch *Strictly Come Dancing*. Somewhere, people are still getting ready and going out to dinner. Did we have that energy back in the day?'

Susie nodded. 'We must have done. And how are you and Paulo getting on? I keep forgetting to ask.'

'It's fine,' I said, trying to sound unconcerned, 'nothing at all to worry about. We are just old friends now, nothing more.'

'Really, Jo? *Really?* That's not the impression I got,' Susie said.

'Why, what impression did you get?' I fired back. 'What did he say?'

It was the same as it had always been, and probably still was. Girls asking their friends what a boy thought of them. *Did he say anything?*

'He hasn't said anything to me. It's just the way he looks at you. As though he is remembering things as they used to be.'

'That's nonsense. There was nothing to remember. He was very happy with Ellen; I know they were. She was much better for him than I could ever have been.'

'Yes, probably, but then – well, life goes on, doesn't it? Raimondo told me she was quite strict about things, an absolute powerhouse, and that's why the hotel was so successful. People change. Circumstances alter. We still have needs and hopes, don't we? Just the same as when we were young. We can learn new things all the time, now we have You-Tube. There's nothing wrong with that.'

11

I thought about this a lot as I lay in bed that night.

Circumstances change; people alter.

Greg had been increasingly predictable over the years. In charge of everything, the one who would sulk if he didn't get his own way or the biggest cake in the box. He was the one who had control of our finances and occasionally, under pressure, the little maintenance jobs around the house. He'd had an impressive collection of tools and gadgets to help too, and a special shed where they were all kept which he liked to call his man cave, and I wasn't supposed to go in in case I broke something or put a screwdriver back in the wrong place.

And actually, he had been pretty clueless. I'd had

more luck putting up roller blinds in my cottage than he ever had, and I was better at decorating too. In the years since we had divorced, I'd had to learn. And none of it was that complicated, even though Greg had liked to pretend things like pressure washing the patio or putting oil in the car were difficult.

Susie's long-term partner Simon had been much the same. Making a big fuss about the smallest of tasks and expecting effusive praise when he did anything.

I wondered what sort of husband Paulo had been. Had he been like that too? Or were he and Ellen more of an equal partnership? He'd always seemed pretty capable to me, and when the kitchen in our student house had flooded because the drains were blocked, he had been unflappable. He hadn't needed lavish praise or special equipment; he'd just gone outside, pulled his sleeve up and stuck his hand down the drain to clear the leaves.

After that night when we had kissed each other, holding each other as though we never wanted to let go, he had kept unexpectedly cool and shown none of the passionate Latin temperament I had expected. And at the time I had found this rather disappointing. I would have liked him to show some emotion.

Explain how he felt. But then it was my fault. He had tried to say something and I had shut him down, unwilling to find out what could have happened next. I must have been mad. But Ellen had been my friend, hadn't she?

* * *

I slept badly that night, and in the morning I woke late to the sound of Susie tapping on the glass door out onto the balcony.

'Come on,' she said. 'It's nine fifteen. If you want some breakfast you'd better hurry up.'

She was looking very bright-eyed and cheerful this morning, dressed in some smart trousers and a jaunty striped T-shirt. This contrasted badly with my bleary appearance. For two pins I would have gone back to bed, but I was starving and there was an exciting day ahead.

We had a quick breakfast of more delicious pastries and coffee while I grilled her some more about Raimondo. He was apparently very nice, attentive and polite and had driven them all over the island in Paulo's sports car. She didn't know what sort, only that it was blue with leather seats.

There were staff everywhere that morning. The

doors to the huge ballroom were thrown open and in there we could see an array of round tables covered with white cloths, and people putting out place settings and glasses. As we watched, some florists appeared with the most ravishing displays of white flowers. Roses and lilies, peonies and dahlias. The scent was intoxicating.

This was what Ceci had wanted, wasn't it? White flowers.

I was aware Susie was edging away from me.

'See you later,' she said as she made for the stairs.

I wondered what she was up to. And then I realised.

'Good morning.'

It was Paulo, and despite everything, my spirits raised at the sight of him. I shouldn't have been feeling such things; after all, today wasn't just to celebrate Ceci's birthday, it was also the celebration of Ellen's life, her relationship with this man and this place. But somehow I couldn't help myself.

He was carrying a box filled with table napkins, snowy white and crisply ironed.

'We are all busy today,' he said with a little smile, 'but I think we will be ready very soon.'

'Can I help?' I said, wondering what sort of task I was imagining I could do.

'No, not at all. I think my staff have everything under control. They know exactly what to do. I should hope so anyway.'

'If there is anything, I'd love to help,' I said. 'There must be something?'

For heaven's sake, what was I thinking? Why couldn't I just take no for an answer? Leave the poor man alone with his memories and his tasks.

He shifted the box in his arms and looked at me properly for the first time.

'Well, there is always Eric. But perhaps later, we could talk?' he said.

I was silent for a moment. What did he want to talk to me about? And how much later was 'later'?

Perhaps all those years ago we could have had a good talk and cleared the air, but we never had. We had just retreated from each other for a while, and then after I had shut him down that day, we'd sunk into an unspoken agreement that while we were still sharing the student house, we made it work. Over the following weeks and months, we had developed a rather prickly relationship where each of us seemed to annoy the other all the time. Nothing more. And it had seemed okay; well, it had worked.

'I'd like that,' I said, and he smiled, and for a moment it was as though the years fell away, and I had a warm, fleeting memory of when we were young, when just about every problem could be cured by a good night out at the student union. And then I felt odd inside, a peculiar mixture of emotions. Happy but at the same time sort of anxious and sick.

'We have left it too long. We need to say things which were left unspoken,' he said, and the feeling intensified. 'I need to explain.'

My mind was racing. No, I needed to explain. I would apologise; in fact, there was really no reason why...

'Where have you been?' said an accusing little voice at my elbow, and there was Eric, in yet another designer outfit of check shirt and mini chinos. 'I've been waiting ages and ages.'

'I was asleep, and then I had breakfast,' I said, 'and now I am watching as the ballroom is turned into a beautiful place.'

'How are you today, Eric?' Paulo said, smiling down at his grandson.

'I'm bored.' Eric grabbed hold of my hand and pulled me into the ballroom where he stood with his arms outstretched, getting in the way.

'Do Mommy and Poppa know where you are?'

'They said I could come and have a look, but I

wasn't to go outside. This is a party,' he said, 'for my *nona*. And my *bisnonna*.'

'Yes, I know, that's why we are all here.'

Paulo had taken his box of table linens and handed it over to one of the waiters.

'I have a special suit to wear,' Eric said, watching with interest as another waiter put out some glasses on the tables.

'You are going to look very smart.'

'I know,' he said, 'but I wish I could have some jeans.'

'Don't you have any?'

'No. And I need some if I am going to be a cowboy.'

This was surprising; I thought all American children lived in blue denim. Perhaps Raleigh didn't approve of them.

'Maybe we could find some,' Paulo said, 'if we went shopping.'

Eric's eyes widened. 'For me?'

'Why not?'

'Oh.'

He went back to watching the waiters, his face a picture of concentration. Paulo had received another phone call and gone off through one of the service doors at the far end of the room.

'How is Andrea today?' I asked.

Eric slipped his hand into mine, and the gesture made me feel rather sentimental for a moment. He might have been badly behaved but he was only a little boy.

'I don't know.'

'I hope she is feeling all right.'

A white rose had fallen out of one of the floral displays onto the floor and I picked it up.

'You could take her this, and say you hope this makes her feel better.'

Eric looked puzzled. 'Why would that make her headache go away?'

'Well, it wouldn't, but it would show you cared and had been thinking of her. And that would be kind, wouldn't it? You should always be kind to people, especially those who look after you.'

'Oh.'

The waiter he had been watching finished his task and walked out with his empty plastic crate, ruffling Eric's hair as he passed us.

'I think I'll go now,' Eric said, and he let go of my hand and hurried off.

I wondered yet again where Leo and Raleigh were. Perhaps they were still in bed, asleep. No, someone must have got Eric up and dressed.

* * *

I went back upstairs, checking that Susie was in her room. It was nearly midday, and the celebration was due to start at two o'clock. Which meant we had plenty of time to get ready and hopefully glammed up so that Ceci would not give us one of her disapproving looks.

I tried on the three dresses I had to choose from and made my choice. It wasn't that difficult. The blue one was obviously from the sixties and rather short; the yellow one might have looked good on Ceci when she was younger, but the colour just made me look ill. Then I decided to start getting ready.

Why was it, I wondered, that when I was younger it took no time at all to slap on some makeup, run a brush through my hair and drag on some clothes and still look presentable? Now it took much longer, and the final effect was nowhere near as pleasing.

And why did I look reasonable when I looked at my face in the mirror, but every time someone took a picture of me from the side, my face looked as though it was sort of collapsing into my neck? When we were young, why didn't we appreciate ourselves?

I showered and pulled on my robe and, sitting at the dressing table, I stared at my reflection for a few minutes more, trying and failing to see the younger me.

Suddenly, I just looked like my mother. Did we all end up looking like our mothers? Would my daughters one day discover the same thing?

Out of the blue, I had a mad wish that I could go back and do my life again properly. Work harder in school, not focus on being the class clown. Watch less television, read more books. Travel more.

Greg had once said during our divorce negotiations that I needed to work on my anger management. I didn't think I did, I just needed other people to stop irritating me. Things like Greg's mother, substitutions in supermarket deliveries, politicians lying, the way tubs of Christmas chocolates got smaller every year but cost the same.

Oh well. I brushed out my wet hair and dried it into its usual style. Perhaps I should have let Gina loose on my hair too. Which was rather depressingly looking like my mother's too. Short enough to be manageable but not long enough to do anything with. Maybe I would have a pixie cut and pink highlights when I got back home? I sighed. Perhaps I wouldn't.

I put on some makeup, wondering how old it was and whether I should have invested in some new stuff. All those fragrant counters in duty-free at the airport, staffed by glamorous assistants. And I hadn't the faintest idea what to look for or what to buy. I'd just walked past them all, looking for somewhere to sit down.

I tried a smear of brown eyeshadow, a touch of mascara, and I took another look. It didn't matter what sort of dress I wore; this wouldn't work. I looked dull. Something needed to change. I had just been doing the same thing in the same way for years. If I didn't do something different soon, it would be too late.

I washed it all off and rummaged at the bottom of my makeup bag, hoping to find some unexpected treasures. Which was unrealistic, as most of my things were sample sizes and things ripped off the pages of magazines. Heaven knows how old some of them were.

Triumphantly, I pulled out an eyeshadow palette I had been given for Christmas some years ago, and an eyeliner pencil. Flicky eyes, that was what women did. Perhaps I would give it a try. Then at the bottom of the bag and rather crumpled, I found a pair of false eyelashes and pounced on them with a cry of surprise. I'd tried them when I went to some work event with Greg a few years ago. He had laughed at me and said I looked ridiculous. Thinking back, he had said that a lot. Perhaps I was as bad as Susie, putting up with sarcastic comments for so many years.

I rinsed them under the tap and blotted them dry with a tissue. One of them was a bit creased so I weighted it down with a shampoo bottle. All I needed now was some eyelash glue. Perhaps Susie would have some? She was far more up on these things than I was.

I went out onto the balcony and tapped on her French windows. There was a bit of scuffling about going on in there, and I pressed my nose to the glass.

Susie and the dashing Raimondo were locked in a passionate clinch and broke apart when they realised I was there. I didn't know who was more embarrassed, but at least they were fully dressed. It could have been a lot worse.

'Eyelash glue,' I whispered when she unlocked the door, 'have you got any?'

Susie was looking a bit wild eyed and rumpled while Raimondo had composed himself elegantly into one of the armchairs and was pretending to read a magazine. Which was upside down, although I resisted the temptation to turn it round the right way.

'Of course,' Susie said, her hair even more tousled than it had been earlier. She closed the door and went off to fetch some, returning a few moments later and handing it over with an embarrassed smile.

'Everything okay?' I said, trying to peer over her shoulder.

'Absolutely. Well, see you in a minute,' she said, and closed the door. And then she locked it and closed the curtains.

Well, I never. Good for her.

I wondered for a moment what it would feel like at my age to have a man look at me with passion. To want to sweep me into his arms and kiss me. It was a long time since any of those things had happened.

I peeled back the tissues and stared at the false eyelashes. When I was in my teens I'd worn them almost every day.

'Can't be that difficult,' I muttered.

I messed about with some travel-size cleanser, toner and moisturiser and started on my makeup again.

Susie knocked on my door just as I was massaging some overpriced gloop into my neck, in the hope that it would work a miracle, and came in without waiting.

'What are you doing? Putting false eyelashes on. That's a turn up for the books, isn't it?'

'I'm going to have a go. Have you told Raimondo to scarper, or is he recovering, panting in your bed?'

Susie pulled a face and stuck her tongue out at me.

'Yes to the first question and no to the second. Go on then, I want to watch this.'

'Don't! You'll put me off,' I said.

Actually, I was pleased how easy it was, and I batted my eyelashes at Susie a few minutes later, rather pleased with the effect.

'That was disappointing,' Susie said. 'I was hoping you might glue your eyes shut.'

'Thank you so much. Next time I find you in an intimate situation with Raimondo, I shall burst in and sing 'O Solé Mio' to you.'

'Very funny. Now then, which dress are you going to wear?'

'The long, pale lavender-coloured one with the embroidery. It fits better than the others. I'll have to wear the only smart shoes I've got which are black, which is a pity.'

'Or those very pale blue trainers you bought? That would be chic.'

'I'll see,' I said, testing out my eyelashes again. It

felt very weird. As though I had, well, false eyelashes on. I would have to concentrate on blinking normally and not like one of those wooden puppets that had been popular on children's television programmes when I was small. 'You need to shoehorn yourself into that red dress. Go away and let me get ready.'

I spent the next half hour being a bit more creative with my makeup, trying with the eyeliner and wondering how on earth people did it right. Perhaps I should have sharpened the pencil first?

I used some of the different eyeshadows, and put on some blusher, which was so old it was cracking in the pot. And then a darker lipstick.

I took another look at myself. Well, I looked a bit more exciting anyway.

At two o'clock I was ready. The dress had a hand-embroidered label in the neckline from some designer I had never heard of. I ditched the smart black heels and put on the pale blue trainers. And then another layer of lipstick. Did I look chic? Or like an older woman playing dress up? Would I be better off ditching the lot and going back to my safe black outfit? I wasn't sure. No, I looked fine. And really, as long as I didn't do something foolish or say something controversial, what did it matter?

As I stood there dithering, there was a knock on my door and Susie was there looking radiant in her scarlet dress and some borrowed stilettos.

'You look fantastic,' I said, 'and more than slightly pleased with yourself. What have you been doing?'

Susie giggled. 'Nothing I want to tell you about. Although Raimondo has just sent up some flowers and a rather cheeky note. Are you ready? You look lovely. I went and leaned over the bannisters, and I can see people are arriving. It's time we went downstairs.'

12

Both of us felt very self-conscious and a bit tense as we walked carefully down the staircase. Susie in her unfamiliar heels, and me concentrating on my posture and not tripping over the hem of my dress, keeping my head up, my chin out and not slouching.

'We look great,' I said as we turned the last corner, 'it will be fine.'

'I don't know why I'm so twitchy,' Susie said.

'I could suggest a reason – the lovely Raimondo has got you all fired up.'

Susie tugged at her dress. 'Could be.'

'So have you...?' I asked.

'Have I what? Oh, you mean... No, of course I haven't! What do you take me for?'

'I expect he will be waiting for you, desire in his eyes, love on his mind,' I teased.

'Shut up! I'm nervous enough as it is,' Susie said, 'although he is very attractive. And what about you and Paulo, before you start poking fun at me.'

I stopped and turned round, causing Susie to bang into me and nearly knock me flying down the last four steps. That would have been a great way to make my entrance.

We grabbed at each other to stop from falling and I dropped my bag on the floor where everything spilled out.

'This is all about Ceci and Ellen,' I said, cramming things back into my bag and catching one foot in the folds of my dress. 'Anything between me and Paulo would be in very bad taste indeed.'

'Will we know anyone?' Susie said, resting a hand on my shoulder and adjusting one shoe which had nearly come off. 'I hate going into places where everyone knows everyone else but me. And then I end up standing at the side, nursing a drink with a weak smile on my face.'

'Nonsense, we are strong confident women of a certain age,' I said, 'allegedly. We can go and introduce ourselves to people. But what if they only speak Italian?'

'Just say *meraviglioso* to everything, which means marvellous. Or *interassante*, which means interesting. Or *bene*, which means good.'

I took a deep breath. 'Well, I'll try.'

By then we had reached the reception area, and we could hear the noise of the party coming from the open doors of the ballroom.

Childishly, we tried to push the other forward and it might have ended in an undignified shoving match, but then Paulo appeared as if by magic, and he smiled at us. At me.

'Come and meet some of my family and friends,' he said. 'You both look wonderful.'

* * *

The thing that struck me as we went into the ballroom was the wonderful scent of the flowers. It was quite intoxicating. There were people congregating in little groups, some laughter and hugs. It looked as though they all knew each other already. And the room was warm, even though the wide windows out onto the Mediterranean were all open.

I felt suddenly nervous. And even more unsettled, and I could feel sweat break out on my upper lip, which was a really unattractive thing to happen at any age.

As we moved into the room, the gathering parted for a moment, and there was Ceci, seated at the top of the room on a glorious blue damask armchair, Freddy at her side.

She spotted me.

'There you are, Jo. That dress suits you well. I wore it years ago in Ravenna. Or was it Ravello? Anyway, it was a place with wonderful views.'

Her eyes narrowed as they swept down to my footwear.

'Are you thinking of playing tennis?'

Of course, that meant everyone else looked at my pale blue trainers too.

Susie moved a little closer to my side in a welcome show of solidarity.

I dabbed at my top lip with a tissue and gave a weak smile.

A tall, silver-haired woman next to her shrugged.

'*È molto chic di questi tempi, Ceci.* It's chic these days.'

'*Meraviglioso,*' I said with a bright smile.

Ceci gave me a look, sighed and waved a hand at one of the waiters.

'If you say so. I expect next year women will be

wearing football shorts to the opera. Now then, you need a drink. There's nothing worse than coming to an event where you know no one. And I see Sylvia and Lucia have not made an appearance. I know they are both in the building somewhere. I can sense their negative energies. Perhaps Sylvia has developed some new illness which means she cannot join us. The Lord does indeed move in mysterious ways.'

Moments later, Raimondo appeared with a wide white smile to offer Susie a drink.

'*Carissima, questo è per te.*'

So, he was calling her darling now, was he? That man didn't seem to have a pause button at all.

I felt quite the spare part for a moment but Paulo was suddenly at my side with a glass of crisp refreshing Prosecco for me, and I knocked back half of it in a mild panic. I really should have calmed down. The last thing I needed was to get tipsy. What was causing this?

'Here's to you, Ceci, and to Ellen,' I said, realising too late I should have said that first.

Freddy raised his glass too.

'To my wonderful, beautiful, talented wife.'

I wondered what it would be like to have a husband who talked like that about me. How long had they been married anyway?

Ceci nodded graciously and then Paulo raised his glass to me and smiled.

'Come and meet some of my family. They are not so terrifying as you will see.'

I felt his hand touch gently on the small of my back as he steered me towards a group of cheerful-looking people standing by the open window. One of the women had a painted paper fan and was wafting cool air over her face. What a good idea; I wished I'd thought of that.

We went through the introductions and formalities and fortunately all of them spoke excellent English.

A stout man with a disarming smile and a jaunty bow tie shook my hand and introduced himself as Ernesto, Paulo's cousin.

'So, *tu sei Jo*. You are Joanna. We have heard a lot about you.'

How? And what?

'*Meraviglioso,*' I said. Marvellous. And then I tried to remember the other words Susie had said.

What had they heard? Nice things or the bits about my reckless behaviour when I was younger; my messy divorce? Did they know anything about the feelings I'd had for Paulo? Had he ever told anyone? No, of course he hadn't.

The woman at his side who was resplendent in a purple cocktail dress was introduced as Ernesto's wife Giulia, and she nodded.

'Ellen spoke often of you. You were the clever one, with *una carriera entusiasmente* – the exciting career.'

'*Bene!*' I said, smiling and wondering what the third word Susie had mentioned.

Then I thought back and wondered how my years in teaching could be construed as exciting. Worthwhile, yes, but exciting?

I'd retired when my little school had closed and been amalgamated with a new, glossy, bigger school where everything was colourful and state of the art. Not like Highfield Infants, where the windows were too high to see out of, the heating boiler was temperamental, and the roof had leaked in various places.

'*Direttrice.* A headmistress,' Giulia said. 'So important. Not a job I could do.'

Her admiration made me relax a little and we chatted for a few moments about everyday things: the weather, the wonderful views, and of course Ellen.

'Such a lovely person,' Ernesto said sadly. 'Kind. Generous and welcoming.'

'Always in church every Sunday. And always helpful,' Giulia added.

'And everyone loved her,' Ernesto said.

'Everyone,' Giulia said with a sad shake of her head. 'And now she is no longer with us.'

'*Meraviglioso,*' I said, which earned me an odd look from Giulia.

I began to feel rather strange at that point. Here we all were, celebrating Ellen's life as what sounded like a living saint, and I had been remembering my envy of her, my own failed relationship with Ellen's husband, thinking about him, recalling that night when we had kissed each other; not a friendly peck either, but a full-blown snog.

There was no doubt about it, I was a bad person.

I would make myself stop thinking about the way Paulo and I had occasionally spent Sunday mornings, *not* going to church but waiting for the others to wake up, huddled under the blue and grey blanket at either end of the sofa in the sitting room watching children's programmes on television, eating toast and drinking endless cups of tea. Taking care not to touch each other. Complaining about the crumbs and the work we should be getting on with.

And then Ellen or someone else would appear and we would go to the pub where we would meet up with friends and we would start bickering again. *Give it a rest, you two,* someone would say. *All you ever do is argue.*

We would spread out the Sunday papers, drinking beer and eating toasted sandwiches until someone suggested doing something else. The something usually involved lounging around on the sofa again, watching old films and eating biscuits.

'She was lovely,' I said, hoping to make up for my previous comment. 'Such a loss to us all.'

Then Ernesto and Giulia saw some old friends across the room, made their apologies and wandered off.

Susie appeared at my side looking cross.

'I've just had a phone call from Simon,' she said.

'What the heck did he want?'

Susie pulled a face. 'He said he'd gone back to my house to collect the last of his stuff and he couldn't find the celebration tea towel from the coronation that he bought. I suppose I'm impressed he needs one. Where did I keep them? I mean, he lived in that house on and off for four years, and they have always been in the bottom drawer next to the sink. He says he is going to "have a sort out", which means when I get back I won't be able to find anything and he will have taken some of my things too. I'm only away for a flipping week. I should have changed the locks.'

'Hardly worth phoning you about?' I said.

Susie gave a wistful look. 'I know what it is, he's sorry now and he's missing me. He sounds all grumpy and put upon, but I know. He would never come out and say it, but I can tell.'

'I hope you are not weakening and thinking about getting back together with him?'

Susie smiled, this time with a slightly steely look. 'Not a chance. It will do him good to realise I did a lot more than just buy cake and magically produce clean laundry.'

Which was truer, I wondered? Out of sight out of mind, or absence makes the heart grow fonder. I started down that line of thought regarding Paulo and then stopped myself.

We had been apart for so long, so many years had passed, so much had happened to both of us. Surely the magical attraction we had felt for each other was long gone. But why then did he still make me feel like this?

I had not been like Ellen, gracious and serene.

I had been the one with the temper who criticised the way Paulo left muddy football boots in the middle of the kitchen floor. Who disagreed with his choice of television programmes, who occasionally stamped out of the room when he came in. He had been the one who had pulled all his clothes out from the laundry basket in a fury when he couldn't find a favourite shirt. We had shouted at each other, and then eventually laughed. I'd read once that love and hate were two sides of the same blade, that there is only a small difference between them. The only thing that was worse was indifference. And that was not something I had ever felt about Paulo.

Had he been like that with Ellen?

'Where's your admirer now?' I said, picking a canape from a tray as the waiter passed us.

'Over there surrounded by fluttering women. He's terribly attractive, isn't he? I can see the appeal.'

I watched for a moment. There seemed to be a lot of laughing and cheek kissing going on in that particular group.

I shook my head. 'I don't think I trust a man that age with so much hair. To my mind it usually means he's had a hair transplant or is wearing a wig.'

'Sweeping generalisation, don't you think? But then men fret about losing their hair, don't they? And trust me, that is real hair,' she purred with a cat-like smile. 'And we worry about other stuff. Wrinkles and middle-age spread,' she said, and we both pulled our stomachs in and straightened up.

'I don't much care if we look old; it's a sign we are still alive. And even my son Alex says all the young women on television who are supposed to be attractive look the same. Too thin and the same hair and eyebrows and pouts. And they always seem to be laughing hysterically about something. Perhaps that's what is expected on television these days. And the clothes they wear are always too small.'

'So now what about Paulo?'

'Oh, I expect we will have a proper chat at some point, when he has time. What we have been doing, just like old friends, that sort of thing.'

'You're fooling yourself,' she murmured.

'Oh, stop it.'

We stood sipping Prosecco and people watching for a few minutes. Everyone seemed to be part of a couple, were well dressed, elegant and wearing studied expressions that said, *Yes, I am having a good time, but I'm remembering Ellen so I'm slightly sad as well.*

Funny how people paired up. I watched and wondered what had attracted one to the other. A tall man with a huge voice accompanied by a tiny woman in blue. Another striking woman with a complicated hairstyle clinging on to the arm of a man who looked like a retired banker apart from his shoes, which were brown and white co-respondent brogues.

'Do you think Greg and the Trollop, you know, still—'

I raised my eyebrows at the question.

'Have sex? I expect so. If she ever gets off her horse. What a ghastly image. Perhaps she gets turned on when he mucks out the stables. Or maybe he grooms her with a Dandy brush and Curry comb, whistling through his teeth like an ostler. Oh, who cares? You should try one of these shrimp things, they are delicious.'

I realised that indifference was something I did feel for Greg.

At the head of the room, someone tapped loudly on the side of a wine glass and gradually everyone stopped talking. It was Paulo standing beside his mother's chair. We could have heard a pin drop.

'Thank you, *grazie*, friends and family for being here today. It has been five years,' he shook his head, 'but today we celebrate Ellen's life the way she would have wanted. With joy, and happy memories. Not with tears or sadness.'

Ceci tugged at his sleeve to interrupt him.

'When I die, I expect you all to be inconsolable. I insist on it.'

Everyone laughed at that, and the room relaxed a little.

'And of course we wish a very happy birthday to my mother, the incomparable Contessa.' He raised his glass in her direction, and she nodded and smiled back at him. 'So now, please enjoy yourselves. We marvel at my mother's energy and wisdom, and at the same time we remember Ellen. As we move on into the future we should celebrate both of them, with gladness, with laughter.'

'If anyone laughs at my funeral, they are out of the will,' Ceci added darkly.

* * *

It really was a lovely event. The room was indeed filled with people mingling, greeting each other with kisses and exclamations of delight, making a big fuss of Ceci and remembering Ellen, funny stories, happy memories. I had known her since university, and of course people wanted to hear about her as a young woman, what had she been like. Had she always been such a wonderful cook?

My memories of Ellen were of her having a particular fondness for bacon sandwiches, not gourmet cooking or fussing about with food preparation. Back then we considered finding a clean plate in the kitchen a culinary triumph.

I was standing with a small group of people on the terrace outside the ballroom, the afternoon sunlight casting shadows, the scent from the bougainvillea wafting in the warm air.

I bet it wasn't like this back home. I could almost visualise the rain lashing against the windows of my cottage.

'I remember her when she came to stay with me,' I said. 'She was so happy with her life, so proud of Leo. I don't think I ever knew someone so content.'

Susie nodded in agreement. 'But no one would have called her a wonderful cook. Not then.'

A woman who had identified herself as yet another of Paulo's cousins, and with the sort of manicure that made me suspect she never cooked or did anything difficult, leaned towards me.

'She learned. She tried. She was wonderful. Her *Gnocchi alla Sorrentina* was the best I ever tasted. And she was so welcoming. No one was ever turned away, even if we called in unexpectedly. And she was so kind to the convent in Sorrento, which was a particular favourite of hers. I understand the nuns still pray for her. She is sorely missed.'

'And *bambini a scuola* – the children at the school – they loved her too,' her companion added, placing one hand on my arm.

It came to me.

'*Interassante*,' I said.

They went off again, looking wistful, leaving Susie and me to stare at each other.

'Do you know, I'm beginning to think we didn't know her at all,' Susie murmured. 'I remember her as being friendly, but none of this saintly behaviour. Looking back, I think she was probably quite controlling. She was always telling Paulo what to do. And Raimondo said the same thing.'

Could this be true?

'I feel very unworthy,' I agreed. 'What on earth are we doing here? I'm surprised I haven't been struck by lightning.'

At that moment, Leo, Raleigh and Eric held firmly in between them came into view, all three of them looking absolutely marvellous. Leo and Eric in what looked like matching suits and ties, Raleigh swathed in a complicated pale blue silk dress and stilettos which could have come off the cover of Vogue.

I sighed. 'I wonder how Ellen would have dealt with young Eric?'

'She would, I am sure, have been the perfect grandmother,' Susie said, chuckling. 'Remind me why we liked her? She sounds like Mother Teresa crossed with Grace Kelly.'

'I feel utterly hopeless in comparison. I bet she wouldn't have thrown her husband's wellingtons out into the garden when he stomped through the house with them covered in mud and grass clippings like I did.'

'Probably not,' Susie said.

'Or pretended to have a sprained ankle because she didn't want to go to visit his parents for the weekend.'

Susie laughed. 'Did you?'

'Twice. I said I might have shingles one year when we were first married, so we didn't have to entertain them for Christmas. Chicken pox always goes around primary schools at that time of year, so it could have been true. I did have a sore throat. I bet Ellen wouldn't have done a thing like that. Hang on, I can see that priest is gradually making his way down the terrace towards us. I don't think I can talk to anyone else for a bit about Ellen's humanitarianism and modesty. I am ashamed of myself, I'll admit it.'

We went back into the ballroom where people were starting to take their places at the tables and found some seats near the back of the room.

No sooner had we stashed our handbags under the table and settled down for some people watching than a waiter approached us.

'Apologies, madam, *Permesso*. May I show you to your proper seats?'

Obediently, I followed him, hoping that the next people to sit there didn't mind the crumbs from our breadsticks. He led me, with many apologies, to the biggest table at the head of the room, and then he took Susie off in another direction.

'*Un posto d'onore*. A place of honour for you, madam,' he said.

'Oh good lord,' I muttered.

I scanned the room, looking for Susie, finally tracking her down to where she was once again firmly attached to Raimondo's side, a new glass of Prosecco in her hand.

I wondered how she was feeling. Was it wise for her to plunge into another relationship so soon after Simon? But then what did I know about such things? Look at the way my life had turned out.

I needed to find out more about him, what his prospects were, before he started asking her for money.

No, surely he wouldn't? But I'd read enough depressing stories in the papers about men latching on to a lone woman of a certain age, and before they knew it the man was having problems with their bank, their child was somewhere abroad needing an operation, and Susie would end up in the papers with a tragic expression talking about it.

Susie turned and waved at me and then came trotting over for a quick word.

'Isn't this lovely?' she said, her cheeks rather flushed. 'I'm having such a fabulous time. It makes life with Simon seem even more dreary, looking back. Raimondo has a villa near Amalfi. And a boat. He's just been telling me all about it. It sounds gorgeous.'

'Yes, are you sure?' I murmured. 'Has he got a daughter abroad, doing good works?'

'I don't think so,' Susie said, looking puzzled.

'Have you asked?'

'Well, no. That's not the sort of thing that comes up in conversation, is it?'

'Well, I'm going to ask him,' I said, 'and find out.'

'He'll think you're mad,' Susie said, looking irritable.

'We aren't going to watch as he empties your bank account and you end up in some documentary about older women being dogfished,' I said.

'I think it's catfished,' Susie replied waspishly.

'That too.'

Susie raised her chin defiantly.

'He has asked me to come back soon to Amalfi. To stay with him in his villa.'

'Are you sure that's a good idea?' I said. 'For all you know he has a titchy little flat somewhere on the outskirts of town, and the boat is a dinghy covered in barnacles.'

Susie chuckled. 'I don't know. I mean, this is enormous fun, but in my experience real life is badly planned, under rehearsed and a bit worrying. Still, I'm enjoying the moment.'

'So you won't be rowing off into the sunset with him?' I asked. 'You're sure?'

Susie spluttered with laughter.

'I'm not daft. But why shouldn't I bask in the warmth of his attention? It's been a flipping long time since anyone said anything nice to me. I'm having a lovely time. Did you know my eyes are the same colour as the waters of the blue lagoon? No, nor did I. He was telling me Ellen started up a charity in Sorrento, I think, rescuing abandoned animals and rehoming them.'

Of course she did, I thought.

Perhaps Susie had been right and we hadn't really known her at all. Seeing Ellen for a few days every so often didn't mean quite the same as the friendship I had with Susie, who I spoke to nearly every day, or even Juliette who had become a friend in almost no time in comparison.

What was a real friend? Someone to do something or nothing with and still have a good time? Why didn't Ellen just drop me when she moved away? Was it just to show me that I hadn't ruffled the surface of her perfect life? To prove to me that she didn't care what I had done, that I hadn't mattered?

13

Up on the top table I settled into my allotted place, where I had a great view of everyone else in the room. The talk was well-modulated with the occasional gentle laugh. It almost looked like a film set. Smartly dressed people, wonderful flowers, the lights from the chandelier glinting off the gleaming cutlery and shining glasses. Although in all the films like that I'd ever seen, something unexpected happened and there were long-buried revelations of infidelity or suspicious death. Or possibly the police arrived or a masked gang with machine guns burst in to kidnap someone.

Even Eric, wandering around between the tables looking for spare breadsticks, provoked only affectionate comments and smiles. But then he was lucky; Italians were well known for their acceptance and love of children. Across the table, Raleigh was busy trying to impress me with how difficult her life was, fundraising and socialising, and on the other side were those whose coming had been foretold. Ceci's sisters, Sylvia and Lucia.

Sylvia had arrived just as the priest was about to stand up and say a blessing. She came in with much ceremony, on the arm of a companion, pretending and failing to be quiet, clattering a walking stick on the stone floor and apologising loudly to everyone for her late arrival. I saw Ceci on the other side of Raleigh stiffen and roll her eyes.

'*Santo cielo*. Good heavens, can't my sister do anything properly? I thought we were going to be spared her nonsense.'

Sylvia, resplendent in turquoise taffeta and what looked like all her jewellery, sat down next to me with a long sigh and then addressed the room.

'I am all right, everyone. There's nothing to worry about. Please carry on. Just ignore me.'

'As always, we will try,' Ceci said.

Of course, then Paulo had to get out of his seat and introduce her to everyone, ask after her health and her comfort.

Sylvia looked up at him with a brave smile. 'I have been unwell, but there is nothing to concern you now.'

'Then I will sleep tonight,' Ceci growled, fingering the handle of her butter knife.

A few seconds later as everyone was settling down again, Lucia came into the room, pausing in the doorway for maximum effect. She was a short, voluptuous woman in a stylish pink dress which even at seventy-eight made the most of her fabulous legs.

'*Oh, mio Dio,*' she said loudly. 'Dear me, am I the last to arrive?'

'As always,' Ceci growled. 'I could set my watch by you.'

Lucia ignored her and allowed herself to be escorted to her seat opposite me. She inclined her head graciously towards me in greeting.

'*Meraviglioso,*' I said.

She smiled. '*Sì,* yes, *sono una donna meravigliosa.* I am indeed a marvellous woman. How clever you are.'

Sylvia snorted at this and I thought Ceci muttered something under her breath that didn't sound flattering.

Quiet restored, the blessing was said and the meal began.

'So have you come far today?' I asked Sylvia, realising too late that I sounded like the Queen at a Buckingham Palace garden party.

She looked up from her *minestra maritata* soup and thought about it.

'I flew in from Brussels yesterday, where I was visiting my son Ralph at the European commission. He is an assistant administrator in the Personnel Selection Office. A very important post. *Molto importante.*'

'How marvellous,' I said.

'*Scribacchino,*' Ceci muttered.

Sylvia was busy dabbing at her nose with a lace-edged handkerchief, but she caught the tail end of this comment, and her nostrils flared with indignation.

'Indeed, Ralph does not wear chinos. He wears a suit and tie every day.'

'I meant pencil pusher,' Ceci murmured.

'My hearing is not what it was,' Sylvia said. 'Old age takes no prisoners. It was a miracle I got here at all. Travel is so exhausting these days.'

'Yes, it can be very tiring. And to do it on your own, I do admire you,' I said.

Ceci wasn't having this.

'Your son drove you to the airport and got you on a plane, and my son made all the arrangements for you to get here from the airport. So basically, you have been sitting down. And you still are.'

Sylvia looked tragic, her voice quavering.

'These days, at my age, even sitting down is a trial. My arthritis.'

'We all have arthritis,' Ceci fired back.

'I don't,' Lucia said cheerfully. 'I am blessed with our father's genes.'

'And his nose,' Sylvia said.

Lucia sent her a hard look and lifted her chin.

'You are just jealous because I have aged so well. And however old I am I will always be the youngest. Papa always said I favoured his side of the family. You two on the other hand are beginning to look like *zia Maria*, Auntie Maria. I remember her after she had that bout of pneumonia and lost so much weight, her face collapsed. You can keep your face or your figure after sixty, that's what I read somewhere.'

'You *read* this?' Ceci said with mock astonishment. 'In an actual book?'

'And which one did you choose?' Sylvia purred.

Lucia pursed her lips and turned away.

I was suddenly in the middle of an increasingly

heated squabbling match. I leaned forward to distract them and started talking to Raleigh about the lovely weather. Even so, I heard Ceci give a little growl in the back of her throat, which suggested she was far from satisfied.

Luckily, Freddy distracted her, asking her whether he was going to be allowed some dessert, and they checked on his iPhone to see what his glucose levels were.

The main course was chicken, cooked in a delicious creamy sauce. Eric, by then safely corralled between his parents, looked at it suspiciously and then asked me if he was allowed fries, but when I shook my head he sighed and tucked in.

I watched Paulo as he moved around the room, chatting pleasantly with people, being the perfect host. How time had changed him.

As a young man when it had been his turn to cook, he had been known to just place a huge metal bowl full of spaghetti and sauce on the coffee table between us all and hand out the cutlery. It had been Ellen who insisted we clear all the books and discarded clothing off the dining table so we could eat there.

Ceci, her sisters and a couple of other older

ladies were bickering gently about the world and everything that was wrong with it.

'My son Ralph has dedicated his life to public service,' Sylvia said. 'I would have done the same if my health had allowed it.'

'How sad for us all,' Ceci said. 'The world is a poorer place for you not being able to *personally* check all the chocolate truffles coming out of Belgium.'

Sylvia wasn't listening. 'Only two days ago, Ralph introduced me to the Deputy Commissioner. Imagine that! We saw him when we took a short cut through the executive car park. *Un uomo affascinante.* Such a charming man. He waved as he passed us and said hello. I think he took quite a shine to me.'

'What with? A duster?' Lucia asked.

'Don't be silly. I could tell he liked me,' Sylvia explained patiently. 'I sometimes wonder if you are quite all there. I've met all sorts of people from different walks of life and got along with nearly all of them. I once passed a plate of biscuits to Georgio Armani, at a garden party. Such a charming man. Such wonderful trousers. And what have you been doing since I saw you last, Ceci? Still living a life of luxury? Not a care at all? How wonderful to just have yourself to think about. And a man to do all the difficult things. I have always felt the world's worries very deeply.'

'I can tell. Worry is so ageing,' Ceci said with a sympathetic look. 'And if I waited for Freddy to do all the difficult things I would still be at home waiting for the car to take me to our wedding.'

'And how long have you been married?' I asked.

Ceci looked blank. 'I've no idea. Freddy, how long have we been married?'

Freddy looked thoughtful.

'Thirty years? Maybe? I'm not sure. I've forgotten all the years I lived without you, my darling.'

He leaned across and kissed Ceci's cheek and she smiled with pleasure.

'What an old flirt you are,' she said.

'Oh, for heaven's sake,' Lucia snapped, 'don't encourage her.'

I bit back a smile as I turned away, afraid I was going to laugh.

Ceci's eyes brightened then as she saw her favourite tiramisu being brought to the table.

'This is good,' she said after her first taste, 'but perhaps mine is better.'

'I've always thought this is so unhealthy,' Sylvia muttered, tucking in. 'What is it after all? Cream and coffee and stale cake?'

'It's far more than that,' Ceci spluttered, indignant.

'If you say so,' Sylvia said, unconvinced.

'They should have used my recipe, which was passed down to me by our mother. Don't you remember? She used to say, "Give a woman tiramisu and she will be happy for ten minutes, but give her my recipe and she will be happy for life."'

I watched, astonished and slightly delighted, as Lucia took a dollop of cream on her spoon and flicked it at Ceci. It landed on her nose, and Ceci wiped it off and gave her sister a withering look.

'*Sei troppo vecchia* – you are too old for that sort of behaviour!'

Lucia shrugged. 'You might be, you old woman.'

Ceci took a spoonful of her own dessert and struggled for a moment, obviously considering returning the gesture, before eating it instead, and Sylvia laughed.

Unobserved by his wife, Freddy finished off his dessert in record time and then quietly signalled to a waiter for more. I watched Raleigh dabbing politely at the edges of her dessert with a teaspoon, and I could almost hear her brain totting up the calories as she did so.

'It's fabulous,' she said after a tiny taste, and then

proceeded to push the rest of it around her dish with a look of fear in her eyes.

Eric sat with his chin over the table, inspecting the bowl, asking what it was and looking doubtful.

'Enjoy it,' Paulo said, 'it's *Bisnonna's* favourite. She will eat yours if you aren't quick.'

Eric did his usual trick of sliding off his chair and wandering around the table inspecting everyone else's food.

'I don't want it,' he said furiously, at last. 'It's got spiders in it.'

'Nonsense,' Leo said cheerfully.

'Hers has,' Eric said, pointing.

I realised he was looking intently into my dish and, looking down, I saw one of my false eyelashes peeking out from behind a dainty chocolate shard.

I hastily peeled off the other one, wondering what on earth I must look like. And then I burst out laughing. So much for my attempts at new glamour.

Horrified, Eric watched me and then after a moment burst into tears.

'I'm never eating that again!'

* * *

The meal had finished by four thirty and we had all moved outside into the sunshine for coffee. Eric, having recovered from the false eyelashes episode, scuttled between the tables sneaking petit fours. Despite the threat of bad behaviour from the sisters, the event had all gone very well indeed.

'So how did you enjoy the meal?'

It was Paulo. Walking through the gardens, he had found me and Susie sitting in the sunshine. Beneath us, the Mediterranean spread out, a blue silk sheet under a hazy sky.

'Lovely,' I said. 'Everything was marvellous.' *Apart from losing one of my false eyelashes in my dessert and giving Eric a fit of hysterics.* I decided to gloss over those two issues. It might be easier to pretend I'd forgotten about them. 'I've met some really charming people and had a great time. I am so pleased to have been a part of it.'

'I was glad to have you here,' he said.

Susie suddenly stood up and darted off, muttering vaguely about some things she had to sort out. I didn't think she was very convincing at all.

Paulo and I, alone in our sheltered spot, looked at each other, neither of us really sure what to say.

'Everyone had such nice things to say about Ellen,' I said at last. 'Everyone seemed to love her.'

Paulo sat down with a sigh and rubbed his hands over his face. He suddenly looked tired. There were dark shadows under his eyes. An expression on his face that I didn't recognise.

'You must be pleased it's all gone off so well,' I said, 'despite your aunts' behaviour.'

He gave a short laugh. 'Them? They are always squabbling; I hardly notice it any more. And do you mean I must be glad it's all over?'

'Well, not exactly, but yes, I suppose so.'

'I am,' he said. 'It's been difficult. I could sleep for a month. It's been on my mind for so long and I didn't seem to have the same grasp of things as Ellen did.'

'Perhaps you need a holiday,' I said, 'to get away somewhere and relax.'

He shrugged. 'And you? What will you do?'

'Go home at the end of the week, I guess. Think about what to do next. Home seems a long way away. This place is so lovely. I wish I'd come here more than just once.'

'Why didn't you?'

'You know why,' I said.

We were silent for a few minutes then.

There. I had touched on the history between us. I didn't know what he was thinking, but my mind was busy with memories of him, of us.

He turned towards me, searching my face for my reaction.

'We liked each other, didn't we, all those years ago? Despite all the arguments. And the misunderstandings.'

Ah yes, that.

There had been an incident around Christmas. We had all agreed we would do a Secret Santa, to keep the costs down. I had drawn Ellen out of the hat, and she had drawn me.

I supposed it had been the build up to Christmas that had made us all so prickly. There was always someone in the house arguing about something. Ellen's ideas about Christmas decorations were quite subtle and tasteful, whereas mine were the exact opposite. We'd had a disagreement about whether fairy lights were a good idea above the fireplace, which I had won, and then, out of sheer devilment, added more and more. By the time I had finished it looked like Santa's grotto and Ellen had tutted every time she came into the room.

On Christmas morning I had felt quietly confident because I had found Ellen a brand new, very expensive makeup case in a charity shop. She had bought me a foot spa which had been heavily promoted on television and must have cost a lot more than the limit we had all agreed on. Every time the advertisement appeared we had all scoffed at it, saying what a horrible thing it was, how it was almost insulting to consider that a suitable gift for any woman, and yet that day, there it was.

Ellen had watched me unwrap it with a little smile on her face.

'I thought you needed one. You were complaining about your feet only the other day. You said they were like hooves. Apparently you can get special abrasive things to get rid of really bad bits.'

And of course, everyone looked at my feet and laughed and I had clenched my toes inside my socks with embarrassment. And then *How generous*, everyone said, forgetting that we had all thought it was a horrible thing.

My annoyance had continued unspoken all through the day, until we had drunk a few too many tequila sunrises, and in the end, I had taken myself off to bed early to avoid saying what I really thought. That she had pretended to be generous, but in fact had just been unkind. But of course, I couldn't say so out loud. Everyone thought it was a nice gesture, but I knew different.

I got you back, her smile seemed to say. *You won't tangle with me again.*

She'd said sorry the next day, she hadn't meant to upset me, and she sounded so sincere that I had believed her. A week later she had put a multipack of Crunchies on my dressing table by way of an apology.

Now my mind was more focused and not wafting in the sentimental haze I had constructed of the past, other memories were resurfacing and somehow making sense. It had taken a long time for us to properly reconcile after that, and somehow she had made me feel that the whole thing was my fault.

I remembered her insistence on the loo roll being hung a particular way, her wanting the kitchen window open, me wanting it closed. If we had a disagreement she would later act as though nothing had happened and be very friendly, whereas I would sulk, once again putting me in the wrong. And then she would hug me and say something nice about my outfit or congratulate me for a meal I had made and there would be a truce between us until the next time. Had I just maintained that friendship with her over the years because of Paulo?

So, in answer to his question, had he and I been happy back then, despite all that?

'Yes, I think so. You and I liked each other.'

My mouth was dry, my heart beating erratically. Perhaps it was the Prosecco, and maybe it wasn't.

What a terrible answer. *I think so.*

'And were you content,' he asked, 'after you married Greg?'

'On and off,' I said. 'I have three smashing children, two lovely granddaughters. A nice home. Shouldn't that be enough? And of course, I had my job and a home to run.'

'I understand,' he said.

I looked up at him in astonishment.

'Don't be ridiculous! How could you possibly understand? Greg was difficult, rather selfish and unkind. Ellen was such a marvellous person in every way; I've heard nothing else all day. Everyone loved her. She thought the world of you. And Leo. Everyone said what a wonderful wife she was, what a great friend. All the tales I have heard about her today. The charity work, rescuing pets, helping the local school.'

'Yes,' he said, 'she did all those things. And more.'

'I bet she wouldn't have nearly fallen down the stairs on the way to this event. I bet she wouldn't have lost her false eyelashes in her food,' I blurted out. 'Is Eric okay now?'

Paulo gave a little chuckle. 'Yes, he's fine. And if that's the worst thing that ever happens to him, he won't have much to complain about. I think he has recovered enough for Andrea to take him for a swim in the pool.'

There was a burst of laughter from a group somewhere in the garden. I looked over to see Ceci, Sylvia and Lucia, heads together in a huddle. Perhaps it was possible to argue and disagree and still really be friends after all. Instead of pretending, as I had with Ellen.

'You asked me and I gave you an answer, so I'll ask you the same question. Were you happy?'

He didn't reply for a moment and then he sighed.

'Sometimes, in the beginning. Ellen was a good person, but there were a lot of things I never really understood about her. There were things we couldn't discuss. She had little contact with her own family, and she was the sort of person to have many acquaintances but few true friends. There were parts of her life she would not share with me.'

I wondered what on earth he meant, but then I supposed it was true of a lot of marriages. There was always some small, dark corner into which the other person could never see.

'What sort of things?'

'Sometimes, in the end, I felt that the only thing she really cared about was this hotel. To make it successful, to make sure it was run properly.'

'She did a good job,' I said.

'She did,' he said, looking down at the table between us.

I felt so sad for him at that moment. Despite outward appearances, life in the last few years for him must have been very different from what I had imagined.

In a way, I could see it had been easier for me and for Susie too, I supposed. My marriage had ended in a burst of relief. But I had exchanged a cheating husband for a rather isolated life and for a long time had held on to my feelings of anger and betrayal like a comfort blanket.

'Forgive me, you don't seem very happy now.'

'No,' he said, 'I guess I'm not.'

I thought of all the useless things people said under those circumstances.

Things about time being a great healer. Tomorrow is another day. When you're going through hell, keep going. Remember the happy times. All that stuff.

And yet at that moment, sitting in the sunshine, the sky clear and blue above us, the gentle noise of people chatting, enjoying themselves. The lovely meal we had eaten, the wine, the glories of the occasion; those platitudes didn't seem appropriate.

I reached across and put my hand on his arm, the fabric of his suit jacket warm under my fingers. My feelings were so intense it was almost as though I could feel the individual threads in the cloth. The warmth of his skin beneath it.

'You must miss her so much. Give it time,' I said. 'It will be okay.'

He looked at my hand.

'Will it?' he said.

'Of course it will. You still have your friends and family here. And your son and his family are only a plane trip away. You must be so proud of him.'

'Yes,' he said, and then he turned away and looked back at the hotel, which was gleaming white in the afternoon sunshine. 'I'm very proud of Leo. I wish we could have had more children, but then – as I said, Ellen didn't want them and it never happened.'

'But your life here, in such a lovely place, must have been wonderful.'

He nodded slowly, glanced at me and then looked down. And then he stood up, walked away a few steps, deep in thought.

I waited in silence, hardly breathing.

At last, he came back.

'I never wanted to do this; did you know that? This life was not my choice. Ellen was the one who insisted we stay when we had a chance to leave. It was the closest we ever came to a proper argument. And then she did what she always did – she shut down and wouldn't talk about it. As the years went by, she came to need this place far more than I did. And eventually, more than she needed me. She worked so hard; she was efficient and clever. Almost obsessive about every little detail. Which of course is why she was so successful. But gradually, over the years, this place seemed to become smaller and smaller to me. Until our lives were bound by the layout of the dining room, how the napkins were folded, the way a sprig of redcurrants was placed on a dessert.'

I was astonished then. Could this be true? Had I been wrong about their marriage? I started to feel tense and breathless, quite lightheaded. He had ad-mitted something which would affect my memories of Ellen and our relationship once and for all. It would explain why she never mentioned her own family and seemed to have no attachment to Eng-land and the old days other than me and Susie.

She'd had this strange ability to be warm and generous and at the same time distant and self-contained.

'Sometimes I thought about you, remembered the way you made me feel. When we lost touch.'

'I told you; I lost your address that night,' I blurted out. 'I put it in my pocket and when I looked, it was gone. And the next time I saw you, you were with Ellen. It wasn't like today when people have emails and mobile phones and tracking devices. I didn't know how to find you. I would have done.'

'Would you?'

'Of course I would. I looked for you everywhere.'

'I looked for you.'

He had looked for me. He hadn't forgotten me after all. But then he had found Ellen instead. Or perhaps she had found him. I had settled for Greg. How different things might have been.

'When I saw you again that day, when I came to move into the attic room, I was so happy. But it couldn't be the same,' he said.

'Because of Ellen.'

'Of course. I didn't know what to do. But I knew how much my father had hurt my mother over the years, and I was determined not to be that sort of husband. And you said something about not hurting either of you, so in the end I did nothing. Which was also wrong.'

'How can it have been wrong? Look around you,' I said. 'It was all okay in the end, wasn't it?'

We sat in silence for a while, and the hotel cat, a sleek tabby, came and wound its way around his feet, and Paulo reached down to scratch its ears.

'I suppose so. I'm beginning to remember so many things about that time, things I thought I had forgotten. But it could have been different, couldn't it?'

'Everyone's lives could be different,' I said.

He reached out and took my hand, and it felt warm and safe in his.

'Look, I have an idea,' Paulo said at last. 'Today is busy with all these guests and visitors. But by to-morrow things will be calmer. If Susie is – how shall we say – busy, then I want to be with you. I don't care if the whole place slides off the cliff into the sea! I'll take you somewhere, show you more of the island than just this place. There are so many delightful spots to visit. But the main thing is I want to spend some time with you.'

His mobile rattled with a text and he checked his phone, frowning as he read the message.

'Oh, *non di nuovo questo*. Not again. I really can't

do this any more. I'm so sorry – you must excuse me. Another emergency. Do you see what I mean about having too much wonderful?'

He started to walk towards the hotel, but then he turned and came back. And then in the shade of the lemon tree, he pulled me to my feet, took me in his arms and kissed me. And for a moment I was back in the dark damp night when we had first met, both of us young, our optimism and energy undefeated by life.

'Don't go away,' he murmured.

'I won't,' I said.

I sat down again, my heartbeats skittering. I touched my fingers to my lips where he had kissed me, with the hand he had held. And then one of the young waiters came quickly towards me, a drink on a tray.

'Compliments of Signor Massimo,' he said.

And he placed a tequila sunrise on the table in front of me.

Unexpectedly, tears sprang into my eyes. Paulo had remembered.

14

Susie was nowhere to be found when I went back to my room to change and so I expected to spend the rest of the evening alone, and for some reason, I didn't mind. It was somehow quite pleasant to choose solitude rather than having it forced upon me. I had a lot to think about.

The day had been so busy, so full of meeting people and making small talk, which could always be exhausting, and then the conversation with Paulo, which had set my thoughts racing.

I was a grown-up. I didn't need a sidekick or partner or companion this evening. For once I felt comfortable in my own company. There was absolutely no reason why I shouldn't have a quiet drink, perhaps just a small snack later on, because I was still full from the lunchtime meal. And then I could think about the day, remember the sights and sounds in peace. And try to think what to do next.

And so I changed into some more comfortable and forgiving clothes. Designer dresses were all very well, but they did mean one had to maintain perfect posture for the evening and not just prepare to slump in a chair in my room, mulling over what I had said. What he had said. How he had looked. The way he still made me feel.

I found a table in a delightful little nook on the terrace. The evening was still warm enough; there were even little pipistrelle bats swooping about in the still air above me. The little girl with the rope was still skipping. The hotel cat was still sleeping, this time curled up in a flowerpot. Perhaps I wouldn't come back as a glamorous redhead next time; maybe I'd come back as a cat. They seemed to do pretty well.

Jess had sent me a picture of Violet at a nursery school trip to a local wildlife park and there was a text from Alex asking what the pin code was for my Netflix account, which I ignored.

I checked the weather app on my phone to see

what it was like back home and saw to no great surprise that it was raining.

I gave an unexpected sigh of pleasure that I
wasn't there and relaxed a little.

A waiter appeared at my side. 'May I bring your
usual, madam?'

I had *a usual*? I looked up at him rather blankly.

'Pinot Grigio, madam?'

I agreed that would be lovely and sat back in my
chair, feeling decidedly chic and cosmopolitan. Perhaps I should have had a cosmopolitan to celebrate
the event? Maybe I was drinking too much?

No sooner had I taken the first sip of my wine
than there was a bit of a commotion behind me and
Ceci, Freddy, Lucia and Sylvia appeared, Sylvia
leaning heavily on a stick and making a lot of fuss
about the shallow steps down onto the terrace, until
one of the waiters came and lent her a hand.

The sound of their conversation increased as
they came closer, and they sat with me. Lucia and
Sylvia had obviously been in the middle of a full-
blown argument, I thought it was about their blood
pressure, and I was sure their bickering wouldn't
have helped either of them. It was obvious my pres-
ence wasn't going to stop them. I wondered why they

sought each other out so much if they found the other so annoying.

'I told you before, there is no pleasure greater than being with family. I saw so many members of my family here today, it warmed my heart. And I am sure it reduced my blood pressure. Great happiness can do that. And stroking a cat apparently,' Ceci said.

'Well, try stroking that cat then,' Lucia said, jerking her head towards the tabby which was about to jump up onto a nearby table where there were some abandoned plates. 'It will take your arm off.'

'Cats always recognise a kindred spirit. And what a pity *your* son could not be here to accompany you,' Ceci said.

Sylvia fussed a little with her turquoise pashmina.

'*Sì*, it would have been nice to have him here, but you have to understand my son's time is not his own. He is essential for the smooth running of his department; well, for the whole European Commission actually. If they don't employ the right people, no department can work at all.'

'Even so, your dear son Roger is Paulo's cousin,' Lucia said silkily.

'Ralph. His name is Ralph,' Sylvia snapped, 'as you very well know, after Ralph Waldo Emerson the famous poet. My late husband was a renowned expert—'

'Not after Ralph Lauren? No, of course not, not having seen that picture of him in those shorts. You don't mind if we join you, do you?' Ceci gave me a charming smile. 'Freddy and I came out feeling in need of some pleasant company, but then we met Sylvia and Lucia in the hallway.'

'Of course,' I said. 'Can I order you a drink?'

The waiter was already standing to attention by my side.

'Holywell Malvern spring water,' Sylvia said, casting an eye over my wine glass. 'It's what the late Queen of England used to drink. And I'm sure we have all had more than enough alcohol for one day.'

'Yes, probably,' Lucia said. *'Sembra molto arrossata.* You're very flushed.'

'It's the company,' Sylvia said crossly.

'I'll have a gin and Dubonnet. I'm sure the Queen used to like that too,' Ceci said sweetly.

'Anche io – me too,' Lucia said. 'Don't worry about me, my liver is younger than yours and can cope with it.'

'And my husband will have...'

Ceci stopped to look at Freddy with a questioning eyebrow and he checked his glucose levels on his iPhone.

'Whiskey,' he said with a smile. 'I have a feeling I'm going to need it.'

Ceci sat back in her chair and sighed. 'Now then, *che giornata deliziosa* – what a lovely day we have had. Everything so well organised by *my* son. You see, Sylvia, the world doesn't just need bureaucrats.'

Sylvia nodded. 'No, that's true. Inn keepers are important too.'

'I'm sure César Ritz and Waldorf Astor would agree with you. And wasn't the food delicious? Last year, Paulo lured his chef away from the Cipriani in Venice.'

'Venice is sinking, isn't it?' Lucia said smoothly. 'I expect he was glad to leave.'

By that point, I wasn't sure if I was going to laugh or have a fit of the vapours, being in the middle of all this.

The three ladies took a break from their verbal jousting for a few minutes as their drinks arrived on a silver tray, accompanied by much deferential bowing from the waiter.

'Nuts,' Ceci said, which caused Sylvia to jerk her head round at the anticipated insult. 'I think I would like some cashew nuts.'

The waiter hurried off to find some and Sylvia dabbed at her throat with a handkerchief.

'It's been a splendid celebration of Ellen, someone who was much admired and loved,' I said, hoping I was going to defuse the situation.

'She was indeed,' Ceci said, 'very much admired. But strict. Very disciplined.'

'Isn't it wonderful when our children succeed in the world? My son Ralph is very much admired too,' Sylvia said. 'He has been told he may well be in line for a promotion soon. He was told by the assistant to the acting deputy leader of the department. Although I shouldn't be telling you this, *è molto confidenziale* – it's very confidential.'

'Oh, I promise we won't breathe a word,' Lucia purred. 'I mean, who would want to know?'

I looked over at Freddy, who was sipping his whiskey with a little smile on his face. He might be used to all this bickering, but I wasn't.

'Is Ralph married?' I asked.

'He is. To a lovely English girl. Cressida. Her father used to work for the government, so she is no stranger to a political life at the highest levels. He is an assistant director, which I'm told is the equivalent of a captain in the navy.'

'I love to see a man in uniform,' Ceci purred. 'Do

you have any recent pictures? All that braid, all those medals.'

'Not with me,' Sylvia said icily, 'and it doesn't work like that.'

'*Che peccato* – what a shame.'

I pressed on. 'And do they have children?'

Sylvia dived into the depths of her handbag and brought out a little book of photographs.

'This is Quentin, who is six, and Amelia, who is five. He is so bright, and she is going to be a beauty. The most delightful children.'

'Goodness me, is that blood?' Lucia asked, peering over my shoulder.

'Spaghetti sauce,' Sylvia said tersely, flipping the page over, 'and here they are on their first day at school. They go to the European School, such a wonderful place. Probably the best in the world.'

'I thought that was Carlsberg?' Freddy murmured.

Sylvia ignored him.

I looked through the pictures. From what I could see, Quentin and Amelia were a pair of perfectly ordinary-looking children who needed help with their table manners. But then Sylvia was a proud grandmother and perhaps I could cut her some slack. Violet and Maud were after all more than capable of wreaking similar carnage at the dinner table.

'How lovely for you,' I said.

Sylvia sipped daintily from her water glass.

'Do you have grandchildren?' Ceci asked me politely.

'Two, Violet and—'

Sylvia wasn't really interested. 'Yes, I am sure Quentin is destined for a career in the civil service; he is such a peacemaker. And he has always shared his toys with his sister. She on the other hand is very spirited. Quite self-absorbed on occasion.'

'I wonder where she gets that from?' Lucia mused, gazing at a picture of Amelia dressed as a fairy and clocking her brother over the head with her wand.

Ceci took a sip of her drink and dabbed her mouth with her napkin.

'So what are you going to do with the rest of your time here?'

I wished that people would stop asking me that. It made me realise that actually I had no plans at all. Everything had been about Ceci's birthday and re-membering Ellen, and now that was over I was be-ginning to feel like one of the extras in a film, just wandering about in the background pretending to be talking or doing something and enjoying myself.

'I'm not sure,' I said, trotting out the usual answer. 'It's such a lovely place, it's a treat to just be here.'

'Have you been to see the Salto di Tiberio?' Freddy asked. 'It's well worth the trek.'

Ceci nodded and turned to Sylvia. 'I really must take you there.'

Sylvia frowned. 'I've been there. Not for many years. That's up on some cliffs, isn't it? Lots of steps, I remember that. I don't think I would be able to manage now with my arthritis.'

'Oh, don't worry, I'd be happy to come along and give you a push if you needed it.' Ceci smiled.

* * *

I went to bed that evening feeling even more as though my part in this event was over and I should start thinking about going home. Susie still hadn't appeared and I hadn't seen anything more of Paulo. And yes, I did realise she was having fun, and naturally he was busy. He had a job to do and other people to worry about.

But even so, I was feeling exactly as I occasionally had when I was younger, out for the evening with my friends perhaps, and enjoying myself with my latest date. Sometimes, out of nowhere, a terrible feeling of being alone had washed over me. The noise, the people, the pounding music, the giggling queues for the ladies; I would somehow stop being part of the fun and instead would stand, struggling with the feeling that I didn't belong.

I could remember it so clearly, sitting at a sticky table, swigging back a drink I didn't want, not sure what to do. But then, on other occasions, I had also been quite happy to go out on the dancefloor with or without a partner and spin and twirl to the music, so I couldn't have been completely hopeless. Perhaps that had been the effect of the alcohol?

That was how I met Greg. I'd just broken up with my latest boyfriend, so I didn't have a plus one to take with me to Ellen and Paulo's wedding. Looking at all those other happy couples, watching Ellen and Paulo so much in love, exchanging their vows, her beautiful dress, the emotional speeches, the champagne, the applause and the excitement of the day. I realised that this was it; he had married someone else and I was probably going to be alone forever.

The evening DJ had been playing what I thought were called 'floor fillers', the sort of music that was irresistible. I had been slightly tipsy, still in my pale green dress which was made of some synthetic material, and I had collided with Greg as he crossed the dancefloor. There had been an actual spark of static electricity as he grabbed my hand to pull me back to my feet, and he had chuckled and made some comment about instant chemistry. Eight months later we were married.

I'd believed then that I wouldn't feel lonely again. I'd had a family, a career, a busy life, a husband. But gradually I'd realised that even that didn't really take away all those feelings, of not quite having got my life right. It wasn't supposed to feel like that, was it? There was still a gap in my life, one that I couldn't quite name. And surely I should have sorted it out by now? Weren't women my age supposed to feel confident and satisfied with their lives? Not restless like a cat trying to fit into a cardboard box that was too small.

I thought about Juliette then, finding happiness with Matthew, or Ceci with Freddy, and I wondered what it would take for me to feel the same level of contentment.

But was Juliette right. Should I take the chance to tell Paulo how I felt? How I had probably loved him for decades without even realising it? Not acknowledging it to myself. Never confessing it to anyone, not even my closest friend. It seemed pathetic, to admit that a piece of my heart had been given irrevocably to a man who had married someone else.

But surely this was not the time or the place to do so.

But if that was the case, when would be the right time?

* * *

'Raimondo wants to take me out for the day,' Susie said the following morning over breakfast.

'Again? Where to this time?' I said. I realised I sounded a bit irritated, and the last thing I wanted to do was to upset her when she was so cheerful. 'What's he got in mind?'

'Oh, I'm not sure,' Susie said, running a careless hand through her curls.

'And where did you get to last night?'

'Nowhere particular. I could see Paulo wanted to talk to you so we went off down the road to a little wine bar Raimondo knows and had a lovely time. I don't think I have talked to a man so easily for ages. And he doesn't try to sort my problems out like most men do, he just listens.'

She was looking very happy this morning, more so than I had seen her for years. Perhaps this was the effect her new admirer was having on her, and I was genuinely pleased for her. Heaven knows I had seen her often enough looking worried thanks to Simon and his gaslighting.

'We might take the ferry over to Amalfi today. I mean, you could come too if you wanted to?'

'What a dreadful idea.' I laughed. 'I'd be a real third wheel. No, you go and have fun.'

Susie fidgeted with the clasp on her handbag. 'I do feel a bit mean, leaving you on your own. But then we will be going home in a few days—'

'Then make the most of it,' I said.

'What will you do?'

'There's nothing wrong with just relaxing,' I said, 'enjoying the sunshine and the views and – well, everything.'

And Paulo had said he wanted to spend the day with me. So where was he?

She left an hour later, Raimondo picking her up in Paulo's car, and I watched them from my window as they drove off down to the harbour, looking very jaunty and windswept.

I spent some time emailing my son and daughters and sending them some photos of the previous day's events. And a picture of Paulo and me which Susie had taken, while I was dressed up in my designer finery. I sent that to Juliette too and within seconds she had replied.

You both look so happy. Why don't you tell him how you feel? We're all a long time dead. Sorry if that's insensitive, but I haven't seen you smile like that before. And he's gorgeous. Faint heart never won fabulous hunk!

I looked hard at that picture again. I had a wide smile; so did Paulo. I could almost remember the feel the light touch of his hand on my shoulder as we stood there. My borrowed dress had suited me; even my hair had been behaving and looking sleek. Behind us I could glimpse some of the lovely flowers in exuberant displays. It almost looked like a wedding picture.

The path not taken.

How would my life have been if we had been together, I wondered. Would we have been happy? Would we have learned not to argue? Would we both have been faithful and content?

That was it, I realised; the thing I was seeking. Not just to be coping, to be running my life efficiently. It wasn't just a case of mowing the lawn or paying the bills on time. Remembering birthday cards and meter readings. Getting by. Not falling down the stairs.

I wanted to matter. To matter to myself. But above all, I wanted to be able to do things I enjoyed, just for me. To be content.

That was what I wanted. To fill the void in my life that somehow had always been there, and still remained empty. But how?

15

I went for a stroll in the grounds of the hotel, going down the shallow terraces which were cut into the cliff and admiring the glorious views and taking deep breaths of the clear air. I had just a few days left of this trip. And I was determined to be independent and not wait for Paulo to have a few minutes free, like a forlorn fan at the stage door, hoping for a glimpse of a pop star. My new life was going to start today. I was going to do something impetuous and fun.

As I passed the reception desk, I picked up a bus timetable. There were buses into the town of Capri fairly regularly and it took just thirty minutes to get there. Result. I just had to find Anacapri station.

That must be a bus stop. It couldn't be difficult. From the map it looked like a short walk, and that would do me good. I'd done an awful lot of sitting about and eating since I had arrived.

Twenty minutes later, I set out along the road towards the town, wishing after a few hundred yards that I had a water bottle. And I had an awful feeling that they might be chic, but one of my new trainers was going to rub my heel. Perhaps I should have put some socks on. At least I had remembered my sunhat, and it was pulled low over my brow.

I'd only been going for ten minutes and a bus to Capri had just passed me, which meant I would have at least a thirty-minute wait.

I heard a vehicle pull up slowly behind me.

'Want a lift?'

This was it. The moment when I would get into a stranger's car and never be seen again. Or perhaps my body would be discovered at the foot of the infamous Salto di Tiberio, my handbag clutched to my chest, empty apart from a packet of breath mints and my reading glasses.

When had I become so suspicious of everyone? So cautious of life?

I turned round, trying to look tough and remember what *no thank you* was in Italian.

It was Paulo, smiling that wonderful smile behind the wheel of a little truck-type vehicle.

Despite my expectations of a solo trip, relying on my own wits, I felt a wash of relief. Or was it excitement at seeing him again?

I stood, dithering. 'I was going to get the bus into Capri.'

He leaned over and opened the passenger door.

'No need,' he said, 'I was going anyway. I was going to invite you to come with me. I have a small bit of business to attend to but it shouldn't take long. I was looking for you. I always seem to be looking for you, and I was told you had gone out. Hop in.'

Driving in a small open-top van meant it was noisy and dusty as we went down the road to the town. Which meant we didn't do much talking other than a couple of shouted comments about the stupendous views.

Really, I thought, I couldn't remember ever seeing anywhere so beautiful.

It was like a film set from some impossibly glamorous movie, where a troubled but attractive woman in chic clothes was whisked around in an Aston Martin by a handsome but slightly dangerous man in an Armani suit who might have been but possibly wasn't a secret agent.

The craggy cliffs and rocks provided an astounding contrast to the softness of the clear sapphire skies and the bright blue sea beneath it. There were other vehicles on the road, of course: buses negotiating the hairpin corners, delivery vans chugging up the hill with sacks of vegetables in the back, a builder's van with stepladders strapped to the roof.

It made me realise that although this was a holiday destination, it was also home to a lot of people. Thirteen thousand, Ceci had told me, and about half a million visitors every year. I tried to imagine the road in front of us filled with people, grabbing their children out of the way of the traffic. They would have to move round by numbers if those figures were correct.

We pulled into a parking space and Paulo stilled the engine. We walked through a few narrow streets until he stopped.

'Over there is the Piazza Umberto, better known as the Piazzetta. Shops restaurants and cafés. Now then, I will see you for lunch later, about one o'clock? But now as I said, I have to go to see someone' – he looked at his watch and frowned – 'and I am late.'

'Sorry, that was probably my fault.'

'If it is anyone's fault it is mine. You always did

try and blame yourself for everything. There's no need to do it now,' he said, exasperated. 'I must hurry, she doesn't like to be kept waiting. And she's not usually there today; she's made an exception for me.'

Ah yes, there was a *she* involved in all this. Of course there was. Why had I not thought of that?

A single man as good looking as Paulo, I expect the word had gone out all over southern Italy.

He pointed to a delightful-looking café with a blue awning and tables set out underneath it in the shade.

'I would recommend that place.'

'Please don't feel you need to organise me, I'll just wander around for a bit first,' I said, 'and then I might have coffee.'

'Later on you will find everywhere busy, but the owner is a friend of mine, and Genero will look after you.'

'I don't need looking after,' I said with a short laugh.

'Don't be so defensive; I know you don't. I mean he will find you a decent table,' Paulo said.

Suddenly he put an arm around me and kissed my cheek. I could feel the warmth, the strength of his body against mine, and it was intoxicating.

'Try the *crema al caffee*. The *Zeppole di San Giuseppe* is the best anywhere. Genero is pretending to be wiping down the tables, but he is watching, and now he has seen you are a friend of mine, you will be fine.'

I turned and a large man with an elaborate waxed moustache gave a wide grin and waved his cleaning cloth at Paulo.

'Genero! *Come stai?* Now I really must go,' Paulo said. 'I will see you later.'

I jolly well hoped so, or I would have to catch a bus. And how would I know which one or where it went from? And how much would it be? Did they need the right amount? I had some euro notes, but no coins.

Perhaps I would worry about that later. After all, this was a sort of adventure. I had to remember my new determination to do things differently.

As I walked towards the café, Genero came forward and ushered me towards a lovely table in the shade, set with a white cloth.

'Café crema and—' What was the word? 'A zeppelin.'

'*Ah sì, certo, signora,*' he said, and moments later a large cup of coffee topped with what looked like whipped cream appeared in front of me, swiftly followed by what possibly was a zeppelin, filled with cream patisserie and cherries.

Both were utterly delicious, and I quelled my first instinct which was to hoover it up as fast as possible and instead made a point of savouring every sip and every bite. That way from my shady corner, I could prolong my visit and people watch and wonder about them.

There were couples hand in hand, a few older people with backpacks and walking poles, families with pushchairs, young girls in giggling groups. Everyone seemed to be enjoying themselves. And actually, so was I. Apart from the niggling thought at the back of my mind which refused to be silenced. Who was 'she'?

Perhaps Paulo had a lady friend in the town. Someone sophisticated and supportive. A woman who provided a shoulder for him to cry on, and who knew what other body parts?

No, I wouldn't allow myself to think like that; it was none of my business.

Genero returned with his trusty cloth and pretended to clear up the table next to mine.

'*In vacanza?* On holiday?' he said.

I nodded and tried to dredge up some Italian words.

'A special occasion. *Un'occasion speciale.*'

That didn't sound terribly convincing, and I thought I had made it up, but Genero nodded and smiled and flicked some cake crumbs off the table onto the ground, where a couple of sparrows swooped in to pick them up.

'*Non così occupato.* Not so busy today,' he said.

'It's a beautiful place,' I said.

Genero looked pleased.

'And you are *un'amica*, a new friend to Paulo?'

'*Oui.*' No, that was French. '*Sì*, yes,' I agreed, not sure if that was true or not; after all, I'd known him for decades, but my Italian wouldn't cope with that. So I might as well use what little language skills I had.

'Nice. Nice,' Genero said, smiling broadly. '*È un brav'uomo. Mi amico.* Good man.'

'Yes,' I said, stirring some sugar into the remains of my coffee.

'He will be... *Sarà con Stephanie*, always. Many times.'

So, was he with someone called Sara or Stephanie?

I had visions of an actress I remembered from my childhood, Stephanie Powers, tossing auburn curls and a pocket rocket figure, and felt mildly discomforted.

'*Allora*, enjoy!' Genero said and went off to escort a new couple to a table inside.

I took another taste of my zeppelin cake, enjoying the tang of the sour cherries on my tongue. Paulo had been right; it was sublime.

Then I wondered again where he was and what he was doing.

The Piazzetta was filling up by the time I had finished. I'd had a text from Alex asking if he could use my washing machine as his wasn't working again. In a spirit of rare assertiveness, I sent him the phone number of the local odd job man and went inside to use the loo, because I never passed up the opportunity, and then I paid my bill.

I strolled over to the end of the square where there was a clock tower covered in scaffolding, a building housing the funicular railway, and a row of columns framing another fabulous view.

I sat down on a bench and a middle-aged couple sat at the other end, taking pictures, arguing about where to go for lunch and complaining about something. He was wearing shorts from which he had forgotten to remove the price tag, and it dangled just beneath the edge of his shirt. He looked like a weather-beaten dog. She had a face which

was all angles, her mouth a steel trap of dis-
approval.

What a shame, to be wasting time grumbling
when they could be simply enjoying the lovely day
together. Would they rather be home, in the rain?
She complaining about something else and him es-
caping to work with a sigh of relief? At least they had
each other for company. Perhaps they should appreciate that and make the most of it.

They moved on, physically together and yet emo-
tionally far apart. I supposed it made me a bit sad
because in a way it reminded me of how Greg and I
must have appeared to a casual observer. Would it
have been better to just be alone rather than hang
on to a relationship where neither one seemed to
like the other?

And yet what did I know? When push came to
shove, he might be the sort of man who would fight
off a bear, throw himself in front of a bullet or a car
in order to save her, although I couldn't for a moment imagine Greg doing any of those things. The
most I would have expected from him would have
been an eye roll.

She might have been putting the loo seat down
and picking his socks off the floor for the last thirty
years and at the end of her tether. But on the other

hand, she might be the only woman in the world who understood his moods and fears. Appearances could be deceptive. Had I understood Greg? No, not really. But I had tried. He was just one of those men who compartmentalise their lives. Wife and family in one box. Work and everyone else in another.

I had been like that woman not so long ago. Irritated and dissatisfied. Perhaps now I was learning how to enjoy life, to accept it and to make of it what I wanted. I was single again; no one else was going to do it for me.

I sat there for a while and all around me was the chatter of people, admiring the view in various languages, complaining about the heat and the prices in the cafés.

I wished yet again I had a water bottle. Everyone else seemed to have them. Young people in particular seemed incapable of going anywhere without one. Some of them had massive water flasks which must have held a litre and been incredibly heavy. One of those and I would be searching for a loo all day. It didn't bear thinking about.

I went for a walk, strolling down little streets and alleyways as the fancy took me. I passed a bus station, the orange buses lined up in a row, which made me feel very optimistic and capable. At least I would know how to get home later on if I needed to. There was always a solution to any problem if one looked hard enough.

There were pastel-painted hotels with brightly coloured shutters, ice cream parlours and pharmacies. Further on, some fashion shops, some of them open, others closed until later in the afternoon. There were high-end names displaying unusual handbags and dresses, presumably catering for all the wealthy, woodlice, celebrities when they ventured forth into the evening.

I wondered what Paulo was doing. Where was he? How long would his appointment take? What was he doing?

I saw a young woman dart into a café and return almost immediately with a carrier bag laden down with paper-wrapped sandwiches. Perhaps Paulo and Stephanie were having a business lunch?

Or maybe they were in bed together, lying languorously on rumpled sheets, smiling at each other as the sun shone through the slats of the closed shutters.

He had been on his own for years. What had Ceci said? No one should be alone.

I had no right to be jealous or suspicious.

Maybe Stephanie was a management consultant

who was stepping in now that Ellen's capable hand had gone. She would be grey haired and sensible, sitting in a dingy office with piles of cardboard folders blocking her view out of the window to the sea below. She would be smoking a cheroot and talking very fast about hand dryers or chill cabinets and Paulo would be reading documents and signing paperwork and looking perplexed.

What had he said? *I can't do this any more.*

16

By the time I returned to the Piazzetta, the day had warmed up, and even though I had been trying to stay on the shaded side of the streets, the sweat was trickling down between my shoulder blades. I wished I had brought some suncream. And my sunglasses. But then in England these things never seemed to be high up my list of priorities. Whether to take a coat or an umbrella were the things to consider.

The crowds were bigger; queues were forming for the funicular railway. And people were obviously thinking about lunch. I watched them, stopping outside the cafés and restaurants, reading the menus pinned up outside. Occasionally the waiters would appear from inside, to encourage people in.

Suddenly a small child ran straight into me at speed, stopping and throwing his arms around my legs so I nearly fell over.

It was Eric, and a few steps behind him Andrea hurried up, her progress hampered by a big back-pack in one hand and Eric's iPad in the other.

'Where have you been?' he said to me.

'Nowhere,' I replied.

Eric shook his head. 'Everyone is somewhere. I've been swimming and then we got the bus which was very exciting, and now we are looking for Nonno. He said he would see us here for lunch.'

'We are ten minutes early, Eric,' Andrea puffed, dropping the backpack onto the floor. 'Nonno said one o'clock.'

'I want him to be here,' Eric said, pouting.

'How is your headache, Andrea?' I asked, ignoring him.

'*Estoy mucho major*. Not too bad, very good.'

'I gave her that rose,' Eric said, 'and it worked.'

Andrea put an arm around him and looked at him with genuine affection.

'*Un buen chico*, a good boy,' she said, and Eric beamed up at me.

'Can I have an ice cream now?'

'Maybe after lunch,' I said, 'and you will find that if you ask nicely and say please, you tend to get better results. But first you need some proper food to make you grow as tall and strong as Poppa and Nonno.'

Eric looked annoyed.

'I am as tall as Poppa and Nonno.'

'No, you're not, not nearly as tall,' I said.

Eric wanted to argue with this.

'I'm strong.'

'You will be even stronger when you have eaten your lunch,' Andrea said, and Eric looked thoughtful.

He took a deep breath ready to resume the argument and then his face suddenly cleared.

'There is Nonno!'

He darted off, dodging around people until he reached Paulo, who swung the boy up onto his shoulders.

'Now I am taller than Nonno,' he called triumphantly.

'Lunchtime, I think,' Paulo said. 'Follow me if you are ready?'

He went over to a restaurant in the corner of the Piazzetta where there was a queue of about ten people waiting to get in, but as we got there, he headed for a small side alley, lifted Eric down and went through a blue beaded curtain. We followed him up a narrow staircase where the air was dark and scented with garlic, eventually coming out into a room where light flooded in through the glass walls. It was breathtaking, the new view out over the sea crystal clear in the sunshine. A refreshing and cooling breeze too, which was very welcome.

I wondered for a moment how on earth anyone could clean that expanse of glass, and then sat down at a table set for four.

'My friend's place,' he said by way of explanation. 'The food here is very good.'

'Can I have fries?' Eric asked.

I raised my eyebrows and sent him a questioning look.

'Can I have fries, please?' he added.

I was happy to see that the little talk we had shared had made a small difference. Paulo looked at me and a little smile twitched at the corner of his mouth.

'Were you good for Andrea this morning?' Paulo asked, looking stern once more.

'I was good, wasn't I, Andrea?' Eric said. 'I didn't run away, and I was kind like Jo said.'

'*Eso es cierto*, it's true,' Andrea agreed.

'Then you can have fries and ice cream as well.'

Eric beamed at me.

'You see? I was right, wasn't I?' I said.

That was the thing I remembered from my teaching days. The constant need to reinforce good behaviour and then go home and sort my own children out. It had got exhausting after thirty years.

Once we had ordered food, Andrea and Eric went off to look out of the windows at the square below, pointing at a dog running after some pigeons.

'How did your meeting go?' I said, too curious to keep off the subject any longer.

Paulo nodded slowly and thoughtfully.

'Good. We made progress.'

This effectively told me nothing at all.

Progress with what, for heaven's sake?

'So, everything is good?'

'Quite good, I think.'

He was different from the way he had been yesterday. He was more reserved, almost formal. I wondered how to draw more out of him.

Are things going well? Are you up to date with your taxes? Are your investments okay? Did you order a stack of new towels? How old is Stephanie? Is she younger than me? Well, probably. Recently I've been realising most people are. How long have you been friends with her? Are you more than friends? What are your intentions?

'That's great,' I said.

'It's a weight off my mind,' he replied, 'or it will be.'

What could that be then?

Perhaps he was embroiled in a court case which had been going on for years, paying back money to the government, fighting to clear his good name, while Stephanie – now a lawyer in a tight, black suit and stilettos – retrieved documents and made ringing challenges across the courtroom. It made me realise that there was still so much about him and his life of which I knew nothing, and suddenly I wanted to know everything.

'I had to go to court about six years ago,' I said. 'It was very frightening.'

'What did you do?' he asked, obviously amused. 'First degree murder? Arson? I remember you setting fire to a litter bin outside the café we used to go to. What was it called? The Green Door? Or was it Betty's?'

'It was Betty's, and I didn't set fire to it, it *caught* on fire because I threw a cigarette end into it.'

'Drunk driving then? Shop lifting? Fighting in the streets?'

I gave a deep sigh. 'I'm so pleased you think all these are things I might be capable of doing, but no. I was on jury service. For a week.'

'Anything interesting?' He chuckled.

'No. Someone who was disputing a parking fine, or it might have been council tax. I can't remember now.'

Two waitresses came through the door at that point with our lunch and a large bottle of chilled water, the condensation running down the sides. Sorting all this out meant that by the time we started chatting again, the subject of going to court and solicitors and legal business was forgotten.

Instead, we were on to an Eric-centric discussion about who would win in a fight, a dinosaur or a robot, and would we rather be stuck in a lift with Bingo or Bluey? Not having much of an idea who they were, it turned into Eric explaining his preferences, while he swung his legs under the table and munched away at his pizza slice and fries.

After that he settled down by a table at the other end of the room by a window to do some colouring, thanks to a book and some crayons from Andrea's backpack. Soon afterwards followed by a bottle of

water, Andrea produced some shape-matching picture cards, wet wipes and a book all about cowboys.
I'd forgotten how much stuff one needed to take
with a child on even the shortest trip. And finally,
Andrea took him to find the loo, and then go downstairs to find ice cream at one of the gelaterias in the
square.

'So tell me more about your life now,' Paulo said.

At last we had a few minutes alone.

'I live in a small town. My son Alex has been
living in London although he is staying with me at
the moment. I'm hoping he will be moving out soon.
I see Jessie and Kat as often as I can, but of course
they don't live nearby. Sometimes I go and visit
them, particularly when their husbands are away on
business. Not because I don't get on with them, it's
just a bit easier and I can help out with my granddaughters.'

'Ellen was the same,' he said, 'you know that. She
got into the habit of only inviting friends to stay
when I was away. For company. Or she would travel
to see them. Particularly you.'

'I don't understand. Why particularly me?' I said,
puzzled.

Paulo paused for a moment, thoughtful, and
then he lowered his voice.

'Surely you remember? I don't think she wanted... how can I put this? Well, she didn't want me to question my decision. My choice. At the time it was hard to make any other. We got engaged. She planned her life around me.'

'Surely you didn't regret it?' I asked. 'You can't have done. What happened between you and me was—'

I was glad there was no one else around to overhear this conversation, and I knew from experience that children heard and could repeat the most embarrassing things. Seven-year-old Jess had once loudly asked me in the middle of Sainsbury's if Daddy knew I had thrown out his comic with the lady on the front.

Paulo looked at me but didn't speak for a second.

'I used to feel different, as though I had the power to go anywhere, do anything I wanted to. You made me feel like that when I first met you. But after we married, Ellen was absolutely focused on our life here. She had such great ideas; she was so good at what she did. And that was the difference. How could I turn my back on that, on seeing her so fulfilled? After a while, leaving, not running the hotel, was something that we would not, could not, talk about.'

'You never did build any roads or bridges?'

He shook his head. 'Not one. Not yet.'

There was something in his brown eyes that worried me then, and at the same time I recognised the meaning, the expression. He had turned his back on leading the sort of life he'd expected to, just as I had. I began to understand why Ellen had kept her life with Paulo so separate from her life with us over the years. In case he suddenly felt he wanted to change things, to make his life different, just as I had.

I'd assumed that she preferred to come to England for a break from running the hotel. A change of scene and climate that meant she could shop in different places, catch up with old friends and their families. Even on one occasion go with me to a university reunion.

She'd seemed to enjoy that, telling everyone about Capri and the hotel. She had looked fabulous too in a blue velvet dress, her hair pinned up in a chignon, and all eyes had followed her that evening. Everyone had envied her. She had blossomed under people's admiration. She'd explained Paulo's absence; such a shame, he was too busy, he didn't like to leave Capri. It had never occurred to me that she might have wanted to keep Paulo away from us, or more specifically from me.

I thought about this for a few moments and suddenly it made sense.

Greg had always been a bit embarrassing when Ellen came to stay with us, paying her extravagant compliments, admiring her style, her flair for fashion. Pulling out a chair for her at the dining table as though he was a waiter. Always angling for an invitation to stay with them that had never materialised.

'It's been a lovely visit,' she'd said one time as she was leaving, 'and Greg is so unlike all your other boyfriends. I do hope you're just as happy as Paulo and I are.'

My mouth was suddenly dry, and the pasta salad which I had enjoyed for my lunch now sat like a rock in my stomach.

I took a sip of water.

'I never did or said anything about it,' I said.

'Nor did I,' he replied, 'but she knew. We never discussed it, but she always knew.'

'Knew what?'

Behind us there was a sudden clatter as Eric came back into the room, still clutching the remains of an ice cream cone. He came across to lean his surprisingly sharp elbows heavily on my knee.

'Can we go and buy some jeans now, please? So I can really be a cowboy?'

I took a deep breath and closed my eyes for a moment.

I felt Paulo's hand on my shoulder and we stood up together.

We exchanged a long look, while Andrea on the other side of the room cleared up all the debris into Eric's backpack and wiped his hands with a wet wipe.

'We must talk about this later,' Paulo murmured, and my heart gave a little leap of anticipation.

'Yes,' I said, 'I think we must.'

17

Well, we found some jeans for Eric in one of the very upmarket designer shops, where Paulo was greeted as a valued customer by the young assistants, and Prosecco was offered before we were led to a chaise longue, waiting for Andrea to wrestle Eric into some new trousers behind some tasteful linen drapery.

My mind was spinning with all sorts of thoughts. Paulo had broached the subject of our feelings for each other. All those years ago. All that time, when it seemed he had felt something for me too. Was it even possible?

I used to feel different, as though I had the power to go anywhere, do anything I wanted to. You made me feel like that.

I felt a little twinge of pride then, as though I had done something very clever. Something that Ellen, for all her charm and ability, had not done. She had been a woman regarded by everyone who knew her as a delight. Who, with her undoubted artistic flair, had transformed the hotel into somewhere elegant and successful.

But I had made Paulo feel powerful.

Meanwhile, there was a lot of struggling and complaints and banging about behind the curtain for a while, until at last Eric emerged looking very pleased with himself, wearing a pair of little trousers that probably cost more than my weekly shop.

'Are you sure Raleigh will approve?' I said, rather unsure about what we are doing.

Andrea shrugged but her expression spoke volumes. Mostly of the 'negatory' variety.

'If I cannot spoil my grandson when I see him, then too bad,' Paulo said, chuckling. 'A boy his age should not be worrying about his clothes. He should be climbing trees and getting muddy.'

Trying and failing to imagine such a scenario, I looked at Eric, who was admiring himself in the mirrors.

'I look cool. Like the other boys when they go out

playing cowboys,' Eric said at last, 'and please can I have a T-shirt too? The one with the dinosaur.'

He kicked a contemptuous foot at his shorts and shirt discarded on the dressing room floor, and I foresaw trouble ahead.

Andrea bit her lip and looked agonised.

'I think you should pick those up properly, don't you, Eric?' I said.

He looked puzzled. 'Why?'

'Because someone has to, and you are the one who dropped them there.'

And much to my surprise, he did.

Paulo paid the bill, looking rather amazed that it cost quite so much to satisfactorily clothe one weedy boy, and we went back out into the sunny afternoon, which after the aggressive air-conditioning of the shop, was quite a shock.

'We'd better go home,' Paulo said, and Eric grinned up at me, swinging the glossy carrier bag with rope handles that the assistant had given him for his old clothes.

'Do I look like a cowboy?'

'Absolutely,' I said, 'apart from the stegosaurus.'

* * *

On our return home, Eric was as subtle as a Chieftain tank driving over a watermelon and raced off upstairs shouting to find his mother. Paulo and I exchanged a look and he took my arm, and we escaped into the gardens. Well, it was nearly four thirty and surely time for a cup of tea and one of the delectable little cakes from the kitchens.

We found a table to the far side of the hotel where we couldn't immediately be seen by anyone else and settled down to watch the sun dipping slowly towards the sea. It was very quiet, just a few insects buzzing in the lemon trees, and far off the sound of a car, labouring up the hillside.

This reminded me it wouldn't be long before I would be leaving and driving back down that road towards the harbour and then onwards to get the ferry to Naples and the flight home. It made me feel sad and uncomfortable to think of it.

This place was so filled with light in comparison with my ordinary little town, the gardens here still filled with colour and fragrance, where my little patch would by now be losing its flowers and the leaves would surely be falling from the trees into wet piles.

We drank our tea in a companionable silence. I wondered if perhaps Paulo should be busy doing something behind the scenes inside, but he showed no desire to leave.

'I hope you have enjoyed your day?' he said at last.

'I have,' I said, my eyes fixed on a seabird, which was wheeling above the cliffs.

Were those the same cliffs where Tiberius flung his enemies to their doom? I had no idea. And I realised that even after a few days I knew nothing of this place. I was just a tourist, like thousands of others.

'The history here must be fascinating,' I said. 'Weren't the Romans here? I've heard about Tiberius.'

Why was I talking about that when I wanted so much to resume our previous conversation?

'The Phoenicians and the Greeks too,' he said. 'The legend is that the Faraglioni rocks were created when Polyphemus threw them at Ulysses. I must take you there, so you can see. There were rumoured to be angry mermaids who lived there and lured sailors to their death. But Greek legends are very variable and other stories exist. But there were more ancient people before them. Then there were pirate attacks and the French under Bonaparte. The Spanish, the English; a lot of people wanted to control

Capri until it was given back to Ferdinand of the Two Sicilies.'

'I would have thought one Sicily would have been enough for any king?'

He chuckled. 'But yes, Tiberius was the most infamous. I should take you to see some of the villas he built. And the Faraglioni rocks I mentioned earlier. They are very beautiful.'

I gave a deep sigh. 'Everywhere here is beautiful.'

'It is, isn't it?'

There was another long silence between us then, and my thoughts began to race. Was this it then? The moment when we would not be interrupted by Eric and his endless questions, or guests wanting to ask about buses or boat trips, and we would actually talk properly to each other?

'I'm sorry it took so long for you to be here,' he said. 'I would have liked to see you, but then time passed, things happened.'

'Perhaps you were right and Ellen did that on purpose,' I said, 'and perhaps I would have done the same in her position.'

'I don't think you would. You were always more...'

I waited while he found the right word.

'...easy going. More trusting. Ellen knew that I

had feelings for you which were different from what I felt for her, and I respected her reluctance to let the past into our future.'

He had feelings for me.

'I was married with a family, and so were you.'

He nodded. 'But she knew.'

'Knew what?' I wanted to be sure that I wasn't getting this horribly wrong.

'That I loved her. That I was glad I had married her. But what was between us, between you and me, that had always been something different.'

My mind wrestled with this. Of course they had loved each other. In a way it would have been easier if he has said their marriage was a disaster, but obviously it hadn't been. Anyone who ever saw them together had accepted that. They had been a gloriously good-looking couple, with a certain glamour about them. All of us, all our friends had accepted that they were going to be together forever. She was so perfect for him.

Paulo and I had been a fiery, fleeting friendship. Something very different and surely not something that would last or bring him the sort of contentment he had found with Ellen.

And my marriage to Greg. That too had been a relationship of – of what? One where we settled for each other and the life we had led. Not blissfully happy, but enough.

At that moment, it seemed a dull, unsatisfactory word.

But perhaps that was what most people did – settled for enough?

Was that what my life had been all about?

I felt a sudden unexpected surge of despair. We all had one life, and I could see only too clearly that I, like many other women, had changed and adapted, had accepted a life of predictability. I was the one who was the homemaker, the carer, the appeaser, the one who put up with things. Peace at any price.

I was sixty-five. I might have just a few years left; I might have many. The one thing I was sure of was that I wasn't going to settle for 'enough' any more.

'What a fool I have been,' I said.

'What?' he said, turning to look at me.

I didn't think I realised I had spoken those words out loud, but now they were out there, I felt a new sort of bravado.

I didn't quite know how, but I was going to change things.

While I still had my health and strength I was going to enjoy my life. Barely an hour had gone by since I had arrived here when I had not wondered what Alex was up to, how Jess was dealing with Maud's new tantrums, if Kat had recovered from her cold. I was not going to carry on the way I had since my marriage broke up. Constantly focused on everyone else. I was going to – frightening phrase – please myself.

'I think I loved you for years,' I said. I had a sudden mental image of Juliette giving me an enthusiastic thumbs up. 'With Greg it was more of a partnership. With you it was something else, something I haven't felt since.'

'We were very young. What were you? Nineteen? Twenty? That's no age to settle down with the first man who falls in love with you.'

I was silent then, turning his words around in my head.

'You fell in love with me?'

He raised his eyebrows as though the question surprised him.

'Of course. You were special, not like anyone else. Your friendship meant everything to me. I tried not to feel that way but I couldn't help it. You were so passionate about everything. So sure of yourself.'

'Trust me, I wasn't. I didn't feel that at the time,' I said.

'But you were. It was all a part of you. All those arguments we had, the way your eyes sparkled, the way you teased me. The way you never took me seriously. I enjoyed it all. You made me laugh at life, feel alive.'

Somewhere in the garden someone laughed, and another voice called a greeting.

'I don't know what to say,' I said.

He took hold of my hand.

'You don't need to say anything,' he said.

'I always say something,' I said. 'I never did learn to shut up.'

'Which, believe me, is so refreshing. It may sound a good thing, but it's hard to live without discussion or disagreement. Maybe I am just a product of my family. You have seen how we love to quarrel about the silliest things.'

I sat there, enjoying the feeling of his hand in mine, wondering what twist of fate had brought me to be in this place at this time with this man. It was the last thing I had expected. I was, by anyone's standards, too old for this sort of nonsense.

But was it nonsense? And if so, why?

If I was forty or fifty, would it still be foolish to be talking like this, with the widowed, lonely husband of one of my oldest friends? At what age did a woman, or a man for that matter, become too old for affection or compliments or love? Ceci obviously didn't think like that. Or simply – in a world dominated by pouting, self-important young people – what did it take for older people to be noticed? Did I just need to resign myself to playing a significant part in other people's lives, but not in my own?

'I have had a good life, a happy life,' he said at last, 'but this life – what you see – was never, ever what I wanted. I told you the first time we met, I did not want to stay here for ever, I wanted to see the world. Seeing you again makes me realise my life is not yet over after all. I have not achieved many of the things I wanted to.'

'What things?'

He laughed. 'Building a road or a bridge for one thing. Well, that's how it started, wasn't it? No, seriously, I mean things for myself. Not for other people,' he said. 'Does that sound selfish?'

'Not at all, I have been thinking much the same. I have spent my life working and looking after my family, and now most of the time they don't need me. Well, apart from my son, who seems to be regressing into teenage years again. But I'll support him and help him to move on with his life. And he will.

Which is great, of course it is, but in the grand scheme of things I feel a bit superfluous.'

'I'm sure that's not true,' he said.

'I don't want to be left behind,' I said. 'I want to keep moving forward. Like a shark, I suppose, they have to keep swimming, don't they? Or they drown.'

He laughed. 'What goes on in your head?'

'I mean I want to have a life of my own for the first time. I went from living with my parents, going to school then to university and then to marriage. This is the first time in my life I have ever lived alone and it is taking some getting used to. Not having to answer to anyone.'

He nodded in agreement. 'My father was never a big part of my life. My mother remarried and lived in Rome, so I spent my childhood here with my grandparents. When they died I was already married to Ellen, and she was making such great changes here. My grandfather always thought she was wonderful. Suddenly there was no question of us leaving. But it was never what I wanted, not at all. You knew that. I had dreams of seeing the world, of doing something momentous or important. Doesn't that sound ridiculous now? But Ellen made it impossible to break away; she refused to discuss it. She had good business ideas. She could see the details much better than I could. She had a flair for design; she was artistic and imaginative. And so we just carried on, doing this, year after year, and of course it got easier. We made improvements and she transformed this place. It worked so well. But sometimes I felt so trapped, so desperate.'

'And now?'

'I am restless to find out. To find out about the world, not just stay in this little corner. I told you that the night we met. To escape. And now, well, maybe it is too late. Perhaps I should be grateful for what I have, not wish for the things I lack.'

'I've been feeling the same way but that's not the way I want to live. Not any more. It's not too late for either of us, Paulo. We could have many years left to enjoy doing the things we want to do.'

He laughed. 'I have been thinking about it.'

'So, what is stopping you?'

He thought about this for a while and then he took a deep breath.

'I have a good life here, anyone can see that. So why am I so restless?'

'You sound like me,' I said, 'wanting to strike out and find new things to be excited about. But not having the courage.'

'You were the bravest person I ever knew,' he said.

'I didn't feel like that,' I admitted. 'I was just pretending. Life can get in the way of our courage. I suppose I want to feel needed again.'

'I need you,' he said, and we looked at each other then.

'Do you?' I said, hardly able to breathe.

'I always did.'

There was a pause then, and he leaned back in his chair, stretching his long legs under the table.

'Can I tell you something? Something that no one else knows?'

'Yes, of course,' I said.

I tried to sound calm, but inside my mind was racing, my thoughts tumbling over each other. *He needs me.*

He lowered his voice. 'I have been making enquiries over the last few months. Finding out about selling the hotel. I was able to convince myself life was good here when Ellen was alive, but since she died, I realise I am not happy. I am just – how would you put it – treading water. Marking time.'

I took a deep breath. 'Selling it! I had no idea.'

'It's early days. I have been speaking to

Stephanie, who works for an international firm of estate agents who deal with this sort of thing. Without any sort of commitment.'

'But what would your family say?' I whispered.

Paulo shook his head. 'Leo made it quite clear he never wanted to run this place. I did ask him a few years ago but his life and his family are in America. One of the reasons he left was because he could see Ellen was expecting him to take over from her one day, and that's not what he wanted either. She always believed he would return, but then he married Raleigh, and he told us that he would never live here again. Of course she was devastated but I'll be honest, I was relieved. He had the determination to do what I never did and I admired him for that. Since Ellen died, the same team have been running the hotel as she ordered. Ellen put all that in place. It's as efficient as it can be. But what will happen when I am gone? That is what I have been thinking for a while now. My grandparents started the hotel. I went to university for a few years, but then my grandmother died, I came back with Ellen and she gradually took over and we carried on when my grandfather died. Ellen was the perfect partner. She made her life here, she had ideas and vision and as you know, she was very determined. But then, nothing stays the same. Time moves on, and we must move with it.'

'I suppose so. It seems a shame,' I said, 'but what about Ceci? What will she do?'

'You don't need to worry about her, but how kind of you to think like that. My mother and Freddy have a beautiful house in the country outside Florence. She has friends there, a good social life and all the help she needs.'

'But you haven't told her your plans?'

'Not yet, but I will. I don't think she will be terribly surprised. Who knows, I might go and stay with her for a change. It will be just like your son coming to live with you,' he said, grinning.

'I'm sure you would know how to work the washing machine, and not to spill red wine on the carpet.'

He leaned back and linked his hands behind his head.

'I hope I would. Today I just have this wonderful, restless feeling inside me, which is growing. And what you said was true. It's not too late to do something different, is it? Something for me.'

'No, it's not,' I said. 'So, Stephanie – the person you mentioned – is an estate agent?'

'Yes, and she is well past the point of retiring too.

I am one of her last clients, so perhaps it would be a good time to change things, for both of us.'

So, Stephanie was probably not a glamour puss with flowing auburn hair and sleek, designer suits.

'Genero said he thought you were meeting her. I thought perhaps she was a girlfriend.'

He burst out laughing. 'No, nothing of the sort. She wanted to see me to bring me up to date. She has had some interest from buyers of a hotel chain in Rome.'

'Wow, that would be quite a change for you,' I said at last.

'You won't mention this to anyone?'

'Of course not.'

He gave a little smile. 'No, I know you won't.'

His mobile buzzed on the table in front of him and he picked it up.

'Another problem I need to deal with.' He threw me an apologetic look. 'I won't miss it nearly as much as you think. I must go.'

He hesitated for a moment and then bent and kissed me very gently.

'Don't let me lose you for a second time,' he said.

'That works both ways,' I said.

I watched him as he walked away, my heart

singing with an emotion I didn't properly understand. Joy and love and an unbelievable excitement. I
wondered if he was feeling the same way.

What would I do next? What would he do?

He wanted to travel and explore the world away
from this tiny island. To realise some of his long-
held dreams. So why shouldn't he? And for that matter, why shouldn't I?

I felt proud for a moment that he had confided in
me. That he would trust me. And we were friends.
We were a great deal more than that. Time would
tell. I needed to take things slowly, wait and see what
happened next. Not trying to do the right thing, always doing what people expected of me, making decisions in my life which, as I now realised, had so
often been wrong.

The terrace was busier then, perhaps some new
guests coming outside to admire the setting, or for a
cocktail before dinner. I should go back to my room
and perhaps start packing my case. Depressing as it
might be, I was due to fly home the day after tomorrow. My adventure was coming to an end, and all of a
sudden it felt strangely unsatisfying. To know that
Paulo was beginning to plan a new adventure of his
own. One which might this time, despite what he

had said, take him further away from me. Somewhere I couldn't follow. And suddenly I didn't like
the idea of that one bit.

I stood up and walked towards the hotel, where
the golden lights from the windows were beginning
to gleam in the dusk. I had no right to even think
that Paulo and I, having reconnected after so many
years apart, would have any future connection. But if
we did...

Deep in thought, I got to the top of the shallow
staircase and suddenly a small figure darted out
from behind some bushes. There was a cry of *yee
haw*, and something hit me on the back of the legs.

The next thing I knew, I was falling, letting out a
gargling scream, tumbling painfully to the bottom of
the steps, landing on my side and banging my head
on the ground. For a moment I lay still, dizzy, the
wind knocked out of my lungs, a horrible pain in
one shoulder.

Then I heard someone shout.

'*Mio Dio!* Oh Eric! No!'

I looked up to see Eric standing over me, the end
of a skipping rope in one hand, the other wrapped
uncomfortably around my ankles. Andrea had
grabbed on to his free arm.

'I told you I was going to be a cowboy,' he said, and his lower lip trembled.

And then I think I burst into tears. And so did he.

It was one thing to fall over when one was younger and still had the ability to bounce. At my age it felt very different.

18

I wasn't really sure how I got there, but a few minutes later I found myself lying on my bed.

There was a strange man peering at me. He had an enormous, rather ruddy nose and a stethoscope hanging around his neck, so I assumed he was a doctor. He was standing by the side of my bed, his hand on my forehead. Something I wasn't very happy about, as I had a thumping headache. I flinched away from him.

'Ah, *bene*, good, you are back with us,' he said.

I think garlic had featured heavily in his last meal, and I recoiled from the aroma.

'Is she all right? Do we need to take her to hospital?'

That was Paulo.

I struggled to sit up, feeling bruised and embarrassed. People were always talking about 'having a fall' at my age, and I'd had several contemporaries who had sported surgical boots or arm supports after just such a thing. Had I broken anything? I moved my limbs cautiously. Only my shoulder seemed to have suffered any injury. And my face felt sore on one side.

'What happened?' I said, feeling distinctly fuzzy and confused.

The doctor shone a bright light in my eyes, and I held my breath to avoid his.

'Not too much damage,' he said, sounding slightly disappointed. 'You don't feel *nauseabonda* – um, nauseous or faint?'

'No.' I tried to push myself upright and a horrible pain shot through my shoulder.

There was a bit more discussion in Italian, all of which went completely over my head, and then Paulo and the garlic-loving doctor went into a huddle in one corner, while Susie came to sit on the edge of my bed, her eyes wide with concern.

'What on earth happened?' I said.

'Eric tried to lasso you,' she said, 'with a skipping

rope. And apparently you went down like a sack of spuds.'

'Oh God,' I groaned.

'He's been taken away for a proper telling off, probably the first one he's ever had, which will probably do him a great deal of good, and Leo and Raleigh have been rowing ever since. Leo says this 'no no' business has to stop, that Eric is turning into a brat, and it's no good blaming Andrea. At first Raleigh even tried to blame the sous chef's daughter who let Eric borrow her skipping rope, which is just ridiculous.'

I put up a tentative hand to my cheek. 'Have I done much damage to myself? My face hurts.'

'Just a graze on your face. Maybe a bruised shoulder. But nothing serious as far as I could understand. Paulo is furious of course.'

'I shouldn't have encouraged Eric to get those jeans,' I said.

Paulo broke off his discussions at that point and came over.

'Don't be ridiculous,' he said firmly. 'There's no excuse for this. None at all.'

'Oh dear,' I said, feeling rather weepy and a bit foolish. 'I'm so sorry.'

'Stop trying to blame yourself. He's a boy, doing

what boys do,' Paulo said, 'no matter how much his parents try to overprotect him. The doctor thinks you will be fine. He says we should keep an eye on you in case of concussion. Other than that, some nasty bruising and a sore shoulder. He prescribes painkillers and bed rest. Perhaps for a week.'

'But I have a flight booked to go home the day after tomorrow,' I said.

Susie balled up her fists and pressed them to her face in anguish.

'Well, I'm not leaving you, not like this! I couldn't possibly. I booked the flights and everything. It's all set up for our return too. We were going to have a bottle of bubbly at the airport, and perhaps some of those sour cream pretzels. I love those. And they never taste the same at home.'

'Then you must stay too. Forget about the practicalities for now, just give me your booking details,' Paulo said. 'I'll sort everything out.'

I sank back down onto the pillows with a sigh of relief, and then tried to get comfortable, which was almost impossible. Painkillers seemed like a very good idea indeed.

* * *

For the next hour I had a steady stream of visitors, people poking their faces nervously around the door to see if I was awake and decent. Leo brought Eric in to apologise, which the boy did, accompanied by tears and what looked like genuine remorse. He had brought me a single white rose which he placed on my bed.

'It made Andrea better, I want you to be better too,' he said. 'I'm sorry. I'm not going to be a cowboy any more. I'm going to be a doctor.'

'That's a great thing to do,' I said.

Then Raleigh came in dressed very soberly in a dark blue dress with white cuffs and collar, which almost gave her a nurse-like appearance. She brought me some extravagant flowers and a box of truffles, to ask if I needed anything, and by the way, did I need their insurance details.

She evidently thought I might be seriously considering suing Eric for causing my injuries and she burst into tears when I assured her I wasn't.

'Of course, Leo and I will cover all your medical costs. I understand there is an air ambulance if you need to go to the mainland. You know, in case you get a brain haemorrhage or a deep vein thrombosis.'

'Let's hope it doesn't come to that,' I said, patting her hand, and she started crying again, which was something she did very attractively and didn't go red and blotchy as I always did.

'I would make you some soup,' she said, sniffling a bit and blowing her nose, 'but I'm not allowed in the kitchens. And I'm not actually sure how to do it. I'll ask Leo what he thinks I should do. Meanwhile, would you like me to read to you? I had a look in the bookcase in the hall and they are all in Italian, but I do have a few of Eric's books with me.'

The prospect of Raleigh reading *The Cat In The Hat* to me, while tantalising, was one on which I was prepared to pass, and I reassured her I would be fine watching television. Or ideally just sleeping.

'I'll bring you some magazines,' she said. 'I have this month's *Harper's*. There's a strange picture of someone in a black dress on the cover. To be honest, I can't think of a single occasion where I would wear it. But there is quite an interesting exposé on blusher you might enjoy and a feature on leather trousers.'

'Sounds ideal,' I said, and Raleigh smiled with relief.

'I'd better get Eric to bed. It's well past his bedtime and it's been quite a day.'

Moments after she had left, Sylvia, Lucia and Ceci appeared, barging past each other in the doorway like some sort of comedy act.

'You must have absolute and complete rest,' Sylvia said. 'I have brought you the last of my special Belgian chocolate. My physician recommended it to me. It is full of iron. Practically a health food.'

She fished a half-eaten bar out of her handbag and put it proudly on the bedside cabinet. Then Lucia offered me a much-thumbed paperback with a very risqué cover illustration of a shirtless man grappling with a nubile woman whose clothes seemed to be falling off.

'*Mio libro preferito* – my favourite book. It's in Italian but it may teach you some new words. It's about an Italian nobleman who is a pirate and also an artist. And he falls in love with a woman who refuses to let him paint her portrait, so in the end he takes her off on board his ship and – well, never mind. I don't want to spoil the story. Always cheers me up, especially chapter twenty-one.'

Ceci countered with a sneer and produced a gift of Venchi truffles in a tin designed by Dolce and Gabbana. Lucia narrowed her eyes.

I defused the situation by giving a little croak of pain.

'Are you taking your medicine?' Ceci asked sternly. 'It's no use waiting to take painkillers until you are in agony.'

'I am,' I said. 'In fact, I have just taken two.'

'But you don't want to become too reliant,' Sylvia added. 'One hears such terrible stories. I was watching a documentary only the other day. A man who injured his back in work and became dependent on them. I think it was fanto, or it might have been futon. Lives ruined, the slow descent into addiction...'

Lucia scoffed. 'Well, your back might be ruined by a futon, but I hardly think—'

'...or was it benzene?' Sylvia said.

'I promise not to take anything dangerous,' I said.

'And if there is anything you need, you only have to ask,' Sylvia continued. 'I will make it my number one priority. Ralph always said I could have been a nurse. I would have been a wonderful nurse, if I had ever trained, but my father wouldn't allow it because of the indelicacy. Men and bed baths, that sort of thing. But I am going back to Brussels later today. I will leave word with the entire staff that you must not be left on your own for a single moment. In case you fall out of bed and break something.'

'That's very kind,' I said with a huge yawn as the tablets began to take effect, 'but I am going to get up tomorrow and try to get moving again.'

'Very wise,' Lucia said. 'Deep vein thrombosis.

Years ago I knew a woman who had a medical episode on a flight I was on from Athens to Bergen. The plane had to divert to Munich, and it was most inconvenient. And it was raining.'

'Was she all right?' I asked.

Lucia pulled a face. 'I think so. When they lifted her out of her seat, a gin bottle fell out of her pocket. Perhaps she was just a nervous traveller.'

'You said it was vodka the last time you told that story,' Sylvia protested.

Lucia flapped a dismissive hand at her. 'Well, whatever it was I'm sure she suffered no more than a headache.'

Sylvia sent me a searching look. 'Have you still got a headache?'

'My doctor has advised sleep now, would you mind?' I said, and the three ladies scuttled around picking up each other's handbags by mistake and bickering for a few more minutes before they left.

I gave a sigh of relief at being left alone in peace and closed my eyes. Then I realised I needed the loo. How was I going to accomplish this?

I poked my feet off the bed and tried to slide out, all the time my sore shoulder screaming in protest. I slid down and bumped inelegantly onto my bottom, knocking against the bedside table so that the tin of expensive truffles fell off and hit me on the head.

I rested back against the bed behind me and realised to my horror that I didn't have the strength to pull myself to my feet. In fact, having got down there, I wondered how I was going to make any progress at all. I shuffled forwards around the bed, whimpering with every movement and wondering if I was going to be discovered by the next person to visit me in a heap on the floor.

'I've found something for you to read. What on earth are you doing?'

Mercifully this time it was just Susie, who was standing open mouthed in the doorway clutching two paperbacks.

'I need to get to the bathroom,' I said, 'but I'm a bit stuck. I don't seem able to pull myself up.'

'Oh for goodness' sake! Why didn't you call for some help?'

She came around to scoop me up and pull me back against the side of the bed.

'I didn't know who would come, and I don't think Ceci or Sylvia would have been much use.'

'You never know, some of those old ladies can be very tough,' Susie said. 'Look, if I stand next to you, you can pull yourself up.'

'I'll try,' I said, grabbing hold of her arm. 'I think the painkillers are working. I'd better get to the loo soon or I'm just going to fall asleep on the floor and wake up in a puddle.'

'That would not be elegant,' Susie said. 'Perhaps if you sit on this rug I can slide you across the floor-boards to the bathroom? Or shall I bring you a bucket?'

I clutched at her arm and winced. 'Don't make me laugh, it's agony.'

Little by little, we reached the bathroom, much to my relief. As I stood, bent almost double, washing my hands, I looked at myself in the mirror.

I looked absolutely terrible, there was no doubt about it. My hair was sticking up at all angles, there was a big graze on the side of my face and possibly the beginnings of a black eye. Added to this dark shadows under my eyes and I looked almost as though I'd been in a bar room brawl. Perhaps it would be best if Paulo didn't visit me. I should tell Susie to keep him out.

I hobbled back out of the bathroom and found Paulo was there already, helping Susie straighten up my bedclothes.

'Oh please,' I said, 'don't look at me, I look dreadful.'

Paulo grinned. 'Not as bad as the time you wrapped your head in bubble wrap and fell down the stairs while you were carrying a pot of blue paint. I know it was a fancy-dress party but I never did understand what you were aiming for.'

Oh God. He did remember.

'Come on, get back into bed,' Susie said comfortingly. 'We all thought it was a great attempt. It's not everyone who could pull off Marge Simpson.'

I thought at that moment I might die of embarrassment, but instead I fell back into the comforting embrace of my bed and closed my eyes.

'We'll leave you to it,' Susie said. 'See you later.'

I waited for the sound of the door closing behind them, but just before it did, I felt someone kiss me gently on the forehead. And I knew it was Paulo. Even after so many years, I knew the touch of his lips and the scent of his skin. I fell asleep with a daft smile on my face.

19

The following day was Sunday, and when I woke I could hear church bells in the distance. I lay in bed, listening to them for a few minutes.

I hadn't been for years; church had become a place where people went when they needed verification for something. A wedding, christening or funeral which really seemed to be just an excuse for a party most of the time.

The changing face of Sundays. I remembered when I was a child, in the days when there were only four television channels and not much on any of them. Sunday was a boring day, for doing homework, getting my things ready for Monday, that day of gloom because the weekend was nearly over and school was looming large again.

And then when I was in my twenties, Sunday had become a day of lounging in bed, reading the papers, eating toast and not really doing much. Move on a few years and Sunday was a day for household chores, getting the children ready for school, cooking a Sunday roast for the family, thinking about work again.

More recently it seemed Sunday had reverted to my childhood memories. Nothing much to watch on television, nothing I really wanted to do, no one to cook for, a day filled with long hours.

It wouldn't be long before I was repacking my bag. I wanted to do something different that day, not just wait until someone needed something from me.

I tottered into the bathroom to inspect the damage to my face. I had a big ugly graze across my forehead and my black eye was shaping up nicely to look terrible for a few days.

My shoulder was still bruised and sore, but I was getting some movement back into my right arm, which meant I was able to cope with my morning ablutions without assistance.

I got back into my room, opened the curtains and unlocked the door, something which took some effort because my right arm still didn't seem to have much strength in it. Sitting on a chair outside the window, evidently waiting for me to make an appearance, was Susie.

She sprang up when she saw me and opened the French doors.

'How are you? Are you okay? I've been waiting for you to wake up. I kept wondering if you were unconscious. I got really worried. I even thought about using the fire extinguisher in the corridor to smash the glass. But I thought you might be lying on the floor on the other side. Anyway, I was about to go and ask someone to find a master key or break the door down.'

'Good job you didn't, I'm fine,' I said.

'You look like you've been fighting and you lost,' she said, inspecting my bruised face. 'Ceci has left some arnica cream which she says will work miracles. It's in my room somewhere. Do you want some breakfast? It's nearly ten thirty but I'm sure the kitchens will sort something out for you.'

'Just some tea,' I said. 'I'm absolutely gasping, but I'm not really hungry.'

She darted off, returning a few minutes later with a tray holding some tea and a selection of Italian pastries on a porcelain plate.

'I told the chef you didn't want anything to eat, but he insisted,' she said. 'He was on the point of making you some poached eggs and looked like he might cry when I said no. Everyone is very worried. Apparently the doctor is coming later to check up on you.'

'Honestly, I'm much better,' I said, 'just feel a bit bashed about and sore.'

Susie looked longingly at a particularly fine *bomboloni*.

'In which case, do you mind if I eat that?' she pleaded, 'I only had coffee.'

'Help yourself,' I laughed. Which was a bad idea as it made my face and my ribs hurt.

'And so we aren't going home tomorrow,' she said, wiping a smear of cream off her mouth. 'Paulo says he has sorted everything out. He even got a letter from the doctor, and he said I had to stay too because I was needed to look after you. Don't look like that, I brought you tea, didn't I? I'll go and find that arnica cream. Ceci is bound to ask.'

She went back into her room, still clutching the remains of her pastry in one hand.

I sat sipping my tea and looking out of the window at the morning. Another bright, sunny day. And I had the same feeling I'd had as a child when school was cancelled because of snow. Rather excited, not sure what I was going to do with this unexpected extension to my holiday but pleased about it all the same.

'Here it is,' Susie said, holding out the arnica. 'Ceci says you should apply it three times a day. Or was it twice? I can't remember, and the instruction sheet is in loads of different languages but the print is so small I can't read any of them. Anyway, I'm sure it will be fine whatever you do with it. Do you want me to help you get dressed?'

'No, not at the moment, and I'm not in a coma. I'm sure I can cope.'

'Good, I know we are dear friends, but I don't really want to hoist you into your knickers. By the way, Paulo wanted to know if he could pop in later. He said he would quite understand if you didn't want visitors.'

I had mixed feelings about this. Yes, of course, I desperately wanted to see him, but I knew I looked terrible. Perhaps I should see him after I'd had the chance to sort myself out.

'By the way, Ceci has asked if you want Gina to come in and do your hair,' Susie said. 'It's almost impossible to use a hairdryer with a sore shoulder.'

I agreed that would be a great idea.

'I've already turned Sylvia away from your door. She wanted to come and see you before she left to catch the ferry back to Naples. I'm sure she meant well, but she was going on about pulmonary embolisms and facial paralysis in a way that I am sure you would not have found reassuring.'

'I'm very grateful,' I said, 'and no, I wouldn't.'

'So, Paulo?'

I ran my hands gently over my face, realising I needed a shower, and there was probably still some blood and grit in my hair.

'Tell him to come a bit later,' I said. 'I need to freshen up, and I really don't want to stay in bed any longer than I have to.'

Susie laughed. 'Gosh, remember when we were kids, it was my idea of heaven to stay in bed all day. When I had a cold, my mother used to bring me comics and cardboard dolls with clothes to cut out, with little paper tabs over the shoulders. Would you like me to find you some of those?'

I shook my head. 'No, not really. Look, go and find something else to do and I'll sort myself out. I'm sure Raimondo must be wondering where you are, isn't he?'

Susie blushed. 'He's downstairs reading the newspapers. Oooh, which reminds me...'

She hurried off again back to her room, returning with a massive wicker basket of pink and white flowers.

'I've been keeping these in my bathroom. They are from him, and he says he hopes you will feel better soon.'

'How lovely,' I said. 'What a kind thought.'

Susie fussed about with the flowers, putting them by my bedside, and then moving them to a table in the window.

'He is, really thoughtful, and very generous and kind. I can't think why he has been single for all these years.'

'Perhaps he was waiting for you,' I said, and Susie blushed even pinker.

'Don't be daft.'

'Now go away and find him, and I'll get myself into the shower.'

Twenty minutes later, a timid tap on my door announced the arrival of Gina, who scurried in with her canvas holdall full of brushes and combs.

She took her scissors out and clicked them open and closed a few times with an enquiring look. I shook my head and she put them away.

It was quite nice that we couldn't communicate very easily, because it meant I could spend a restful hour with my eyes closed, while she tweaked and dried my hair. Occasionally she would mutter something. *Mio Dio.* Or *assolutamente no*, which showed me she was having some problems. Eventually she took her scissors out and with a lot of gesturing to assure me she wasn't going to do too much, she did a bit of snipping and shaping while I held my breath and hoped she knew what she was doing.

Then she took out a massive hairdryer, which seemed too heavy for a woman her size to wield, and blasted hot air into my ears.

When I opened my eyes, there seemed to be a lot of my hair on the floor, far more than I had expected, and my hair had been dried into a wide bouffant style reminiscent of Mary Tyler Moore in the 1980s.

I stared at my reflection for a moment while Gina got out her hand-held vacuum cleaner and hoovered the carpet and me.

I tried to think what to say while Gina watched anxiously for my reaction, but the only thing I could remember was *Eccelente*.

So I said that.

20

I stayed in my room, just venturing onto the terrace outside my window where I sat in a chair and Susie fussed about, asking me if I wanted a rug over my knees. Which I didn't because it was still quite warm.

I sent an email to my family explaining what had happened and reassuring them I was fine. Although I did receive a couple of panicking calls from my daughters when I sent them a WhatsApp selfie of my bruised face.

Alex sent me an unexpectedly long email; he had apparently been busy with work and reassured me he had definitely not had any friends round. Apart from a couple who wanted to watch the football. And a colleague from work who had just broken up with his girlfriend and needed a place to stay for the weekend. And he promised he would touch up the paintwork on the bannisters when he had a moment.

My daughters sent video messages from their children who, despite it still being early October, were asking if I could make them some Halloween costumes. When did that become such a thing, I wondered. I didn't remember trick or treating when I was a child.

Jess, who was married to a solicitor, asked if I was going to sue, and Kat asked what on earth I had done to my hair and if I would be better by Christmas.

Then I began to worry about how everyone would fit in to my little house now that my grand-daughters had both outgrown their travel cots, and then firmly pushed the problem from my mind. It was a long way off, after all. Who knew what I would be doing by then?

I might be off on a Christmas cruise or staying somewhere snowy, which was always something I had wanted to do. Vermont, perhaps, or Austria. The possibilities were endless if I just opened my mind to them.

Having finished my rather pleasant daydream of

sitting in a log cabin by a roaring fire with a mug of hot chocolate in my hand with floor-to-ceiling windows overlooking some suitably festive scenery, I then sent them some more cheerful views of Susie carrying two glasses of wine towards me with a big grin on her face, a beautiful sunset and another reassuring selfie after I had borrowed some of Susie's Touch Eclat concealer.

'Would you mind awfully if I went out this evening?' Susie said. 'I mean, there are lots of people around in case you need something.'

She was standing in the doorway fiddling with the handle and not quite meeting my eye.

'Of course not,' I said. 'You've been fussing around me all day. I'm guessing this is for an outing with your admirer?'

'Well, he did say he would like to take me out to dinner. And you really are looking better. Not the black eye, of course. I mean, that's going to take a bit of time to go, but you don't seem quite so battered. Did you ask Gina to do that to your hair, by the way? It's a bit different. I've never seen you with big hair before. You look like you're going to take off.'

'I'm absolutely fine,' I said, trying to pat my hair down and make it look a bit less exuberant, 'and I really don't need people to fuss or keep my company all the time. And Gina just did what she felt like.'

'Ceci wanted to come and see you. I think now Sylvia has gone, she is feeling a bit out of sorts. I know they squabbled all the time, but I have the feeling they both secretly enjoyed it. Lucia is still here but they don't seem quite the force with only the two of them. And Raleigh and Leo wanted to come and say goodbye too. They are off tomorrow, back to America with the boy wonder.'

'Poor Eric, how is he?'

'To be honest he doesn't seem quite as bad. He was sitting between his parents looking very chastised at breakfast this morning. Not running about and not arguing either. And I did see Andrea sitting with her feet up by the pool having a quiet hour to herself for once. I think your accident really shocked all of them, not just Eric. It's about time something did in my opinion. All that "No No" parenting nonsense, I think they have given up on that.'

'Good job too,' I said. 'They do say kids push their boundaries, and he didn't seem to have any.'

'So wise. So, what do you say about this evening? Are you sure you don't mind?'

'Not at all,' I said, 'and I hope you have a wonderful time.'

Susie grinned. 'I'll try. Well, I won't have to try too hard, because he's such easy company. Right then, if you're okay for a bit, I'll let him know and then go and get ready.'

'You mean he's still around?'

Susie blushed. 'He's downstairs. He's waiting to see what you say before he books the restaurant.'

* * *

Just as I was wondering if I could face going downstairs that evening for something to eat, there was a knock on my door. I opened it to find Paulo there with a little metal trolley which he pushed into my room.

'I have brought you some supper,' he said. 'Pasta carbonara, because it used to be your favourite.'

He bent and kissed me and brushed my cheek gently with his thumb.

'You poor thing.'

'I'm fine,' I said. 'Getting better by the minute.'

I watched as he whisked off the metal covers to reveal two steaming bowls of pasta. It smelled divine and my mouth watered for the first time in a while. How wonderful that he had remembered.

'I hope you don't mind if I join you?' he said. 'My

son and his wife have gone out for the evening, Andrea and Eric are packing ready for their journey tomorrow. My mother is sulking because Lucia has met up with an old friend and they are having dinner together so she doesn't have anyone to argue with, so you can see I too am at a loose end.'

'Can't she argue with Freddy?'

'They never do, he just let's her get away with everything. You're sure you don't mind me staying?'

'I'm absolutely delighted,' I said, and we sat outside on the terrace in the warm evening air, while below us the lights from the garden glowed in the dusk.

'It feels like the end of things,' I said after a while. 'People going home, and the gardens look less busy too. I know that the season is finishing. Isn't this the time when you should be taking a break?'

He didn't answer for a few moments as – having reassured himself that I was no longer on any medication – he opened a bottle of Pinot Grigio and poured out two glassfuls.

I held my glass up to look at it.

Even the wine glasses here were things of beauty. Elegant narrow stems and lovely engraved bowls, not like the supermarket versions I was used to. Perhaps in future I would do things more stylishly. I had seen something similar in a local antique shop for a ridiculously low price, and I decided I would buy them if they were still there on my return. There was joy to be had in such things. There was nothing wrong with making life better in small ways.

I had already decided that from now on I would wear my new clothes and decent underwear instead of keeping them 'for special occasions', and at my age who knew when that would be? What if the opportunity to do so never came? I was determined to take pleasure in every day, not keep putting things off until the future.

'I have had news from Stephanie,' he said at last. 'There is a new bid on the table from the hotel chain. They have increased their offer.'

'An offer you can't refuse?' I said, taking a sip of my wine.

He gave a little laugh. 'Quite possibly.'

'So what will you do?'

He picked his cutlery up and then put it down again.

'I think I will accept. It will be the end of an era; I can see that. But I told you, I don't want to do this until the day I die. I need to do something else.'

'Good,' I said. 'And you're sure?'

'As sure as I can be,' he said. 'What is the alternative, after all? To hang on for more years, until one day I cannot carry on and the problem falls on my son to deal with?'

'Have you told him? You really should, don't you think?'

'I have. I told him this morning, and my mother too. I'm sure she has something to say about it, but to be honest after she and my father split up she hardly lived here at all. She left me with my grandparents, and then Ellen and I brought the place up to date, made changes and improvements while she settled in Florence with Freddy.'

'She's a lucky woman, finding someone so compatible,' I said.

'She says it took her fifty years to do so, but it was worth the wait.'

'You must have so many memories of this place. It might be more difficult to leave than you think.'

He sprinkled a little more parmesan onto his pasta and then looked across at me.

'There are things I will miss,' he agreed, 'but a lot of things I won't.'

He picked up his wine glass and held it out towards me.

'A toast, to the future, to life and to us.'

He held out his wine glass towards me, and I suddenly couldn't meet his gaze.

So this was it. He was talking about us.

Us.

Our lives had gone in such different directions. He had moved on and so had I. So many years had passed; neither of us were the same people we had been back then. He had been here in the land of sunshine and colour and warmth, with Ellen and his family, and their friends, while I had taught at little schools, and raised my own family in the damp English countryside.

The thought struck me, despite all those differences and all those years apart, that perhaps there were also still things we had in common. I knew when I was younger I had been stubborn and argumentative. And so had he. Perhaps that similarity was what had attracted us to each other back then, but maybe the decades that had passed had brought changes to both of us. If nothing else I knew now which battles were worth fighting and which weren't. Maybe I had grown up after all.

I realised he was still waiting, and I clinked my glass against his.

'To all those things and more,' I said at last.

My phone buzzed with the arrival of a text. It was from Alex, of course.

> I've been working from home and there's no milk or bread left. I've looked in your freezer and I can't find any. When is the next supermarket delivery?

'Is there a problem?' Paulo said.

'There certainly is,' I said, biting down my irritation.

And then I knew there was something I had to do, and soon.

'I'm so much better now, I certainly don't need any more time in bed, and you have some decisions to make. About the hotel, and the future. And so do I. Well, not the hotel bit because obviously I haven't got one, but we both have plans to make and ideas to sort out, don't we?'

He topped up my wine glass and then he nodded.

'I will arrange some flights for you and Susie. It will be up to you to drag her away from Raimondo. I know one thing – when all this is sorted out, I don't want to lose you for a second time.'

I didn't think I could breathe properly for a moment and then I took a deep breath and I smiled up at him.

'No,' I said, 'nor do I.'

'I would like us to start again,' he said, 'to find our own contentment. To remember the past but also learn from it. You had your life, and I had mine, and I do not wish them away, not at all. And I do not regret the choices I made. But I do want something else now. I want to get to know you again. I don't want to remain stuck in the past.'

'No,' I said, with a huge smile, 'nor do I.'

And suddenly those things seemed possible. There were opportunities for both of us. How marvellous that felt, to know that we both had new chances to explore the future, new lives to find.

* * *

We talked and talked about the past. He even went to find a couple of photographs in his desk, not of just us two because that would have been rather strange if he had kept them, but of all our friends. Parties we went to, picnics on the beach which went on for hours while the sunset faded, and the only light on our faces was from our driftwood bonfire.

It was strange looking at us back then. The

colours from the photographs had faded with age. There was Susie with her shock of pale, red-gold hair. Ellen, beautiful, and aware of the camera, posing her long legs like a model. Me, head thrown back in laughter, a beer bottle in my hand. I could almost feel the warmth from the fire, hear the chatter, the terrible guitar playing from a young chap I'd dated for a few weeks whose name I couldn't remember.

We had thought we were invincible back then. Old age and illness and mortgages and relationship difficulties were for other people. We were different, weren't we?

Perhaps every generation feels the same at that age – ridiculously confident, invulnerable to the problems life might throw at us. We thought we were special, that we knew so much more than everyone else, didn't we? And yet we hadn't; we were wrong, of course.

Those decades had gone by in a heartbeat. We'd both had careers, triumphs and disappointments. Our children had grown up, relationships had come and gone, marriages had failed, illness had come for some of us after all.

We laughed and exchanged memories and agreed we had been so young back then, so foolish.

And yet after all that time we still liked each other – wasn't that what Ceci had said was the most important thing? And because of that, there were still possibilities. For what, I wasn't sure. Friendship? Companionship? Something more maybe.

There was a part of me that was enthusiastic about the prospect, and a little part of me that held back. This was not the time for reckless declarations. To take our relationship any further. There was time for that. Apart from anything else, my ribs were still sore; I didn't think I would be very alluring when I was covered in scratches and bruises even if I did put my best underwear on. And yet the prospect of it was so exciting. I'd waited for so long to feel like this, to want to be close and intimate with him. To be able to touch his skin, be near to him.

He needed to get his life in order, and I needed to do the same. Thinking about that in this place, where life seemed warm and easy, where every corner revealed a new, wonderful view was impossible.

I needed to go home to my funny little house where the front door stuck in wet weather and the garage and the attic were full of my children's junk. Boxes of schoolbooks, unwanted furniture, a mountain bike in pieces, skateboards and tennis racquets.

You can't throw that away! Just hang on to it for a bit, and I'll sort it out one day.

Well, that day was coming sooner than they thought.

* * *

'Do we have to go home?' Susie said mournfully at breakfast the next morning when I told her my decision. 'It's so lovely here. And Raimondo really does have a boat and a beautiful house. He wasn't stringing me along, and he has mentioned no interest in my bank account or my pension, so you can stop worrying about that.'

'Paulo is going to arrange our flights, and yes, we do need to go home,' I said firmly. 'There is nothing stopping you from coming back.'

'True,' Susie said, brightening up, 'and I've realised I want to sort out my flat. I've been meaning to redecorate for months, but I kept putting it off because Simon said he couldn't bear the disruption and we could never agree on colours. And of course, Raimondo could come and see me, couldn't he? I'd better clear out the spare room. It's full of junk at the moment.'

'Spare room? Really?' I teased.

Susie blushed. 'Maybe.' She fiddled a little with her cutlery and then took a bite of her Danish pastry. 'It's years since I've felt this happy. Since a man has been kind to me and made me feel good about myself. It will take getting used to. I'm not being silly, am I? My track record with choosing men isn't great.'

'Of course you're not being silly, but look at the practicalities. You still haven't got all of Simon's stuff out of your flat. In the grand scheme of things, you've only just broken up with him. The other woman, remember her? You need time, to properly finish off one relationship before you go dashing into another one. You've only known this man for a short time. You can exist perfectly happily without someone for a bit, you know.'

Susie sighed. 'I know you're right. But I don't like being on my own, I never did. What if this is my last chance? I've made such a mess of things in the past.'

'Last chance for what? Can you hear yourself?' My voice got a bit squeaky with indignation at that point. 'Last chance to be happy? In these last few days, I've realised I have to be happy with myself first. It's taken me a long time to see that. For the last few years I've been plodding on, doing the same things, putting the bins out on the right day, cutting the hedges back, balancing things and budgeting because that's what I always did. There's more to life than just carrying on, there has to be.'

'What things?'

'Living. Learning new things. We always considered ourselves liberated women, didn't we? Going to university, having the sort of careers our mothers never could, buying our own car, changing phone providers. I don't know – doing the things we always put off because we chose to put someone else first. Now we don't have to. Now we really can just do what the heck we like. Go to Paris in the spring, paint our nails blue, sit in bed all day and eat cake, redecorate without having to ask for someone else's opinion. Isn't that the ultimate liberation?'

'I'm not really enjoying this pastry. I wish I'd had one of those almond croissants instead,' Susie said, eyeing the buffet table.

'Then have one,' I said, and we both laughed.

21

'We've come to say goodbye,' Raleigh said. 'I hope you really are feeling better. Your black eye doesn't look quite so bad.'

'I've been using some concealer,' I said with a grin.

'We will be leaving for the airport soon. I could get some more there and send it on to you?'

I had been in the middle of my packing, sorting out my things into the depressing groups of dirty laundry, things I had brought and not worn, and the few gifts I had bought for my granddaughters. How was it that my belongings never fitted into the cases as easily on the return journey?

I realised I was being careless with none of the

special folding and rolling techniques I had used, and my shoulder and ribs were still sore, so that didn't help. Packing a case to go home was never very enjoyable at the best of times. Perhaps I would have to take everything out and start again, which would be even more annoying.

Leo and Eric stood next to her in the doorway of my room, Eric still wearing his new jeans, but this time teamed with a check shirt. Evidently the stegosaurus T-shirt was a step too far for Raleigh. Leo was smart in well-pressed chinos and a white polo shirt; Raleigh looked as though she was going to a fundraising event in a grey silk dress and heels. I could only assume they were flying in the posh seats, otherwise she would look like wreck by the time they got home. Or maybe rich people's clothes didn't crease and stain like mine did?

'I'll be fine,' I said. 'Honestly, my shoulder feels so much better already. Come on, Eric, there's no need to look so tragic.'

'Well, I disagree,' Leo said firmly. 'It could have been a lot worse, and Eric needs to know that. Actions have consequences.'

I held out an arm to the boy and after a moment he raised his head, ran to my side and buried his face in my waist.

'I'm sorry,' he muttered, his voice muffled.

'I'm fine, really, I am,' I said. 'Just don't do any-thing like that again. Do you promise me?'

He nodded silently.

'Then that's okay.' I looked across at Leo. 'I take it your dad has told you his plans?'

Leo nodded. 'He has. He explained everything and I'm glad for him. And more than a little relieved. It's been something that has been worrying me for a while. Leaving a management team in charge is never the same.'

Raleigh agreed. 'We knew we wouldn't be able to take over. I mean, what do I know about running a hotel? Although I'm good at staying in them. And I have so much to do when we get back. There's a black-tie dinner for St Xavier's to celebrate the school's tenth anniversary which I have to help plan.'

'What do they need now? A Hadron Collider?' I said, and Raleigh giggled.

Eric looked up at me.

'Can't you come with us? Please?'

'No, I have my own little boy to sort out,' I said firmly. 'Have a safe trip home, be a good boy on the plane and look after Andrea.'

He nodded again.

'Promise?'

'Promise. When are you coming to see us?' he said. 'Mommy said I could ask you.'

'I don't know,' I said, 'I'll have to see.'

'You could come for my birthday,' he said, 'that's in February. I'm going to be six.'

'Well, maybe I will,' I said.

'I hope you have a safe trip,' Raleigh said, 'and come and visit us very soon. We have plenty of room, and Eric will be asking on a daily basis, if I know him.'

She gave me a very gentle hug and murmured in my ear.

'Thank you, for everything. You may not know it but you have made such a difference. Come and see us, you are always welcome.'

Leo kissed my cheek, and then with a bit of last-minute fussing about boarding passes and passports, they were gone.

I wondered for a moment if I ever would travel to visit them, and then I thought yes, why not? This, after all, would be part of this new independence I had been thinking about, doing exciting things.

Then suddenly, as was usual for him, Eric came rushing back and he threw his arms around me again, making me wince a little as he crushed my sore ribs.

'You've got to look after Nonno now we are going home,' he said, 'otherwise he won't have anyone to talk to. And you could come to my party together. He said he would like that.'

I laughed, delighted at the prospect of doing just that with Paulo at my side.

'We'll see,' I said, giving him a last hug. 'Now hurry up, you don't want to miss your plane.'

* * *

The following day was our last in Capri. Now that Leo and his family had gone, it seemed as though our holiday really was over.

Susie, despite our agreed talk about our new-found independence, decided she was going to spend it with Raimondo, having lunch at some delectable restaurant he wanted to take her to, high on the cliffs above Amalfi.

I had retreated to my favourite spot in the gardens and was enjoying my coffee in the company of the hotel cat, who was scowling at me from a safe distance up a tree.

'So now that Susie has gone off for the day, I suggest we do the same,' said a voice behind me, and I turned to see Paulo. And despite my feisty statements to Susie, my insistence that we, as mature sensible women, didn't need anyone's approval, my spirits raised at the sight of him, and I felt happier than I had for years.

We understood each other better than we had before. It was as though a line had been drawn in the past behind us, and we had stepped over it into whatever the future had to offer.

'What have you got in mind?' I asked with a huge smile.

He sat down in the chair next to me and stretched out his legs in front of him. And then he gave me a grin that was so friendly, so familiar, and somehow tinged with mischief that I felt myself relax.

'As long as you feel up to it I suggest a boat trip. I promised you one, didn't I? The sea is very calm. And it's going to be a lovely day.'

* * *

The feeling that this day was really the end of something, but also the beginning of a new chapter, intensified. And although I felt rather sad, there was also something inside me that I didn't immediately recognise. Not excitement, exactly; something deeper than that. There was something else to look forward to, a different sort of life. One for me.

* * *

Half an hour later, we pulled away from the jetty at Marina Grande in our boat – a *gozzo caprese*, I was informed, a traditional wooden boat that would have held several people, but this time we were the only ones on board.

The captain, a grizzled, silent man, steered us expertly over the rocking water as we left the harbour, and I hoped I was not going to be seasick. That really would have spoiled the experience, but after a few minutes of concentrating on the horizon, I began to feel better.

The charm of the string of pastel-coloured houses clinging to the cliffs above us was more apparent as we went further out to sea. Other boats passed us and the ferry from the mainland bringing new visitors to the island. There were passengers waving, cheerful, looking forward to their own adventures and experiences.

How different I felt compared to when Susie and I had arrived. Then I had been so anxious, worried sick about meeting Paulo again after such a long time. Knowing that in all the intervening years I had never really forgotten him and had often wondered about him and his life. I had tried and failed to leave him firmly in my past; but now, none of that mattered. I believed in myself, and I realised he did too.

Perhaps I had never expected to see him again, but after everything, Ellen, most ironically, had brought us back together. And things between us were good, better than that, which was something I hadn't even considered might happen.

Maybe I had hoped for a tentative acknowledgement of what we had been to each other. I had never for a moment anticipated that old feelings might resurface. That we might look at each other and remember what had been. What might have been.

The rocky headlands, some of them covered in tumbling vegetation, reared up above us, and across the water we could see caves and rock falls on the shoreline, the waves busy at the foot of the cliffs. And then we rounded a corner of the coastline, and there in front of us were some huge monoliths sticking out of the water. I gasped to see them, and I felt Paulo take my hand.

'The Faraglioni rocks,' Paulo said, 'the ones I told you about. Stella, Mezzo and Scopolo. Centuries ago, fires were lit on the top, to warn sailors away from the dangers of the coast.'

'How on earth did people get up there?' I asked.

Paulo laughed. 'I can't imagine, I would not like to try. But look, this is the most wonderful part. The arch through the Mezzo. Many people come here for just this view. When I was a boy, I swam through it. I don't think I would like to try that now either.'

I sat back in my seat and looked up at the towering rocks above us, and I felt the boat slow as we got closer. It was as though all my senses and feelings had been awakened, the warmth of the sun on my shoulders, the freshness of the breeze, the sound of the sea birds high above us, the rocking of the boat and the slap of the water against the sides. And Paulo's hand in mine again, warm and familiar.

We waited for a few minutes while another boat went through in front of us, and we could hear the cheers and whoops from the passengers.

'You know the legend?' Paulo said. 'When you go under the bridge, you kiss for luck and for happiness. And you can make a wish, and maybe the sea gods will grant it.'

We exchanged a look, both of us smiling, and as the boat inched forward under the rocky arch, he put an arm around my shoulders and pulled me in towards him. And then he kissed me.

'I have made a wish. Have you?' he said.

I looked at his face, once so dear and familiar, and now that feeling returned.

And I did.

And then I leaned my head back and looked up at the sky, and I wondered if this was possibly the best day of my life. And tempting as that thought was, I didn't want it to be. I wanted there to be other good days, other adventures, other best days to look forward to, not back on.

Paulo closed his eyes for a moment and frowned, as though he was trying to get his thoughts in order. At last, he spoke.

'I have been happy, and sometimes sad, like most people. But my life has not ended, I can see that now. After Ellen died, I wasn't sure if I should just carry on, waiting until the end, not sure when or how I would die too. But now, perhaps life – and you – have taken me on a different path.'

'I was just thinking the same thing,' I said. 'I want there to be things to look forward to. I want my best days to be ahead of me.'

And at that moment I remembered what I had

said to Susie: *lots of water under lots of bridges. There's nothing to tell.*

But this time was different.

The beauty of this place, the air, the sunshine, the colour and the sea and Paulo. They all brought a long-buried sensation back to me. And I realised what had been missing from my life for so long. Those things he had said about me.

Passion. And courage.

* * *

We drove back to the hotel just after four o'clock, my face slightly windburned and glowing from the hours we had spent out at sea. On the way, we stopped in a little wine bar perched on the edge of a rocky promontory where the waitress was beautiful enough to grace any catwalk in Paris, and the wine came in a carafe with two glass tumblers, scratched with age and use, and it was perfect.

'Now then, there is something I have been meaning to do ever since you got here.'

'Yes?' I said, slightly breathless all of a sudden.

He pulled out his mobile phone and handed it to me.

'Please, will you put in your phone number, your

email, your address, and any other way that I can contact you. Social media, carrier pigeon, anything!'

I laughed and did so, my fingers trembling. How silly to feel like this at my age. Like the same insecure and rather unsophisticated person I had been when he first met me. And yet somehow, I liked the feeling. The hard outer shell of being an adult had softened slightly, and I could almost remember what it felt like to be young and optimistic. To be wanted and valued just for myself.

'I will let you know what happens,' Paulo said, 'about the hotel. I will go and see Stephanie tomorrow to see if there has been any progress. After you have gone.'

After I had gone.

It was sobering to think that this place, no matter how important it had become to me in the last few days, would continue perfectly well without me. The sun would rise, the shops open, fish would be caught, meals eaten, sea birds would wheel in the sky above it.

'I'll miss this place,' I said, 'and I'll miss you terribly.'

'I will miss you. But this will not be goodbye. It cannot be.' He put his phone away and tapped the pocket. 'We both have too much to do.'

'Do we?'

'Indeed, we do. If nothing else we have been invited to another party, this time in America. Where I am assured by my grandson that we will dress up as cowboys, but I have it on good authority that we will not be lassoing anyone.'

'Well, I would hope not,' I said, 'and if he is anything like my children were, by the time his birthday comes around, it may have changed to spacemen or dinosaurs. And he did tell me he wanted to be a doctor.'

'Well, let's wait and see, shall we? And you, Joanna. What next?'

I sighed. 'I have to deal with much more mundane things. The first thing I need to do is go back and get all the kids' junk out of my garage, and the attic too. I'd forgotten about that. It's over ten years since any of them actually lived at home. And when I moved, I just took all their unwanted stuff with me, and over the last few years they have been adding to it, which is ridiculous. Whatever I have been storing for them, they obviously don't need most of it. Then I need to make sure Alex finds himself a new place to live and doesn't just settle into my house for the foreseeable future. And I need to follow your mother's example and look for things that are fun. I have spent long enough with my life in neutral. I want to make the most of whatever time I have left. And not live with regret.'

He reached across the table and took both of my hands in his.

'I don't want to waste another minute. I told you I loved you then, Jo, and I still do. I think we have something wonderful to offer each other. Something that doesn't happen very often. And this does not diminish the love Ellen and I had for each other. She knew that I loved her, I was loyal and faithful to her, but she also knew you were special to me. Look, I know Susie and Raimondo are out this evening. I don't want you to be eating alone in the dining room, not when you are going home tomorrow. Let's have dinner together in my flat. We can talk some more and I will give you some of the finest wine in my cellar, something I have been keeping for a special occasion. I think this is it, don't you?'

'Oh, Paulo,' I said, tears in my eyes, 'what will everyone say? What will our children think? What about your mother?'

'What about us?' he said firmly. 'Just for once, what about *us*? You and me. Do your plans for the future include a companion? Someone to perhaps help you with your luggage and advise on things? But only if advice was needed, of course.'

'They might,' I said, and I grinned at him, 'if I could find someone who is kind, handsome and available.'

Paulo took my hands and kissed the back of them.

'I like to think I am kind and before too long when the sale of the hotel is finalised, I will definitely be available,' he said.

'You are also still very handsome.'

He laughed and shook his head.

'I'm not sure about that.'

'Well, I am, and I am right, so let's not argue about that.'

He looked up at me, his eyes suddenly serious.

'I have a better idea. Let's learn the lesson that the last forty years have taught us – let's not argue at all.'

* * *

I went to my room to freshen up for dinner, and my mind was in a very different place from a week ago. I was loved; at long last, I was valued. I was not just the shredded remains of my past, an unsatisfactory wife, a mother who was taken for granted. I was, after all, still me. Still wanted and appreciated for who I was. Not for my youth or my charms, or my usefulness, just for myself. It was a heady realisation.

I was standing looking out at that wonderful view again, wanting to always remember it and the way I felt this evening, when there was a knock on the door.

I opened it to find Ceci there, stylish as always in a pale pink dress and white pashmina, the outfit finished off with a dazzling diamond necklace.

'May I come in?' she said. 'Freddy and Lucia are waiting for me in the dining room. I have left them both there with particularly dry martinis, something they both love. And she is doing her best to be pleasant and agreeable. I'm going to miss her. I know we argue a lot, but then we always did. It doesn't mean anything. They will be perfectly all right for ten minutes. And it will do them both good to miss me.'

She went to sit in the most comfortable armchair and fussed a little with the hem of her dress. I began to feel nervous, wondering what she had to say to me. Had Paulo spoken to her? Did she know?

'I've come to interfere,' she said, 'because at my age no one dares to stop me, and to tell you something. It might take me a while. *Per favore, sii paziente* – be patient. I first married when I was nineteen; I've told you a little about that. It wasn't a happy marriage, but it did give me Paulo, which was a blessing. I came back here for a short time to live when that marriage failed, and my parents family who were running this place, took us in. Now, if you wanted to find a couple who argued! *Mio Dio,* sometimes the air was blue with their shouting. But when my mother died, my father gradually lost his zest for life. I didn't want to see the same thing happen to Paulo. I married again, unwisely as it turns out. *Follemente innamorata* – I was madly in love. Or so I thought. Madness like that never lasts and no one wants to live in a state of insanity, do they? It wasn't until I was fifty, perhaps fifty-one, that I found Freddy, the first man who loved me for who I was. A man who always put my happiness first and still does. And as I said to you, a man I like. And just as Freddy always puts my happiness first, Paulo is that sort of man too. So I ask you, do you love him?'

I felt quite giddy for a moment and sat down on the edge of the bed. I looked at her, her gaze focused on me.

'I do,' I said. 'I think I always did. But I came here

to celebrate Ellen. It's not right that this should happen.'

Ceci laughed. 'My dear, when would it be right? He has been on his own for five years, maybe for longer than that if my suspicions are true. I am a mother, just as you are, and I knew better than to ask too much. He is going to sell this hotel, and I do understand why. But what, I wonder, will he do next? I like you, Joanna. And I love my son. I have seen you together this last week. The way you look at each other. It's as though nothing has changed, isn't it, even after all these years. Yes, don't look so surprised, I guessed what you were to each other. And I have seen a sort of sadness in you that I recognise. I may laugh about my failed marriages; I may say things to cover up what went wrong. But I know that you, like I have been in the past, have been in mourning for a lost life. Your hopes that were lost, your expectations and dreams of the sort of life that you wanted but did not achieve. I know exactly how that feels. Was it his fault? Was it my fault? Was it the other woman?'

I could feel myself almost tearful at that point. She was right.

Ceci patted my hand. 'I have told Paulo this. There came a time when I had to let go of the past.

To forget the mistakes I made, the wrong choices, all the time lost. And when I did that, I could allow myself to have a future. Now I am telling you to do the same thing. I asked Freddy this morning why he wanted to marry me all those years ago. I had two failed marriages behind me. I was not a good bet at all. And he said, "I had waited long enough to find you." And I think maybe you and Paulo have waited long enough too. Don't you? Don't let that chance, that precious opportunity, slip away from you.'

'Thank you,' I said, even closer to tears.

Ceci looked at me, more kindly this time, her head on one side.

'Being swept off your feet by first love can be delightful, but it can be wonderful with both feet on the ground.'

22

I got home from Capri to find that in just one week, Alex had spread himself out from the confines of the granny flat all over my house. There was a young man asleep in my spare room ('Mum, it's only Liam from work, you've met him loads of times. I'm sure you said it was okay if he stayed for a few days. He's just broken up with Emily. He's no trouble, you'll hardly know he's there.') and evidence of several takeaways and pizza deliveries sticking out of my overloaded kitchen bin, and the recycling wheelie bin was almost filled with empty beer bottles and cans. My washing machine was full of their wet laundry, which had been forgotten about for days and smelled mouldy.

There was a cracked window in the kitchen which had been repaired with duct tape, the fridge was almost empty apart from a particularly lurid curry stain up the sides and it looked like someone had spilled red wine over the sofa cushions and made only feeble attempts to clean up.

'Look, it was an accident. I could pay for the dry cleaning if you like? And it was Liam's fault the window got cracked, not mine. I told him not to chuck stuff around.'

* * *

Juliette came round for coffee the day after I got home, bringing with her some millionaire's shortbread for us to taste.

'So go on then,' she said as we waited for the kettle to boil, 'tell me all about it.'

'We had a great flight out, and we landed on time. And then we took the ferry—'

Juliette held up a hand. 'Not that bit. I'm not in the least bit interested in your travel arrangements. I have to say, you're looking a lot brighter than when you went away. So, my intuition, which Matthew says is my superpower, tells me something is up. And I want to know what happened with Paulo.'

I spooned some coffee into two mugs and smiled rather sentimentally at them.

'Aha!' Juliette said, clapping her hands. 'I knew it. Was the old magic still there? Did you take one look at each other and fall into bed together?'

I gave her a look. 'Don't be naughty! Yes to the first bit and no to the second part. He was just as lovely as I remembered him, and yes, I still fancied him something rotten. But it took a bit of time for us to talk properly because there was so much going on. Other people and his family. All the things he had to do in the hotel. There always seemed to be something that he needed to dash off and sort out. We hardly had any time alone together until after the party. And then we talked and talked, and there was so much to catch up on—'

Juliette held up her hand again.

'You're getting off the point again. What I want to know is did you snog him?'

'Well, yes, I did actually,' I said, feeling rather proud of myself.

'And?'

'And what?'

'It's okay, you don't need to tell me, I can see from that soppy look on your face. Are you in love?'

I could feel myself blushing. Being in love was

not something I had felt for a long time or expected ever again. It always seemed to be something younger people did. Not people my age.

'Can I be in love at my age?' I said.

Juliette scoffed. 'Why on earth not? What would you call it? Being in really *like*? You've still got a pulse and so does he. When I met Matthew, it wasn't like a bolt of lightning. But I was smitten there and then. Even if he was wearing tweed and I was covered in ice cream, but that's a story for another day. But as we got to know each other, I couldn't sleep, I couldn't eat, and I used to get this most marvellous tingly feeling whenever I thought about him. But we're getting off the subject again. So what happens now?'

'The most important thing is he's selling the hotel. It turns out he never really wanted to spend his whole life running it, but he did because Ellen was so good at it. It's a glorious place. You should take Matthew there. She did an amazing job; everywhere is so beautiful, the staff are great, the views are astonishing. But then after Ellen died, he finally admitted that he didn't want to carry on. His son Leo wouldn't want to take it over; in fact, no one in the family could, and he had to think of the future.'

'He could give it to me, I'd have a go,' Juliette said with a chuckle. 'I mean, I've never run a hotel, but

I've stayed in a lot over the years. And think of all that lovely food and the sunshine.'

'Yes, if you're a guest, but I think it's a very different matter if you are in charge. You wouldn't get to eat the food very often because you'd be serving it to other people and you probably wouldn't see much of the sun either.'

Juliette pulled a face. 'No, probably not. It's like when people say they want to run a pub, but when they do they get cross because people complain about everything and won't go home at a decent hour. Is there really no one else in the family to take it over?'

'His mother is eighty-five and lives near Florence, and his two aunts are in their seventies and have the diplomatic skills of Star Wars stormtroopers.'

'I like the sound of them. Look, are we going to try this millionaire's shortbread or not? If it's okay I'll make some for the Christmas Fair. Janice Newton from The Laurels wants us to call it an *Olde Victorian Christmas Fayre*, with a y, which always annoys me. I asked if that meant we needed to reopen the work-house, have starving waifs in the corner and an outbreak of ye olde typhoid, but she just sat there gaping. Now then.'

She took a knife and sliced into the traybake,

which looked very appetising, but then all the caramel underneath the chocolate slid out in a puddle, dripping onto the table. I grabbed a couple of plates and some teaspoons.

'Hmm, it said condensed milk but I didn't have any so I just used evaporated instead. I don't think it's worked, do you?'

'The shortbread base is nice,' I said.

I went to get some kitchen roll and a damp cloth, and the next few minutes were very sticky indeed.

'Never mind, Matthew will eat it. I'll say it's millionaire's surprise and it's a pudding. Give Matthew a jug of custard and he'd eat bike tyres. Anyway, back to Paulo. So he's gone to sell the hotel and you're back here. How does that work if he's your *trooo lurve*?'

I giggled. 'One thing at a time. Little steps.'

'You need to take big steps at your time of life,' Juliette said, 'no use messing about. Do you think I could have that cloth? This stuff is sticking my hands to the table. I think I've invented a new sort of superglue. Perhaps I should write to the papers.'

'Firstly, I need to get Alex out of the granny flat. He says he has found a place near his work; he just doesn't seem in much of a hurry.'

'You're too soft on him,' Juliette said.

'I know,' I said, licking some caramel off the back of my hand, 'but I have a plan.'

'Oh goody! Tell me all about it.'

* * *

A week later, I organised a family Zoom call, which unbelievably – because my internet was always unpredictable – worked. Bang on two o'clock, Alex logged on from the sitting room in the granny flat and next to his image I could see Kat and Jess sitting in their respective kitchens. I felt a burst of satisfaction and affection for them, all grown up and coping with life. That at least was something to be proud about.

I decided to put my plans into action, or at least put them out there so my children knew what was coming.

'I've decided to make a few changes in my life which might surprise you. And I like to think I'm helping you move on to the next phase,' I said, staring at my laptop screen with a bright smile, which was supposed to calm their fears. 'You're fully formed adults now; all of you are in your thirties. First of all, I want you to know I'm proud of you all, and I love you very much, but I think I am being selfish assuming you are always going to want to come to me for Christmas with your families. Particularly when there are small children involved, you always seem to have to move with a car crammed to the roof with their belongings.'

This was a bit of subtle psychological stuff, gleaned from some magazine article Juliette had read at her hairdressers.

Kat looked puzzled. 'But we always come to you for Christmas. I don't even know where half our decorations are.'

'So do we. I thought it was all arranged? That would mean I'd have to cook a blasted turkey. I haven't cooked Christmas dinner for – well, ever, actually,' Jess said.

'It's very straightforward, just a matter of preparation and timing,' I said.

'Liam says it's just a roast dinner with knobs on,' Alex chimed in.

'How would you know?' Kat scoffed. 'Last time I looked, you couldn't cook a Pot Noodle without assistance. You're the only person I know with a season ticket to Deliveroo.'

There was then a bit of spirited discussion about this, which looked like it was going to degenerate into an argument, and if I knew them, a long-held grievance about a burnt birthday cake was going to be brought up.

I blew a football whistle – engraved with *Best Dad Ever* which I had found at the back of the messy drawer in the kitchen, an item which confirmed my belief about such gifts. And the hubbub ceased.

'But Mum, that would mean you'd be on your own. Well, apart from Alex, and he's not much help, is he?' Jess said. 'It wouldn't make any sense.'

'No, actually, that's the other thing; well, one of the other things. Perhaps I should have started this discussion in a different place. The fact is, I'm going away for Christmas,' I said.

There was a stunned silence and the three of them looked blankly at me for a moment.

'You never go away for Christmas,' Kat said. 'You're always at home. That's what Dad said you both preferred.'

'It's what he preferred,' I said, 'and while you were younger, yes, that's what we did. We had our way of doing things. We had lots of silly traditions, didn't we? But times have changed, and it's only right that they should. You need to make your own traditions now. I'm probably going back to Capri, or I might go somewhere snowy. Possibly Austria or the Dolomites.'

'But why?' Jess asked, looking even more puzzled.

'Actually, I've always wanted to go skiing,' Alex chimed in. 'The Dolomites sounds pretty cool.'

'Well, if Alex is coming with you, then I want to come. Violet has never seen proper snow, she'd love it,' Jess agreed.

'And Maud,' Kat said.

'No, you don't need to come with me,' I said.

'I don't understand why on earth you would want to go to Capri again. You've only just come back?' Kat said.

'Hang on. If you're going to be away for Christmas, wouldn't it make sense for me to stay on here for a bit? You know, there are always bur-glaries. Liam says his dad's shed was broken into the other day. They took Liam's skateboard,' Alex said.

'And how old is Liam? Twelve?' Kat scoffed.

'Thirty-one, same as me,' Alex shouted back. 'It's good exercise, I'll have you know.'

I blew the whistle again and everyone winced.

'That's the other big thing I wanted to talk to you about,' I said. 'I want the three of you to reclaim any of your old junk from the attic or the garage. I'm going to be clearing away a lot of the stuff I don't want any more, and I thought it would be a chance for you to do it too.'

There was another stunned silence and then they all started talking at once.

Kat was first. 'Honestly, Mum, we don't know what's got into you. Why can't my old schoolbooks stay there? They aren't costing you anything.'

Jess: 'Yes, but you don't mean all my dance trophies, do you? I mean, those are family heirlooms.'

Alex: 'And you can't get rid of that mountain bike. I'm definitely going to get it back in one piece. I've even been looking at some clips on YouTube. Next year I'm having a real fitness goal.'

Kat scoffed. 'You'll be telling us you're going to do dry January next.'

'Well, I might do dry February,' Alex said. 'I always think of January as a free trial month. Of course, I'm going to move out if you're absolutely sure that's what you want? After all, I did apologise about the window and the fridge.'

Yes, it most definitely was what I wanted so I didn't engage with any of their disputes. After all, the best way to win an argument was not to have one at all. I'd realised I had been doing some 'no no' parenting of my own in the last few years, and it didn't work with them any more than it had with Eric.

I thought back to Ceci, Sylvia and Lucia and smiled. Some people might like squabbling all the time to show their affection, but I wasn't one of them.

'I promise you I'm not throwing away any of the things you want to keep, but really I think the time has come for you to sort through it, don't you? I'm going to hire a skip,' I said, 'so you can put any of your things in there if you don't want them. I'm going to be having a clear out too.'

'You're not ill, are you?' Kat said, leaning forward. 'I mean, there's nothing you ought to be telling us?'

'No, nothing like that,' I said, 'although it is good at my age to do a bit of riddling out of the junk, otherwise you'll have to do it when I fall off the perch.'

'Are you sure?' Jess asked, looking concerned. 'I mean, perhaps you should have a word with someone. You seem a bit odd. All of a sudden. Out of the blue.'

'I suppose I do,' I said with a chuckle, 'but I have thought it through. Alex, you are getting far too settled in the granny flat, and although I am more than happy to help out in an emergency, I don't think it is good for you to be living with your mother again.'

'I don't mind,' Alex mumbled, 'and it's probably

good for there to be someone here in case you have another fall,' he finished triumphantly.

My daughters murmured their grudging agreement at this.

I ignored them again. 'You have a lovely flat waiting for you in the New Year. I want to clear out all the stuff we don't need. If nothing else I will be able to put the car in the garage for the first time, not leave it out on the road, and this year I definitely want to go away for Christmas.'

'Do we need to do this in such a rush?' Kat said. 'I mean, one minute you are okay—'

'And we just assumed we could come for Christmas,' Jess added.

'—and the next minute you're talking about changing everything and going off abroad. It's like you've suddenly decided to have a gap year, which sounds great fun but who would you go with? You can't possibly go on your own.'

'Why not?' I said. 'I've got all my marbles, I'm perfectly mobile now I've had my knee done, and to be honest, a gap year sounds like a great idea.'

Kat gasped. 'It's Susie, isn't it? She's put you up to this. She's the one putting ideas in your head. Just because she doesn't have any family of her own to consider. It's different for you.'

I was outraged by this. Did they honestly think that my happiness, my interests, were completely reliant on them for the rest of my life?

'Listen to yourself, Kat. I thought you regarded yourself as a feminist. Women can do anything they want to do, wasn't that what you and Jess always say to Violet and Maud?'

'Yes, they can. Just not—'

She stopped talking then and looked a bit flustered.

'I hope you weren't actually going to say *not at my age*?' I asked.

All three of them looked rather uncomfortable at that point.

'I'm sixty-five,' I said, 'not ninety-five. And no, it's nothing to do with Susie. Look, you might as well know—'

'You are ill! I knew it!' Jess wailed. 'Don't worry, we'll get you a second opinion. The best doctors. Have you got health insurance?'

'I'm not ill, and if you would just listen instead of shouting over each other I will tell you something else you need to know.'

There was silence then and the three faces stared blankly at me from their screens, waiting for me to speak.

'When I went to Capri it was for the five-year anniversary of Ellen's death. You all met her; she was
one of my oldest friends. Well, Susie and I stayed at
the hotel Ellen used to run with her husband, who
was also a very old friend from university.'

'Yes, Mum, we know this,' Jess said. 'Paulo someone, you told us.'

'Well, Paulo and I used to be – we are more than
just friends.'

Alex frowned, not really taking this in. 'You
mean he and you...'

'Yes.'

There was a stunned silence. I suppose it was the
same for all children when they realised that their
parent might just have had a life of their own before
they appeared. Or, heaven forbid, any meaningful
relationships.

'Go on,' Kat said slowly.

'Well, we sort of reconnected. There was nothing
tacky about it, we just realised we still liked each
other.'

'Liking each other isn't the same as – you know –
getting back together again,' Jess said, 'as a couple.'

'No, I know. But the fact is, we have. Got back together again,' I said.

'Does Dad know?' Alex asked.

'It's got nothing to do with him!' I said rather heatedly. 'He's got what's her name—'

'Siobhan,' Kat put in.

'He didn't ask me what I thought about that all those years ago.'

Alex tilted his head to one side thoughtfully.

'No, I suppose he didn't. But okay. You're not hurting anyone, Mum, there's no reason why you shouldn't have a boyfriend. He's been on his own for years by the sounds of it, and so have you.'

Jess and Kat gasped at this, and I almost felt like running upstairs to the granny flat to give Alex a hug.

'Actually, it might be a good thing,' he continued, 'for Mum to have a friend to go travelling with' – it was almost as though I wasn't part of the discussion any more, like some sort of difficult child – 'and if he owns a hotel, maybe we could go and stay there sometime?'

'Honestly, Alex. Can you hear yourself?' Kat said, exasperated.

'What?' Alex said, confused.

'Never mind about that, we are talking about this man Mum has picked up?' Jess said.

'She says he's a friend, not just some man,' Alex interrupted.

'Yes, but we don't know anything about him. Is he actually going to look after her? It doesn't seem likely going on what happened last time. Coming back after a week with the remains of a black eye and a sore shoulder,' Kat added.

'That was nothing to do with him, it was a genuine accident. His grandson tripped me up, I've told you all this,' I said.

'So this Paulo is a grandfather? For heaven's sake, how old is he?'

'One year older than I am. Which is not that old, I would like to remind you. And Eric is just a little boy who hasn't been told about his boundaries. And respecting other people's space. Which reminds me a bit of you three at the moment. The difference being that Eric is only five.'

Kat, as the eldest and bossiest, called for silence.

'So let's get this straight. We're not coming to you for Christmas?'

Jess held up her hand. 'I suppose you could come to me, if I get some help with the cooking. I might have a state-of-the-art kitchen, but I have no idea how to use half of it.'

Kat was not going to be sidelined. 'And you are going off with this random man, to Capri or possibly somewhere else, you want to clear our childhood treasures out from the garage, and you want Alex to move into his own place.'

'That's partly correct,' I said. 'Firstly, I think it would be lovely for you all to be together at Jess's house. She's got more room than I do, and a bigger dining room. Secondly, most of the so-called treasures in my garage are actually old stuff you couldn't decide whether to throw out or not; and thirdly, Paulo's not a random man. I knew him before I even met your father, and before you ask, he's a very nice person who meant a great deal to me once. And still does.'

'Oh,' Jess said, 'I see. By the way, you lot, if any of you have any food allergies, you'll have to sort them out yourselves.'

'Wow. Mum's got a boyfriend,' Alex said. 'Don't you think we should meet him? Give him the talk.'

'What talk?' I said.

'About looking after you and being nice to you.'

'I don't need anyone looking after me, but if I did, he would be the one I would choose,' I said.

'What does he look like? Has he got any other kids?' Alex asked.

'Just one son, Leo, who is a successful businessman who lives in Texas. And he and his wife have one son too, who is five.'

'Cool,' Alex said, his eyes suddenly unfocused as he probably started thinking about all the possibilities.

'Yes, but he's just a friend, isn't he?' Kat asked. 'I mean, at your age, you're not going to – you know – have—'

'Shut up, Kat,' Jess shouted, putting both hands over her face.

So, my children were fine with me having a *friend* but nothing else. Amazing, even in this enlightened world where just about anything was okay with the younger generation, the prospect of their mother actually having an intimate relationship with a man was too cringeworthy to contemplate. I sometimes wondered if they thought they had just sprung fully formed from my imagination, or whether the stork or the gooseberry bush actually had some part in their appearance.

'Have what, Kat?' I said innocently.

'You know perfectly well what I mean, Mother,' Kat said stiffly. 'It's not something any of us want to imagine.'

I should hope not, all things considered. And if it hadn't been for my bruised ribs and sore shoulder, there might have been a great deal more to think about.

'Imagine all you like, dear,' I said airily. 'We are all adults here, aren't we? Good, so that's all cleared up then.'

'So, are we going to meet him?' Kat asked.

'Of course,' I said. 'Well, if that's everything?'

'I think we should be asking a lot more questions,' Jess said, 'but I can't think of any that aren't embarrassing.'

'I can,' Alex said. 'So have you actually—'

'Shut up, Alex,' his sisters shouted.

We spent a few minutes catching up with each other's news and then Jess had to go as Violet had a birthday party to attend and Kat was planning to do some ironing, so we signed off, leaving just me and Alex staring at each other.

He hesitated for a moment and then gave me a winning smile.

'By the way, can I come downstairs and see if you have any milk?'

* * *

'Excellent news, I couldn't be more pleased,' Juliette said the following morning when she called in for coffee, bringing with her some lavishly decorated cupcakes. I had just been sorting out the kitchen drawers and the table was covered in bric a brac and unwanted cooking implements.

'Sorry about these cakes. I've been watching some videos on Facebook to try and learn some icing skills, and the girls make it all look so easy. I wasn't nearly as successful. The icing is a bit lurid, isn't it? I think I added too much food colouring. The red ones look like there has been a massacre, and now I look at it properly, that brown one looks like Maurice has done a whoopsie. No one would eat that one.'

We both pulled disgusted faces and Juliette threw it in the bin.

I made some coffee and cleared a space at the table so we could sit down.

'The skip is arriving tomorrow, and then the kids are coming over at the weekend to start the riddling-out process. Alex thinks he can sell some stuff on eBay rather than just chucking it. Although I don't think there is much call for old textbooks, two broken vacuum cleaners and a crate of old towels, which Greg always said he was going to use when he washed the car. Which was never.'

'Wonderful. And there are very good charity shops in the town that take anything useful. And far more interesting, what about your Latin lover? When am I going to meet him?'

'He's not exactly that yet,' I said.

Juliette sighed, her eyes closed. 'How marvellous. Now that's something to look forward to.'

'I think I'll be a bit self-conscious actually,' I said. 'I'm not as sleek as I used to be.'

Juliette laughed. 'I don't expect he is either. He's probably worrying about the same thing. That's the great thing women of our age have going for them. It's not about whether you have a perfect figure, it's about acceptance of each other. Snuggling up. Being kind. Loving the other person for what they are. Knowing if they are feeling insecure and helping.'

'You've got all the answers,' I said, laughing. 'It's difficult to make a new start at our age, isn't it?'

'No one can make a brand-new start. But you can make a brand-new ending. You know, the more I look at these cakes the more I dislike them. Have you got any KitKats?'

'Always,' I said, going to get the tin, 'and I'm going to do that thing about a brand-new ending. You're quite right.'

Juliette nodded and then her face brightened, and she picked up a discarded wooden spoon from the table in front of her and touched me lightly on the shoulder with it.

'As founder and lifetime president, I hereby invest you into the Old Ducks Club,' she said. 'You're part of a select band. Ageing gracefully is an art; ageing disgracefully is much more fun.'

* * *

'So you did it? After all this time and all those years, you actually got everything sorted out,' Susie said, unwinding her scarf.

We were sitting in our favourite wine bar about ten days later and Susie had ordered two glasses of Pinot Grigio as a tribute to our trip to Capri.

She looked bubbly and happy, dressed in a warm woollen dress that only someone as slim as she was could have worn successfully.

'Well, not quite everything,' I said. 'Once the skip gets here—'

'I don't care about the skip!' Susie said. 'I'm talking about Paulo. Him and you. That thing. The one that after so long is back on. I mean, it is back on, isn't it?'

'It seems that way,' I said. 'I'm going back for Christmas, leaving the kids to their own devices.'

'Good, and how incredibly romantic. And talking of romance, I had a phone call from Raimondo earlier on, and some more flowers. I'm going to have to buy another vase to put them in; they are in a wine cooler at the moment and the others are in a bucket. He's coming to see me for Christmas. I was going to invite you over, but I'm guessing you're going to be far too busy.'

I smiled to myself; I was counting off the days until I was due to fly back out to Naples. The more I thought about it, the more excited I became. I had splashed out on some smart clothes too, the sort that ordinarily I would keep for a special occasion. Well, if this wasn't that, I didn't know what was. I had taken a lot of the old garments I owned to the charity shops, and some which were too battered and worn to the recycling bin at the supermarket. As I pushed them through the slot, it felt like such a triumph, as though I was ditching the old me, but more than that, I was accepting that there could be a new me. One who actually wore smart things and decent underwear.

I had to admit, it wasn't easy; it took some time and three trips, because everyone seemed to shop online, and I wanted to go into an actual shop. Perhaps I was unusual? And as I was about to buy some smart black trousers, I remembered what Ceci had said about black being lazy and put them back on the rail.

* * *

A few days later, the skip arrived outside my house and at the weekend everyone arrived to start work. It was surprising how enthusiastically they sorted things out, and yes, they dumped a lot of those *precious and irreplaceable* items into the skip themselves.

We made quite a party of it actually. And we had a lot of laughs about it all. Remembering their childhoods, their hobbies and little dramas.

At one point the day turned into a version of an American legal drama when the prosecution (me) and defence lawyers (Jess, Kat and Alex) haggled and tried to thrash out some sort of plea bargaining to be allowed to leave certain things in the garage as long as they were prepared for me to change my mind at any future date and insist on the removal of, for example:

- A folder of Jess's art coursework, much of which even she couldn't explain, and the corner of it had been eaten by mice.

- Alex's first football boots which, despite the fact that Alex had never played meaningfully in a proper football match at any level, he wanted to save for his own as yet unplanned firstborn son.
- Two plastic boxes of Kat's crafting supplies and wool, in the unlikely event that her daughter Maud might one day want to recreate the Bayeux tapestry.

I said yes to all of them; I wasn't quite as ruthless as I had pretended. We sorted everything out into things that were unsavable, others that could go to the charity shops, and a few that they took home.

But by the time the skip was picked up again at the start of December, I could, for the first time since I had moved into my house, park my car inside the garage. It felt like a triumph.

23

So much had happened since then. I knew I was not the same person I had been; I was certainly not living the same life.

Alex moved out into his new flat at the beginning of December. Jess had made plans for them all to go to her for Christmas celebrations because as she said, she had the biggest house and twice as many bedrooms as I did. That seemed to give them a lot of pleasure, and they were all looking forward to doing something new, making traditions of their own as I had hoped, so perhaps they could see I had been right after all.

I went back to Capri for Christmas, to find that

sun-kissed island was preparing for the winter months. It was raining and a cold wind was blowing in from the sea.

Even the ferry crossing from Naples was different this time. The sea was rough, the boat rocking and uncomfortable. Someone said there had been no crossings at all the previous week because of the bad weather.

The prospect of not being able to make the journey was too awful. But then at last, the ferry reached the harbourside at Marina Grande and I picked up my cases, checking I hadn't left anything behind. All the time I was remembering how anxious I had been last time I'd made this journey, not knowing for a second that it would be a trip that would change my life forever.

What I didn't know, of course, was how it would feel to be back with him. With Paulo. Just us, without the distraction of the hotel to run, the other guests, without worrying about the memory of Ellen.

Paulo was there at the quayside, waiting for me, shrouded in a waxed coat with the hood pulled up, and his face broke into that wonderful and familiar smile as he saw me. As I waited to start down the gangplank, I took a deep breath, feeling as though I might burst with excitement and happiness. This time it would be all right.

Since my first visit, we had spoken on the phone most days, exchanged emails and texts. How different from last time when he hadn't known how to contact me. I had learned so much about him, and about myself.

I knew about the delays with his solicitors as the sale of the hotel went through; he knew about my family, the clearing out of my garage. He knew that Alex and Kat were going to spend Christmas with Jess, that my neighbour Juliette – would be keeping an eye on my house when it was empty. It was surprising how helpful, how kind, people could be if one just asked.

He knew, and perhaps shared, my feelings about this second meeting. Was he as anxious as I was? Did he wonder about how things would progress in the next few days? What level of intimacy we might reach?

'Welcome back,' Paulo said as he swept me into a hug, his cheek cold against mine. 'Let's get you out of this rain. It hasn't stopped for two days.' He stopped then, leaning back to look at me. 'Perhaps you will bring the sunshine back? It's wonderful to see you again. I've missed you so much.'

'I've missed you too,' I said, smiling so much that my face was beginning to ache.

And then someone struggling with an armful of laden carrier bags banged into us, and we realised we were blocking other people. And so we hurried into the car park, where the little Hotel Massimo truck was waiting.

As we drove through the town, I could see a lot of the tourist shops and hotels had closed for the winter, but some shops and restaurants were still open, decorated with fairy lights which blew and flickered in the breeze and many had Christmas trees inside which shone out into the dark afternoon. A couple of the shops had extravagant displays of beautifully wrapped gifts in the windows, which made me want to stop and stare. There were strings of little blue lights strung between the masts of the boats in the harbour and between the streetlights like a sparkling canopy. Everything, me included, felt very different from my last visit.

'The last guests left yesterday,' Paulo said, brisk and businesslike as we drove up the hillside away from the marina. 'Sylvia has gone to England to be with her daughter and taken Lucia with her. My mother and Freddy will arrive tomorrow morning and they will leave after Christmas to spend the New Year with his daughter in Milan.'

'I can't wait to see her again; I like her enormously. She's very wise. She gave me some excellent advice the last time I saw her.'

Paulo turned fleetingly to smile.

'And what did she say, this wise mother of mine?'

'Just girl talk,' I said.

'Girl talk,' he said, laughing.

'I'm still a girl in my head, Paulo. And I am sure your mother is too. I want to see some pictures of her when she was a young woman. I bet she was stunning.'

'I am sure she will show you,' he said. 'She has been looking forward to seeing you. She has been nagging me. I think she had guessed more than I have told her. She seems to think we are well suited.'

I looked across at his profile and grinned.

'I told you she was wise.'

* * *

It was strange to be back in the hotel that once had been bustling and busy and was now so quiet. There were signs that a lot of packing up had been going on, and the doors to the ballroom were open, showing that it was empty. The glittering chandeliers were switched off, the tables stacked in one corner. It was the end of something, but also the beginning.

Just for a moment I could remember it as it had been. All those people, me in my borrowed dress and Susie laughing and happy with Raimondo as he brought her Prosecco and looked at her with the sort of expression of which I didn't think Simon had ever been capable.

She was currently at home, finishing off the decoration of her spare bedroom and waiting for Raimondo to arrive to spend Christmas with her. I didn't think I had ever seen her so happy.

The doors into the garden were all closed, and outside, gusts of rain slanted between the lemon trees. On the terrace where I had sat drinking wine in the shade of the parasols, everything had been taken down, the tables and chairs put away for the winter.

Somehow it looked sad, and I remembered how it had been the last day I was there. So beautiful, the air so bright and clear. The sunlight and that wonderful blue sky.

However, in Paulo's apartment, everything was

almost as I remembered it – comfortable, warm and welcoming. Except this time there was a Christmas tree in one corner decorated with red and green coloured lights – the Italian colours, he reminded me, which were traditional – and a golden star at the top. There was a log fire burning in the grate, a crowd of scarlet poinsettias on the windowsills and nativity figurines on a coffee table.

'It's all a bit conventional,' Paulo said. 'My mother insisted. Maybe a little over the top?'

'It's beautiful,' I sighed. 'Exactly as I would have hoped.'

'Are there enough fairy lights, even for you?'

'Well, not really; after all, you can never have too many,' I said, and he chuckled.

'I will search to find if I have any more, and if not I will scour the shops for some! Those endless arguments about that all those years ago, do you remember?'

'I was a nightmare, I'll admit it,' I said.

'My mother and Freddy are looking forward to sharing a proper Italian Christmas with you, I mean with us. Tomorrow is Christmas Eve, when all Italians have fish, then she will want us to play cards and tell her all our news. On Christmas Day a few friends will be joining us for an afternoon feast, and you had better be hungry because it will go on for a long time. We don't like to hurry such a celebration in Italy.'

'I like the sound of that,' I said. 'At home I spend all morning cooking and then my family tend to race through Christmas dinner.'

'Not here, we have all day. Now then, are you comfortable staying here with me?' he asked. 'There is a second bedroom if you prefer.'

I caught hold of his arm as he turned.

'Don't be daft,' I said gently, suddenly realising that perhaps he was nervous too. Wondering if the feeling between us could be just as real as it had seemed. I looked for a moment into his wonderful brown eyes and then I smiled.

And I put my arms around him and pulled him towards me.

And I kissed him.

I felt him relax and his arms went around me, and he held me tight against him. All the years we had lost, all the last few weeks of text messages and emails, were forgotten. At long last, we were back together. There were no doubts or ghosts of the past between us.

His room was lovely, but a bit spartan. Just a big wooden bed, a wardrobe and a chest of drawers. But there was a comfortable chair in the corner and a small writing desk covered in papers. I supposed that was just his masculine taste. There seemed no trace of Ellen in that room. There were no traces of her ever being in there. No photographs, nothing to show her love of colour or the last faint traces of her perfume. It felt like he had brought me into his sanctuary.

He carried my cases in and left them in the corner and then he turned to me.

'Well,' he said, 'will this be okay? Is it warm enough? I know you always felt the cold.'

I took my coat off and dropped it onto the chair.

'It's fine.'

I suddenly recalled what Juliette had said. *You can make a brand-new ending.* And this moment, perhaps this was when it started.

I went to put my arms around his waist and looked up at him.

'Do you remember?' I said.

'Oh, yes, I remember,' he said. 'I remember everything.'

'Then?'

It was as though we had never parted. The desire we both felt for each other was still there. I thought we were both apprehensive, wondering if our old relationship, such as it had been, would have stood the test of time. But it didn't take very long to realise it had.

The evening light in his room was calm and forgiving. The bed softer still. The sheets like silk under my skin. And he was so warm, so passionate and kind. And there was no rush this quiet December evening as we discovered each other at last. How long had I wanted to be appreciated like that, so cherished, so loved.

It was everything and more that I had ever dreamed of. There was no hesitation, no regret, no memories of the past there to spoil it. Just him and me, absorbed in each other, finding at last the things we had sought. The ice in my heart thawed under his touch, and I knew then what it was to be precious to a man. Important and valued. At last.

Although my heart soared with joy, I could have cried. With happiness, with relief that the wait for him, for this moment, had not been in vain. Nothing in the past mattered any more, none of the difficulties, the problems, the disappointments, the doubts. The only thing I knew in that moment was him and me.

We lay there for a long time afterwards, wrapped in the warmth of each other's arms. The afternoon darkened into night outside and still we lay there, not wanting to disturb that perfect moment.

And then he brought me a soft woollen robe to wear and a bottle of champagne and two glasses from his kitchen. I sat up in bed and watched him, loving the way his muscles moved under his smooth skin. I was filled with wonder at the beauty of his face as he smiled at me. Nowhere could there be any person on the planet who was as happy as I was at the moment, I was sure of it.

* * *

The following day I woke to see him still sleeping beside me and I gave a great sigh of contentment.

'Are you awake at last?' he said, his eyes still closed.

I snuggled up to him and his arm went around my shoulder.

'I'm hungry,' I said, kissing his chest.

He brushed my hair back from my face.

'I bet you are,' he said with a grin.

He brought me coffee, hot and sweet, and a dish of croissants and apricot jam. We sat up in bed talking and just being happy together. How simple it all sounded now it was possible; how difficult to imagine once upon a time.

'And now I have a Christmas present for you,' he said at last, and he handed me a package, beautifully wrapped with curled red ribbons that I was pretty sure he had not done himself.

Inside, wrapped in some designer-logoed tissue paper, was a slim leather box, and inside that, a beautiful gold bracelet with just one charm on it. A little outline of Italy.

'I will buy you others,' he said, fastening it around my wrist, 'to celebrate the things we do, the places we see together.'

'I can't wait,' I said.

'Nor can I.'

He smiled and kissed my hand and then took me in his arms and kissed me, and at that moment I felt truly invincible. Who cared if we were older, less confident? If we had lost the suppleness of our youth, if we had made mistakes in the past?

This was the beginning of something new and special. And whatever happened, for the rest of my life, I knew I would never be lonely again.

* * *

We showered and dressed and cleared away the debris of the previous evening, and then we switched on all the Christmas lights and they twinkled out into the grey day like little sparks of hope.

We stood, arms around each other, looking at the Christmas tree, and he dropped a kiss on top of my head.

'*Buon natale, amore mio.* Merry Christmas, my love,' he said.

'*Beh, era ora*, it's about time,' said a voice behind me.

I turned to see Ceci, arm in arm with Freddy standing in the doorway, both of them smiling. She was wearing a beautiful forest-green dress with a suitably festive crimson wrap. She held out a hand to me with a little cry of welcome and I went forward to kiss her cheek. Then Freddy gave a funny courtly little bow and kissed my hand.

And then after all that formality, we all laughed and it really did feel as though somehow, at last, who knew how, I was ready to face whatever the future threw at me. I was centred in my own life, exactly where I should be.

* * *

MORE FROM MADDIE PLEASE

Another brilliantly funny, feel-good read from Maddie Please, *Sisters Making Mischief*, is available to order now here:
www.mybook.to/SistersMakingMischief

ACKNOWLEDGEMENTS

Thanks are due as always to all the marvellous people at Boldwood Books, for their help and encouragement and hard work.

Special thanks to Emily Ruston my editor who has been unfailingly supportive and positive. Jenna Houston, Nia Beynon, Issy Flynn, Claire Fenby, Jennifer Davies and Arbaiah Aird for sorting out the finer points of my grammar, and of course the inimitable Amanda Ridout.

Thanks also to my agent Broo Doherty of DHH Literary Agency who is always there at the end of a phone call or email when I most need her.

A big thank you to my readers around the world who have enjoyed my books and have left such lovely and thoughtful reviews. You make all the difference.

A special shout out to Rachel Gilbey of Rachels Random Resources who organises my blog tours with such efficiency.

Thank you to Freya Webb for working her magic with my marketing.

And thank you to David, Emma, Claudia, Jon, James and Beth for their encouragement and support. It means the world to me.

And of course, to Jane, the best Bestie anyone could have.

Finally, and most importantly, always remembering Brian without whom none of this could have happened.

ABOUT THE AUTHOR

Maddie Please is the author of bestselling joyous tales of older women. She has had a career as a dentist and now lives in rural Herefordshire where she enjoys box sets, red wine and Christmas.

Sign up to Maddie Please's mailing list for news, competitions and updates on future books.

Follow Maddie on social media here:

facebook.com/maddieplease

x.com/maddieplease1

instagram.com/maddieplease1

bookbub.com/authors/maddie-please

ALSO BY MADDIE PLEASE

BECOME A MEMBER OF

THE SHELF CARE CLUB

The home of Boldwood's
book club reads.

Find uplifting reads,
sunny escapes, cosy romances,
family dramas and more!

Sign up to the newsletter
https://bit.ly/theshelfcareclub

Boldwood

Boldwood Books is an award-winning fiction publishing company seeking out the best stories from around the world.

Find out more at www.boldwoodbooks.com

Join our reader community for brilliant books, competitions and offers!

Follow us
@BoldwoodBooks
@TheBoldBookClub

Sign up to our weekly deals newsletter

https://bit.ly/BoldwoodBNewsletter